S0-FAF-063

ALL IN A DAY'S WORK

Hordefish's defender was about to kick the downed Hunter in the head, but Cimarron kicked backward and his boot struck the shin of one of his captors. The man howled in pain and loosened his grip, enabling Cimarron to break free and grab the Indian. Holding the redskin by the scruff of the neck, Cimarron reached out with his free hand and grabbed another Indian attacker. Then, in one fast and fluid motion, he cracked the skulls of the two men together and then let them fall unconscious to the ground. God, he was tired. . . .

Other Cimarron Books That You'll Enjoy

(0451)

☐ CIMARRON #1: CIMARRON AND THE HANGING JUDGE (120582—$2.50)
☐ CIMARRON #2: CIMARRON RIDES THE OUTLAW TRAIL (120590—$2.50)
☐ CIMARRON #3: CIMARRON AND THE BORDER BANDITS

(122518—$2.50)
☐ CIMARRON #4: CIMARRON IN THE CHEROKEE STRIP (123441—$2.50)
☐ CIMARRON #5: CIMARRON AND THE ELK SOLDIERS (124898—$2.50)
☐ CIMARRON #6: CIMARRON AND THE BOUNTY HUNTERS

(125703—$2.50)
☐ CIMARRON #7: CIMARRON AND THE HIGH RIDER (126866—$2.50)
☐ CIMARRON #8: CIMARRON IN NO MAN'S LAND (128230—$2.50)
☐ CIMARRON #9: CIMARRON AND THE VIGILANTES (129180—$2.50)
☐ CIMARRON #10: CIMARRON AND THE MEDICINE WOLVES

(130618—$2.25)
☐ CIMARRON #11: CIMARRON ON HELL'S HIGHWAY (131657—$2.50)
☐ CIMARRON #12: CIMARRON AND THE WAR WOMEN (132521—$2.50)
☐ CIMARRON #13: CIMARRON AND THE BOOTLEGGERS (134494—$2.50)
☐ CIMARRON #14: CIMARRON ON THE HIGH PLAINS (134850—$2.50)
☐ CIMARRON #15: CIMARRON AND THE PROPHET'S PEOPLE

(135733—$2.50)
☐ CIMARRON #16: CIMARRON AND THE SCALP HUNTERS (136659—$2.75)
☐ CIMARRON #17: CIMARRON AND THE COMANCHEROS (138120—$2.75)
☐ CIMARRON #16: CIMARRON AND THE GUNHAWKS' GOLD (139208—$2.75)

Prices slightly higher in Canada

Buy them at your local bookstore or use this convenient coupon for ordering.
NEW AMERICAN LIBRARY,
P.O. Box 999, Bergenfield, New Jersey 07621

Please send me the books I have checked above. I am enclosing $_____
(please add $1.00 to this order to cover postage and handling). Send check
or money order—no cash or C.O.D.'s. Prices and numbers are subject to change
without notice.

Name _____

Address _____

City _____ State _____ Zip Code _____

Allow 4-6 weeks for delivery.
This offer is subject to withdrawal without notice.

20
CIMARRON
AND THE RED EARTH PEOPLE

by
LEO P. KELLEY

A SIGNET BOOK
NEW AMERICAN LIBRARY

PUBLISHER'S NOTE

This novel is a work of fiction. Names, characters, places, and incidents either are the product of the author's imagination or are used fictitiously, and any resemblance to actual persons, living or dead, or events, is entirely coincidental.

NAL BOOKS ARE AVAILABLE AT QUANTITY DISCOUNTS WHEN USED TO PROMOTE PRODUCTS OR SERVICES. FOR INFORMATION PLEASE WRITE TO PREMIUM MARKETING DIVISION, NEW AMERICAN LIBRARY, 1633 BROADWAY, NEW YORK, NEW YORK 10019.

Copyright © 1985, 1986 by Leo P. Kelley

All rights reserved

The first chapter of this book previously appeared in *Cimarron on a Texas Manhunt*, the nineteenth volume in this series.

SIGNET TRADEMARK REG. U.S. PAT. OFF. AND FOREIGN COUNTRIES
REGISTERED TRADEMARK—MARCA REGISTRADA
HECHO EN CHICAGO, U.S.A.

SIGNET, SIGNET CLASSIC, MENTOR, PLUME, MERIDIAN AND NAL BOOKS are published by New American Library, 1633 Broadway, New York, New York 10019

First Printing, March, 1986

1 2 3 4 5 6 7 8 9

PRINTED IN THE UNITED STATES OF AMERICA

. . . he was a man with a past he wanted to forget and a future uncertain at best and dangerous at worst. Men feared and secretly admired him. Women desired him. He roamed the Indian Territory with a Winchester '73 in his saddle scabbard, an Army Colt in his hip holster, and a bronc he had broken beneath him. He packed his guns loose, rode his horse hard, and no one dared throw gravel in his boots. Once he had an ordinary name like other men. But a tragic killing forced him to abandon it and he became known only as Cimarron. *Cimarron*, in Spanish, meant wild and unruly. It suited him. *Cimarron*.

One

"This just came in," the barber announced, "and it has proved quite popular with most of my customers."

Cimarron, submerged in the hot-water-filled tin tub in the back of the Fort Smith barber shop, took the wrapped bar of soap the barber handed him and studied its label. He sniffed it, shook his head, and handed the soap back to the barber.

"What's wrong?"

"That thing stinks like a rose garden gone wild," he told the barber. "Were I to use that, I'd come out of here smelling like some fancy man folks wouldn't dare trust their daughters with." He grinned. "Or their sons either, for that matter." His grin widened. "Give me a bar of plain yellow soap, and let's have done with it."

The barber took down an unwrapped bar of yellow soap from a shelf and handed it to him. "I heard you caught up with that notorious Red Eye Hilbert out in Indian Territory, Cimarron."

Cimarron, vigorously soaping his body and splashing water in every direction, nodded.

The barber shuddered. "I'd not want to run up against a man like Red Eye Hilbert, no sirree. It would, a meeting like that be sure to scare me out of a year's growth. Is it true he's killed upwards of fifteen men?"

Cimarron nodded again.

"How'd you catch him?"

"That's a long sad story," Cimarron commented, not wanting to go into the details of the time he had spent chasing Hilbert from Creek Nation down into Chickasaw Nation and then up into Seminole Nation. "Let's just say that I pulled his stinger and registered him for a room over in Judge Parker's hotel.''

"I hear the jail's pretty crowded these days," the barber remarked, taking a towel down from the shelf. Cimarron briefly ducked his head under the water and then began to soap his hair.

"But now that the judge is holding court day and night," the barber continued, "and more and more white folks are moving into Indian Territory I guess a man can safely bet that the day's coming down the pike when Indian Territory will be as civilized as our own Fort Smith itself."

Cimarron scooped up water in both cupped hands and poured it over his head to rinse the suds from his hair. "What you say's true enough, I reckon, though there's some who claim that barbed wire and bib overalls are what'll be the ruin of Indian Territory." He rose and took the towel the barber handed him. "One thing's certain. If civilization drives all the desperadoes out of the Territory there won't be a need for a man like me to roam around out there anymore and risk getting a bullet in his belly or balls.''

"I suppose that's true enough," the barber mused, quickly stepping back as Cimarron shook his head and water flew from his long black hair. "But I'm surprised you sound sad when you say that, Cimarron. Don't you ever long to live a quiet life like other folks, as a rule, do?"

"Nope. The fact is, I don't. I reckon I just like living by the law of old Judge Colt.''

The barber shuddered as Cimarron stepped out of the tub, dried his feet, and reached for his clothes.

When he was dressed and his cartridge belt was once again strapped around his lean hips, he strode out of the back room and plopped down in one of the two empty barber's chairs. "Trim my mane for me," he said to the barber as he made himself comfortable in the chair. "And I could use a shave," he added, running his hand over the black stubble that covered his cheeks and chin.

He closed his eyes, barely aware of the *snip-snipping* of the barber's scissors. Later, he almost dozed as the man applied creamy lather to his face, stropped a razor, and began to scrape away the stubble.

"How about a bit of bay rum?" the barber asked after he

8

had wiped the last of the lather from Cimarron's face. "It's bracing, and some customers tell me the ladies like it."

Cimarron shook his head, and after the barber had whipped away the cloth covering his torso, got out of the chair. "How much do I owe you?"

"That's four bits for the bath, two for the haircut, and two for the shave. One dollar in all."

"I'm obliged to you," Cimarron said as he paid and then studied his face in the mirror the barber held up. "I look almost brand-new," he observed as he ran the fingers of one hand over his smooth cheeks.

"Will you be staying in town long this time?" the barber asked.

"Not long, I reckon. It'll soon be time for me to rattle my hocks and ride on out of here again." He patted the barber on one bony shoulder and gave the man a conspiratorial wink. "But before I do I'm fixing to have me a high old time over to Mrs. Windham's parlor house where, I've heard tell, there's a new girl in residence since the last time I had the pleasure of visiting that establishment."

"Her name, they say, is Doe, although I'm not entirely certain about that since I, being a family man and all, steer clear of such establishments as Mrs. Windham's parlor house. I—"

Whatever else the barber had been about to say was drowned out by the sudden thunder of gunfire that erupted in the street outside the barber shop.

Cimarron's hand dropped to the butt of his .44 as he spun around to face the door. "What the hell—"

"Look at him!" cried the barber, wringing his skinny hands. "He's at it again!"

"Who's at it again?" Cimarron asked, peering through the window of the barber shop. A crowd of people were gathered outside the greengrocer's store, where fruits and vegetables were displayed on wooden stands. He didn't wait for the barber's answer, because a Fort Smith policeman fired a shot, causing a strikingly beautiful young woman standing near the officer to shriek. Instead, he grabbed his hat and buckskin jacket from a wall peg, put them on, and raced out of the barbershop and into the street.

"What's going on here, O'Dwyer?" he yelled to the policeman.

The officer turned toward him, sighed, and said, "Ah, is it you now, Cimarron? It's glad I am to see you. Maybe you can lend a much-abused officer of the law a hand here."

"Don't you dare lend that bully a hand!" the young woman Cimarron had noticed earlier shouted at him. "If you lay so much as a single finger on my poor Pierre I'll—*I'll scratch your eyes out!*"

"Who's Pierre?" Cimarron asked O'Dwyer, keeping one wary eye on the young woman. "Some felon you're after?"

O'Dwyer shook his head and pointed to the tiny white poodle that was barely visible as it cowered and snarled behind the skirt of the young woman.

"Shoot the varmint and be done with it!" bellowed a man from the depths of the crowd that had quickly gathered.

Cimarron glanced at the man, who added, "It's the law now! Tell him, O'Dwyer!"

Cimarron turned his attention to O'Dwyer, who explained, "It's a new city ordinance that the town fathers have seen fit to pass, faith preserve us, which requires us police officers to shoot any mutts we see running loose without collars or licenses and—"

"I heard that!" the suddenly stony-faced woman cried. "And I will not have my Pierre referred to as a 'mutt'!"

"Maybe we can settle this peaceably, O'Dwyer," Cimarron suggested as he eyed the young woman's shapely figure, her fine-featured face, big breasts, and rounded hips. "Maybe we can put Pierre in a dog pound somewhere until the lady can buy herself a collar and license for her mutt—her pet, I mean." He gave the young woman an apologetic grin, but her face remained stony.

"Fort Smith may be striving hard to become the cultural capital of the Middle West," O'Dwyer observed, "but it is not yet advanced enough to possess such elegant amenities as dog pounds within its borders. Cimarron, perhaps you could have a word or two with the lady—explain to her that I'm merely an honest man just trying to do my duty under the law."

Cimarron took a step toward the woman. She held up a hand.

10

"Don't come near me!" she warned him.

He stood his ground. "Miss, I'm a lawman like Officer O'Dwyer here is, and I got to tell you that, under the law, what you're doing is you're harboring a fugitive from justice."

"Fugitive from justice indeed!" the woman exclaimed indignantly. "Pierre, I'll have you know, is completely innocent!"

"I know how hard it is for you to understand," Cimarron said sympathetically, his eyes dropping from the woman's face to her breasts, which were heaving with excitement. "But without a license and a collar—and your dog's got neither one nor the other—he's breaking the law, and so Officer O'Dwyer here has to—"

"If you don't put that mutt out of its misery," yelled the man in the crowd who had earlier urged O'Dwyer to shoot the poodle, "I sure as hell will!"

"How dare you talk like that!" shouted a woman standing near him. "The shooting of helpless animals under that misguided city ordinance will lead to a bloodbath on the streets of Fort Smith. Shots will go astray. They may hit innocent people. *Children of tender years!*"

"Save your preaching for Sundays!" the man retorted and drew his gun.

"And if dogs are not killed outright—the howling from the pain of their wounds will—" the woman persisted but then fell silent as the man raised his gun. She plowed through the crowd and lunged at him. He shoved her aside. A man came to her rescue, and another one threw a left hook that struck the armed man on the chin.

"Fight!" somebody yelled from the other side of the street as the crowd quickly became a roiling mass of bodies. Words were exchanged. So were blows, as those men and women who supported law and order boldly battled those whose only cause was compassion for what one parasol-wielding woman dubbed, at the top of her trumpeting voice, "defenseless dumb animals about to be struck down by a cruel and unconscionable law." With one blow of her parasol she managed to disarm the man eagerly hunting Pierre, who still was hiding behind the young woman's skirt.

"You restore order," O'Dwyer suggested to Cimarron, "while I dispatch that foreign French critter."

"Oh, no!" wailed the young woman as O'Dwyer strode resolutely toward her, gun in hand.

The man who had been disarmed picked up the woman who had struck him with her parasol and dropped her on a four-legged tray of cabbages which stood outside the greengrocer's shop.

Cimarron, as the tray shattered and scores of cabbages rolled into the street, watched the young woman back away from the approaching menace that was Officer O'Dwyer. She looks like she's about to faint, he thought. Were I to save her from her predicament, I'm sure she'd be grateful to me.

He was suddenly thrown violently to one side by the surging crowd that had become a mob as each of its two factions fought for its beliefs. He lost his balance and went down. His right hand closed on a cabbage and he looked down at it, then up at Officer O'Dwyer. Before he knew what he was doing, he had thrown the cabbage. It struck O'Dwyer on the right side of the head, and the man went down like a steer under the slaughterer's sledge. Cimarron was up on his feet again and fighting his way through the melee surrounding him. When he reached the side of the young woman, he seized her arm in his left hand, scooped up Pierre in his right, and went racing down a side street and away from the unconscious O'Dwyer and the scene of the battle.

"Oh, let's stop!" exclaimed the breathless young woman when they had gone nearly three blocks.

Cimarron glanced apprehensively over his shoulder. When he saw that no one was pursuing him, he halted, handing her back her dog.

"Mercy me!" exclaimed the panting woman by his side. "I couldn't have run another step even if that frightful policeman had been about to apprehend me and murder my poor Pierre!"

Cimarron put out a hand, intending to pat the woman's shoulder in a consoling manner, but he quickly withdrew it when Pierre snarled a warning and then snapped at him.

The woman smiled and petted the dog. "Pierre is quite protective of me, as you can see."

"You live here in town, do you, Miss—"

"Yes," the woman answered, pointedly failing to give

12

Cimarron her name. "And I really must be on my way. If that dreadful officer should come searching for me—" She shuddered and turned away.

"I'll walk along with you if that's all right," Cimarron volunteered.

"That won't be necessary," the woman said. "Pierre can look after me quite satisfactorily until I reach home and my husband."

"Your husband," Cimarron repeated, his hopes collapsing.

The woman bent down and placed her poodle on the ground.

Cimarron, resigned to defeat, held out his hand to her. "It's been a pleasure."

Pierre snarled and then buried his teeth in Cimarron's left calf.

"Stop that, Pierre!" the woman admonished her dog. "The nice man wasn't trying to hurt mama."

Cimarron howled with pain as he tried to shake the dog loose, but Pierre held on. In desperation, he drew his gun.

"Pierre!" the obviously alarmed woman screamed. *"Heel!"*

The dog let go of Cimarron's calf and obeyed its mistress's command. Woman and dog fled down the street away from Cimarron, who holstered his gun, damned both woman and dog—her for her husband, Pierre for his sharp teeth—and then limped down a side street, heading for Mrs. Windham's parlor house.

The front door of Mrs. Windham's parlor house was opened in response to Cimarron's knock by the proprietress of the establishment herself.

"Cimarron!" Mrs. Windham cried and threw her arms around him. Hugging him to her ample bosom, she said, "It's been a while. I thought my best customer had either up and died on me and the girls or had quit the country altogether!"

He disengaged himself from her strong grip. "Neither one. Been busy out in the Territory is all. I hear you have a new boarder somebody said was named Doe."

Mrs. Windham wagged a playful finger in his face. "She's a caution, Doe is." Then, sobering, she added, "But expensive."

"I've got a pocket full of cash I'm itching to spend."

His statement brought the smile back to Mrs. Windham's fleshy face. She hooked her arm in his, kicked the door shut behind her, and led him into the parlor.

"Sit down there in your favorite chair," she directed him, indicating a chair covered with red plush inside a gaudy gilt frame. When he had done so, she minced across the room to the parlor entrance, and cupping both fat hands around her mouth, bellowed up the stairs, "Company, girls!"

Then, turning back to Cimarron, she asked, "Want a drink? I've got some peach brandy that goes down smooth as cream only a helluva lot hotter!" She guffawed.

"I'll have some."

As Mrs. Windham busied herself behind her mahogany bar, Cimarron tried to make himself comfortable in the chair, but he could not rid himself of the tension he'd been feeling ever since his encounter with the nameless woman and her poodle. The stiffened flesh between his legs that was the legacy of the encounter seemed to throb and pulse, making him decidedly edgy.

"Thirty-five cents," Mrs. Windham said as she handed him a snifter containing brandy.

"That's pretty steep," he remarked. "Last time I was in here a drink cost only two bits."

"That's aged liquor you're holding," Mrs. Windham countered. "Napoleon himself couldn't have bottled finer French brandy. And that's not to mention that it came upriver all the way from New Orleans. Down there I hear it's selling for four bits a shot. So consider what you've got a bargain, Deputy."

Cimarron dug down in his pocket and paid for the drink. "How's business been?" he asked, not really caring, as Mrs. Windham busied herself straightening the antimacassars on the ornate furniture in the room. He paid no attention to her answer as his eyes fell on the young woman who suddenly appeared in the entrance to the parlor. He knew he had never seen her before. He knew he was glad he was seeing her now as he studied her lithe figure that was as trim as an acrobat's but well padded in all the right places.

He swallowed some of his brandy and almost choked on it. He coughed and put the glass down on the table. Look at that pair she's got, he told himself. Like cantaloupes in August,

14

all ripe and waiting to be plucked from the vine. He gave her a smile and she returned it, revealing even white teeth. She patted her yellow hair and then blew him a silent kiss.

He stood up, barely able to restrain himself from lunging at her. She sauntered across the room toward him. He stared deep into her lovely blue eyes.

She stopped and said, "My name is Doe."

He opened his mouth to introduce himself, but all that emerged from it was a kind of hoarse croak.

"Oh, look, ladies!" cried one of several women who suddenly came flooding into the parlor. "It's Cimarron. *And I saw him first!*"

"Girls, girls!" Mrs. Windham admonished as they crowded around Cimarron, all of them talking loudly at once.

"Hello, Cindy," he said to the woman who had spoken. "How you been keeping, honey?"

"Fit as a fiddle and ready for anything!" she replied gaily. "You know me, Cimarron."

"Let us have a modicum of decorum, ladies!" cried Mrs. Windham. "All of you now, sit down and be demure. You know very well I run a respectable house and deplore rowdiness, whether it be practiced by my clients or my employees."

As the women sat down, Cindy gave Cimarron a wink, which he missed because he was still staring entranced at Doe in the doorway. When Mrs. Windham formally introduced him to Doe, he took her hand. When she squeezed his, he almost fainted with the mighty wave of lust that swept over him and left him momentarily weak. They left the parlor in silence, walking hand in hand.

Once inside Doe's bedroom with the door closed, Cimarron lunged at her, his desire stoked in part by a fleeting mental image of the lady with the poodle who had gotten away from him. He held Doe close to him, his fingers pressing into the small of her back, his hips swiveling slightly as they pressed hotly against her pelvis.

"What do you want me to do?" she asked. Not the least bit concerned about the price he would have to pay for it, he whispered his lurid answer in her delicate ear.

Doe drew back, gave him a small smile, and then got down on her knees. She was unbuttoning his fly when the sound of a man bellowing downstairs caused her to freeze.

"*Get out!*" Mrs. Windham's shouted words ricocheted through the house. They were followed by more male bellowing and then the sound of heavy boots striking the stairs.

Cimarron turned sharply as the door behind him was thrown open. "Beat it!" he snarled at the bearded man who stood swaying drunkenly in the open doorway.

"I want her!" the man muttered, his finger pointing at Doe, still frozen in place on her knees in front of Cimarron.

"The lady's spoken for," Cimarron told him. "You want her, mister, you'll have to get in line behind me."

"And I want her now!" the man roared at the top of his voice, as if he had heard nothing of what Cimarron had said.

As Cimarron went up to the door and started to close it, the man's hand shot out and sent it slamming back against the wall. Then he lunged past Cimarron, seized Doe, lifted her up, threw her down on her back on the bed, and straddled her.

Mrs. Windham came panting up the steps followed by her girls. "Cimarron, did you see him? He's drunk as a deacon, and if I don't get him out of here he's going to make trouble. Where is he?"

But Cimarrron didn't answer her. Instead he moved swiftly to the bed and hauled the man off Doe. Holding him by the scruff of his neck and his belt, Cimarron marched him across the room toward Mrs. Windham and her girls, who stood staring speechlessly at him and his captive. He let go of the man's belt and waved the women out of his way. Once out in the hall, he was about to start down the steps when the man elbowed him in the ribs and broke free of him.

He ducked the right jab the man threw at him, but the man's surprisingly quick and agile left uppercut caught him under the jaw and sent him reeling backward. When Cimarron regained his balance, he went at the man and delivered a sharp series of body blows that knocked his opponent backward. His balance lost, the man toppled head over heels down the stairs to the first floor. Cimarron bounded down the stairs after him, hauled him to his feet, dragged him down the hall, and, opening the front door, threw him out into the street. Then he slammed the door and went back up the steps, taking them two at a time.

"I'm grateful to you, Cimarron," Mrs. Windham told him

at the door to Doe's room. "I suppose I should have sent for the police the minute that drunken bum arrived, but I have no love for the police as you and they both no doubt know."

"I'll be getting back to the business I came here about," he told Mrs. Windham. Two of the girls flanking her tittered coyly behind their hands.

When he and Doe were alone again with the door closed, he patted her head as she knelt down before him and completed the task of unbuttoning his fly. Her hot hand slid into the opening in his jeans and seized him. Drawing him out, she made a soft sound of surprise and looked up at him.

"It's huge!" she remarked in an awed tone.

"It's also, as you can plainly see, ready as can be for what you're going to give it."

Doe's lips parted slightly. The tip of her tongue flicked between them. Her right hand encircled the base of Cimarron's shaft. Her left hand cupped his testicles and began to caress them. She leaned toward him, and her tongue touched the tip of his hardened flesh.

He sighed. And then he moaned as Doe's tongue began to tease the entire length of him. He looked down at her and groaned with pleasure as her lips opened wider and she took him into her mouth, inch by thoroughly aroused inch. He clasped his hands, their fingers interlocked, behind Doe's head as she continued servicing him and held her against him for a moment, his shaft thrust deep into her throat.

She made a soft gurgling sound and then another one. His grip loosened as her head began to bob rapidly back and forth, and his knees began to grow weak. They bent, threatening to buckle under him at any moment. But they didn't. He drew a deep breath, closed his eyes, and concentrated on the thrilling sensations sweeping through him as Doe's tongue swirled around his rampant flesh.

Then, as he began to tremble, Doe's lips locked even more tightly on him, and her left hand continued caressing his testicles. In her evident eagerness to please, she drew back too far and he slipped out of her mouth. He groaned. But it was only a momentary lapse in the erotic rhythm that was sending him soaring. She guided his shaft back into her mouth with her right hand, tightened her lips' grip on it, and continued sucking it.

He couldn't help himself. He gave a series of animal-like grunts as he exploded. His hips bucked almost out of control as he came in a seemingly never-ending series of hot spurts.

Doe, swallowing several times in swift succession, kept him within her mouth until his body no longer shuddered and his legs slowly straightened. Only then did she draw back her head and let him slip out of her mouth. She looked up, her lips glistening wetly, her eyes shining.

"Oh, honey," he managed to murmur. "That was sure one fine time you just gave me."

She licked her lips and got to her feet. She stood facing him and then, as he began to soften, she tucked him back into his jeans and buttoned his fly.

"I hope you'll ask for me next time you come calling on us," she whispered, giving his bulging crotch a tender pat.

"I'll be sure to do that, Doe," he assured her. "You can count on it."

"Ten dollars." Doe held out her hand, palm up.

"Ten dollars. Right." He rummaged around in his pocket and came up with a double eagle, which he gave her.

"I hope you'll recommend me to your friends and acquaintances, Cimarron."

He was about to promise her that he would most definitely do that when he heard a woman scream and a man shout, "This way, boys!"

"What is it, Cimarron?" Doe asked anxiously as several pair of boots thudded up the stairs and more shrill feminine screams came from the first floor of the house.

Before Cimarron had time to answer Doe's question, the bedroom door was thrown open and the man who had invaded the room earlier, no longer drunk now, stood with arms outflung in the doorway, two other men standing staunchly behind him.

"That's the son!" the man roared and pointed at Cimarron. As Cimarron raised his fists to defend himself, the man smirked and said, "You haven't got the chance of a snowflake in hell, mister. This time I've brought along reinforcements."

As all three men surged into the room, Doe backed up against the wall and began to whimper.

Cimarron threw a punch that glanced off the shoulder of

18

the trio's leader. Before he could throw another, all three men were upon him, bearing him down to the floor. He grunted as fists pounded his body and a knee slammed into the side of his head. His arms were seized and held behind his back. His face was pressed against the floor. The bearded man, chuckling to himself, got up, drew back one heavily booted foot, and kicked him in the ribs.

Cimarron gritted his teeth, refusing to cry out in response to the searing pain that tore through him. He struggled unsuccessfully to free himself from the two men who were holding him almost immobile. Then, as he twisted his head to get a better view of them, he saw one of them draw back his head as he prepared to sneeze, and he seized the opportunity. He thrust his body upward, at the same time, kicking the would-be sneezer in the groin. The man bellowed and let go of Cimarron's arm. Cimarron hammered his fist into the second man's head, and he too lost his hold. Only now becoming aware of Doe's screams, Cimarron sprang to his feet and sank his other fist into the fleshy body of the bearded leader, who bent over and grasped his gut as the air *whooshed* out of his lungs.

Cimarron raised both fists and brought them down hard on the back of the leader's skull. The blow sent the man to his knees, but Cimarron had no time to gloat over what he had done because at that moment the others sprang at him. As Doe continued to scream, they wrestled him around the room, overturning tables and chairs, and then lurched out into the hall. Cimarron broke free of them and traded blow for blow for a time. Then the bearded man recovered and came storming out of the bedroom to send a fist the size of a ham flying into his face. Cimarron slumped and almost went down.

His vision blurred and he shook his head, trying to clear it. As he did so, he felt himself being lifted up and then hurled forward. He stumbled groggily for several steps and, as a fist plowed into the small of his back and a boot landed squarely on his buttocks, he lost his balance.

He hurtled through the room, hit the stairs and went tumbling down them, pain prodding every part of his body. When his head struck the hard wood of the first floor landing, sparks erupted in his mind, and agony rocketed through him. He tried to move but found he couldn't. He tried to speak but his lips remained motionless. The sparks grew into a blazing red bonfire, and pain was everywhere within him. When the bonfire died, he slipped down into a deep darkness where no pain lurked and where he found blissful, if temporary, peace.

When he came to, the grim world that surrounded him began to whirl. He quickly closed his eyes to blot it out. But he couldn't blot out the pain that raced through his body and head, tormenting him with needles, bruising him with hammers, burning his muscles until they screamed. He groaned and slowly opened one blurry eye.

Iron slats. Little light. The sound of someone merrily humming the tune of an Irish jig. He opened the other eye and saw, beyond the gridwork of bars that formed the cell he found himself in, Officer O'Dwyer seated behind a desk watching him.

"Ah, me boyo!" O'Dwyer exclaimed, "it's awake you are." He got to his feet and strode up to the bars.

Cimarron gingerly sat up on his bunk and winced. His right hand rose to touch the dried blood that had crusted on his broken upper lip. He hung his head and let the pain caused by his movements have its ugly way with him.

"Public brawling," O'Dwyer chirped. "Disturbing the peace," he continued cheerfully. "Those be but two of the charges lodged against you by the three men you so brutally attacked in Mrs. Windham's notorious house of ill repute, Cimarron. I am sure, me bold boyo, you could be charged with conduct unbecoming a peace officer and a gentleman— that is, if such a charge were on Fort Smith's constabulary's books."

"O'Dwyer, do a favor for a dying man. Go away somewhere and shut up. Will you do that? Will you honor the soon-to-be-deceased's last request?"

O'Dwyer laughed heartily and slapped his thigh.

Cimarron moaned and lay back down on his bunk. "I didn't attack them," he protested weakly. "The three of them, they jumped me, the lying bastards!" He slowly sat up again and blinked at O'Dwyer who was beaming at him through the cell's gridwork. "Let me out of here. You can overlook what happened. Wipe it off the books."

"Could I now?"

"O'Dwyer—please." Cimarron dropped his head in his hands. "Did you ever read old Will Shakespeare's play *King Lear*?" He didn't wait for an answer from O'Dwyer. "There's something Lear says in that play that fits me like my Sunday socks. It's—and I quote—'I am a man more sinned against than sinning.' "

O'Dwyer scoffed wordlessly but noisily.

"Give me a break, O'Dwyer," Cimarron pleaded, raising his head and giving the policeman a bleary-eyed glance.

O'Dwyer's feigned cheerfulness vanished in an instant. Leaning close to the bars, he muttered, "I'll not be giving you even the ghost of a chance, you obstructor of justice!"

"I don't know what the hell you're talking about! I told you those three men jumped me, not the other way around."

"I'm talking about the other little matter in which you and I were involved."

"What little matter was that?" And then Cimarron knew what O'Dwyer was referring to. He groaned again.

"Just so, my boyo!" O'Dwyer gloated. "I saw you out of the corner of my eye, now didn't I just? I saw you hurl that king of all cabbages at me, and I felt the skull-shattering impact the weapon had when it struck me down right in the midst of the dedicated performance of my noble duty." O'Dwyer drew himself up and pompously folded his arms over his uniformed chest. "Help you beat the charges lodged against you? After what you did to me earlier today to allow that lady and her lawbreaking mutt to escape from me?" He snarled. "Not on your life will I!"

Cimarron frowned. Then, despite the pain he was feeling, he broke into a broad smile.

Seeing the changed expression on his prisoner's face O'Dwyer turned around, obviously seeking its cause. "What are you doing here, Petry?" he asked when he saw the deputy marshal standing just inside the open door of the city jail.

"Marshal Upham sent me," Petry replied and added, "to fetch him." He pointed to Cimarron.

"He's being held on fifty dollars' bail," O'Dwyer declared.

"So Marshal Upham told me when he sent me here to bail him out."

"Bail him out!" O'Dwyer echoed, his face falling.

"Ah, Petry," Cimarron exclaimed melodramatically, "you are indeed an angel of mercy as is Marshal Upham himself."

"Upham heard about what happened from Mrs. Windham," Petry explained to O'Dwyer. "She came to his office and begged him to do all he could to help Cimarron out of the jam he's gotten himself in. The lady with her, Miss Doe, also pleaded Cimarron's case, according to Marshal Upham."

Cimarron grinned.

O'Dwyer groaned and clapped a hand to his forehead.

Petry continued, "Marshal Upham's in dire need of Cimarron's services. So he sent me here with a blank voucher drawn on the court for the Western District of Arkansas, which he's already signed so I can post bail for Cimarron." Petry proceeded to fill out the voucher, using the stub of a pencil he took from his pocket, and then handed it to O'Dwyer, who reluctantly unlocked the cell door.

"Be seeing you, O'Dwyer," Cimarron said as he strode past the angrily muttering man and out of the jail with Petry by his side.

Marshal Upham looked up from behind his desk as a sheepish Cimarron sidled into his office and sat down.

"You look like death warmed over," Upham commented icily.

"I feel like I've been drawn and quartered and then stitched back together by a blind tailor."

"Maybe I shouldn't have bailed you out. Maybe I should have left you there to rot in that city jail until you learned your lesson. You don't look to me to be able to walk, let alone go on the scout again in the Territory."

"I've learned my lesson, Marshal, I truly have. Next time three bully boys come at me, I'm going to hightail it in the opposite direction as fast as a turpentined cat can run. And I figure I'd best go on the scout. If I stay here in town there's no telling how much more trouble I'm liable to get myself into."

"He's a brawler," Upham muttered mournfully to himself. "A fornicator," he intoned sorrowfully. "A hellion," he sighed. "Cimarron, I can't for the life of me understand how you manage to persuade ladies like Mrs. Windham and Miss Doe to speak out in your favor."

Cimarron gave the marshal a sly wink.

Upham cleared his throat, frowned, and said, "But never mind about all that. Let's get down to business. I'm sending you out to the Sac and Fox reservation to see if you can find out who took a shot at a man named Paul Baldwin."

"Who's Paul Baldwin?"

"A white man who's been leasing tribal land to graze cattle on. He was wounded in the incident, and I want you to bring in whoever did the shooting on a charge of attempted murder. You'll find his place two miles due west of Keokuk Falls on the Canadian River." Upham rummaged about in the pile of papers littering the top of his desk, finally coming up with a signed form, which he handed to Cimarron. "Since we don't know who shot and wounded Baldwin you can use that John Doe warrant in the matter."

"Baldwin filed a complaint with you, did he, Marshal?" Cimarron asked as he folded and pocketed the warrant.

Upham shook his head. "His sister, Miss Miranda Baldwin, visited me here yesterday and filed the complaint. It seems she's worried that the would-be killer might try again to kill her brother."

"Was she pretty, this lady named Miranda?"

Upham drew a breath and then let it out in a rush. "She was pretty, yes, but what the hell's her being pretty or ugly got to do with this attempted murder case we're discussing?" he roared, his face reddening.

Cimarron held up a placating hand. "Don't go getting riled, Marshal. I was only asking." He rose and headed for the door.

Behind him, Upham coughed and then, in a softer tone, suggested, "Maybe you should rest up for a day or two before you ride out, Cimarron. Far be it from me to run my men into the ground. And, as I said earlier, you don't look a bit well."

"I'll head out for the Sac and Fox reservation first thing in the morning, Marshal. But till then—well, I thought I'd mosey on back to Mrs. Windham's and—"

"You intend to return to the scene of your crime?" Upham inquired incredulously.

"—and thank her and Miss Doe for persuading you to show me some of the kindliness I've always known lives in your great big heart by bailing me out of that pesthole of a city jail.''

"No more brawling!" Upham warned.

"None," Cimarron promised. "Not unless you'd call what I intend to do again with Miss Doe brawling."

Upham shook his head in chagrin as a grinning Cimarron left the office.

Two

Cimarron had left Okmulgee and forded the Deep Fork of the Canadian River early in the morning. Now, as the sun continued its daily slide toward the western horizon, his stomach rumbled its hunger. He tried to pay no attention to the demands it was making on him.

He rode beneath a blue and cloudless sky. The wind that snapped the brim of his flat-topped black Stetson and lifted the straight black hair that lay upon the nape of his neck was cool, almost cold. It's almost winter weather, he thought, as his dun plodded on through the sere grass of the Osage Plains. He salivated as he remembered the taste of the goat cheese and brown bread bought at the general store in Okmulgee that he had eaten when he had made his nooning due south of Okfuskee.

Got me a ways to go yet, he thought, before I see sign of civilization again. Keokuk Falls, it's a good fifteen, twenty miles from where I'm at right now with nothing much of anything in between it and me excepting cross timbers and frost-bit grass, neither of which makes for good eating.

He rode through a forest of shin oaks, shivering as the chill wind rattled the leafless limbs of the trees through which sunlight, which seemed to hold no warmth, spilled. Visions of roast venison rose in his mind to torment him. Crisply cooked salt pork. Fried chicken gizzards snapping and crackling in hot grease. The saliva that was filling his mouth threatened to become a flood. He swallowed several times and continued his journey at a steady pace, resigned to tightening his belt a notch or two until he arrived in Keokuk Falls, where he would eat—

The visions returned to him, a tempting army of delights on the march. Creamy mashed potatoes with yellow blobs of melted butter. Steaks, crusted—almost charred—on the outside, and running with blood on the inside. Hot shortbread with brown apple butter spread thickly on each delicious slice.

Should have doubled my goat cheese and brown bread order back at that general store in Okmulgee, he thought. Tripled it, maybe.

He scanned the countryside, searching for game—a jack, a prairie chicken—willing to settle for a skunk. He saw none. He looked up at the sky. No birds flew in it. He was dreaming of a cinnamon-sprinkled apple pie, the sweetest one in the world, and licking his lips over it when he suddenly spotted the dozen or so wild hogs that were rooting about in the distance among a thick stand of loblolly pines. He quickly drew rein and pulled his Winchester '73 from its boot. He raised it and aimed at a lean hog that was, he estimated, less than a year old. He knew it would be succulent when roasted because it was far too young to have started to produce fat. It would be a melt-in-your-mouth-porker, of that he was certain. His finger tightened on the trigger as he squinted through his weapon's raised rear sight, along the barrel, and fixed the gun's front sight on the hog.

Before he could squeeze off a shot, the hogs, as if responding to some mysterious signal, all turned to the right and the young porker that had been his prey momentarily vanished from sight. Moments later it reappeared, and he had a clear shot at it as it rooted, snuffling, along the ground, its folded-over ears flopping back and forth.

The sound of his shot sent the hogs scurrying away into the woods, some in one direction and some in another, until they all disappeared. All of them, that is, except the one that he had wounded but failed to kill. It stood its ground, seemingly stunned, with blood flowing freely from its left haunch. Then, as Cimarron prepared to fire again, it shook itself and went racing away into the woods.

He swore as it disappeared from sight. Booting his rifle, he picked up his reins and put heels to his horse. His dun went galloping away in the direction the wounded hog had taken.

He trailed the hog for a mile and then still another mile

26

before he came upon the animal down on the ground near a stream, breathing its last as a result of the loss of blood. He drew rein sharply as the puma that was standing over the almost lifeless hog drew its lips back over its bright white teeth and snarled ominously, its whiskers quivering.

Cimarron slowly reached behind him and drew his rifle from its boot. He was raising the rifle to his shoulder when the puma, as if sensing danger, snarled again, the sound of a rasp in the otherwise still air. As the stock of Cimarron's Winchester rammed against his shoulder, the puma leaped over the trembling hog and sprang at Cimarron, forelegs thrust out, curved claws uncovered.

The claws of its right paw raked the shoulder of the dun, which screamed, whirled, and went racing away, throwing Cimarron from the saddle. The rifle flew out of Cimarron's hand, hitting the ground some distance away. He rolled over once and then was upon his knees and drawing his .44.

But before his gun could clear leather, the puma sprang a second time. The animal struck Cimarron with the force of a battering ram, knocking him down, and raking his hand with a claw, causing him to drop the Colt. Cimarron paid no attention to the pain in his hand as the puma circled him, still snarling, and prepared to attack him a third time. He reached for his boot and drew his bowie knife. As the puma sprang at him, he shifted to one side. His hand arced upward and, as the heavy mass of flesh soared past him, his bowie raked the puma's ribs. The animal hit the ground and growled. It turned its head and tried to bite the long bloody gash Cimarron had made in its side.

Cimarron rose, the knife in his hand dripping blood, and moved swiftly toward the crouching puma. At his approach, the animal scrabbled backward along the ground. Gnashing its teeth noisily, it suddenly halted its retreat. When it sprang, Cimarron was ready and waiting for it. His knife plunged deep into the animal's belly. Both he and the puma hit the ground hard. He rolled out from under the heavy animal, ready to bury his knife in the puma's body again, but the puma, lying on its side and its whole body heaving, gasped for breath several times, and then died.

Cimarron retrieved his guns and went to the stream, where he washed the wounds the puma had inflicted on his hand.

27

Ignoring as best he could the slicing pains that lived in his claw-raked hand, he went to where the dead hog lay on the ground. Kneeling on the ground beside the animal, he proceeded to gut and skin it. When he had cut off some of the sidemeat, he built a fire. Then, spearing a piece of pork on a stick he had sharpened, he held it over the flames, turning the stick in his hands, until the meat was thoroughly roasted.

Withdrawing the meat from the fire, he let it cool for several minutes before biting into the tender flesh beneath the pork's seared surface. He ate with relish, his eyes moving between the remains of the hog and the puma as he thought how easily it could have been him lying dead on the ground instead of the big cat. But I'm not dead, he thought somberly, and don't expect to be any time soon. That puma, he bit himself off a mite more than he could chew, he thought grimly. Namely me. But he was hell while he lasted. He meant for it to be him eating high on this here hog and not me.

When he had finished eating, he kicked out his fire, packed some of the sidemeat in his saddlebags, and went to where his dun was standing in the distance. He climbed into the saddle, turned the horse, and moved out, heading west toward Keokuk Falls and whatever awaited him there.

Cimarron arrived in Keokuk Falls late in the afternoon. As he rode through the town, he noticed the heavy wagon traffic and equally heavy pedestrian traffic going into and out of an unmarked building that might have been a warehouse or large storage shed. The town hasn't changed a bit since I last rode through here, he thought. The whiskey peddlers are still at it. And all those folks traipsing in and out of that big barnlike place, my guess is they're buying the ardent on the sly.

As if to confirm his suspicion, a man came staggering out of the building, a paper sack clutched in his right hand. He stopped and, leaning against a lamp post, opened the top of the bag to reveal the neck of a bottle, which he uncorked and brought to his lips. He tilted his head, drank, popped the cork back into the bottle, and staggered down the boardwalk, grinning foolishly, his red-rimmed eyes alight.

When he was almost at the western edge of the town, Cimarron drew rein and, addressing a gray-bearded man seated on the stoop of a tin shop, asked, "Old-timer, can you maybe

28

tell me if a man name of Paul Baldwin still has his ranch two miles west of town on the Canadian River?''

The man studied Cimarron for a moment. After spitting a brown stream of tobacco juice, he remarked, "Uh-yup. Baldwin's still out there on the north bank of the river. But who knows for how long?''

Cimarron, his hands folded around his saddle horn, asked, "What might you mean by that?''

"Someone took a pot shot at Paul Baldwin not long ago."

Cimarron said nothing.

The old man said, "Somebody might take another pot shot at him, and this time that somebody might not miss.''

"I'm obliged to you, old-timer.''

As Cimarron heeled his horse and the dun moved out, the elderly man called after him, "You wouldn't happen to be that somebody, now would you, son?''

Without looking back, Cimarron shook his head and rode out of the town, which was situated in the southeastern corner of the Sac and Fox reservation. He followed the sharply twisting Canadian River on his left and soon came within sight of a two-story clapboard house, which he believed was the home of Paul Baldwin. The home of Paul Baldwin and his sister, Miranda, he corrected himself. Miranda, who, he recalled, had been described as "pretty" by Marshal Upham back in Fort Smith. He nodded thoughtfully to himself as he approached the house. Will she be blonde, he wondered, or brunette? Blue- or brown-eyed? He decided it didn't matter which. I like the ladies either way, he thought. The pretty ones along with the plain. And if I've been alone too long, I don't much mind if they even turn out to be homely. A man takes what he can get when he can get it. Grinning, he hoped he would have a chance to "get" Miranda Baldwin. Pretty Miranda Baldwin.

He drew rein and slid out of the saddle when he reached the neatly painted house. He wrapped his reins around the hitchrail that stood in front of the house and then climbed the steps to the porch. Standing under the wide overhang, he knocked on the front door.

It was opened almost immediately by a young woman. She wasn't just pretty, he thought; she comes close to being beautiful. Hair the color of coal hung halfway down her back in a pony tail. Her clear eyes were the color of walnuts. She had a broad forehead, a small nose with narrow nostrils, and full, decidedly sensuous, lips.

And a body, he thought as his eyes roamed up and down it, that could offer a whole lot of comfort to a lusty man like me. Those breasts of hers look to be about to burst through that tight chambray dress she's wearing. So do her hips. She's as long-legged as a cavalry remount. And just about as glossy-complected.

"Yes?" The word was a challenge, as was the appraising look the woman was giving Cimarron.

"Afternoon," he greeted her. "Would you happen to be by any chance Miss Miranda Baldwin?"

"I am. And you are—"

"Name's Cimarron, Miss Baldwin. I'm a deputy marshal out of Fort Smith. Marshal Upham told me you were in need of a lawman to look into what happened to your brother."

Miranda made a sour face. "I suppose I am in need of someone like yourself. A regrettable situation."

"Regrettable?"

"I've heard stories about the scoundrels who ride for Judge Parker."

"Scoundrels?"

"I am well aware of how you deputies have been known to scandalize decent citizens of both sexes with your rowdy carousing and atrocious womanizing in houses of ill repute."

"Well, Miss Baldwin, I suppose some of what you say is true. But what you've got to understand is that deputies, as a general rule, live a hard life while they're out trailing miscreants and malefactors, so it shouldn't come as all that much of a surprise when they kick up their heels whenever they get the chance to. I hope you won't keep on thinking too unkindly of the breed to which I happen to belong."

Miranda's eyes narrowed, and Cimarron decided the encounter was definitely going badly. He was off on the wrong foot, he reckoned, not a doubt about it. Searching for a way to right matters between himself and Miranda Baldwin, he said, "I hope I'll have the chance to prove to you that us deputies, we're not as black as some like to paint us. I hope I can be of some service to you, Miss Baldwin." He made a conscious effort to keep from leering as the word "service"

30

he had just spoken echoed in his mind, and he thought of the many ways he would like to service the lovely Miranda Baldwin.

"Come in, please."

Cimarron followed Miranda into the house, and when she had seated herself in the sunny parlor, he sat down across from her.

"Are you good with a gun, Cimarron?"

Her question took him by surprise. His right hand settled on the butt of his Colt. "I reckon I can hold my own in any gunplay I might get involved in."

"Have you ever killed a man?"

Taken aback by Miranda's blunt question, Cimarron hesitated a moment before answering, "Yep, I have. More than once. In my line of work—well, sometimes killing's a part of it, though I have no fondness for it and try my best to avoid it if I can."

"But you wouldn't hesitate to gun down a would-be murderer?"

"Miss Baldwin, I got to say you sure do ask a man some unsettling questions. What's lying behind them?"

Miranda settled back in her chair, crossed her ankles, folded her hands in her lap, and replied, "A man tried to kill my brother, Paul, but succeeded only in wounding him. His name is Clyde Hunter. He's a Fox Indian. I want you to find him and kill him so that my brother's life will no longer be in danger."

Cimarron held up a hand. "Hold on a minute, Miss Baldwin. Let me ask you a question or two of my own. This Clyde Hunter, you saw him shoot your brother?"

"No, I did not."

"Then it was your brother who saw him do the deed."

"No, it wasn't."

"Then how come you're so sure this fellow Hunter's the one who shot your brother if neither you nor your brother saw him do it?"

"Clyde Hunter, Cimarron, is an educated Fox Indian, which is, in my opinion, one of the worst kind of Indians. They tend to think they know it all, and they like lording it over other Indians and any white men with whom they come into contact. Hunter has been an enemy of my brother—and other cattlemen—almost from the moment he returned from the East, where he attended school.''

"Enemy?''

"Hunter has a notion that it is wrong for any Fox land to be leased to white ranchers for grazing purposes. He has spoken out—most volubly and often—against the prevailing practice in tribal councils and in any other forum afforded him. He has made threats against cattlemen like my brother. He has urged that the Indians band together and run such men as my brother off what Hunter is pleased to call Fox land. Fox land indeed! My brother applied for and received a perfectly legal permit from the Indian Bureau through the Indian agent here on the reservation, Mr. Abel Garth, which allows him the use of the land on which he has been grazing our cattle.''

"I hope you don't mind me being a bit blunt, Miss Baldwin, but what this thing looks like to me is you've got nothing but a suspicion that it was this Clyde Hunter who shot at your brother and not even a little bit of proof to back up that suspicion of yours.''

Miranda's eyebrows rose. "But I've just explained it all to you in as simple and straightforward a manner as possible. Surely you can understand that Hunter has to be the one who tried to kill Paul.''

"Maybe your brother has other enemies he don't know anything about. Do you think maybe that's possible?''

"Well, of course that is possible . . .''

Cimarron smiled.

". . . but not at all probable. My brother is a very well-liked man, Cimarron, by both Indians and whites alike. You can ask anyone. Paul is an easy man to get along with. He's friendly. He's not a troublemaker.''

"I'd like to have a talk first with your brother himself, Miss Baldwin. Where might he be found, do you know?''

"He's out on the range making hay with the hired hands. I'll be happy to take you to him.''

When Miranda rose, so did Cimarron. She excused herself and returned a little while later wearing jeans and a blue cotton blouse. He followed her outside and, leading his dun, walked with her to the barn some distance behind the house.

When they reached it, he left his dun ground hitched

32

outside it and, after entering the barn, offered to saddle the mare Miranda had indicated she intended to ride.

"I can manage on my own quite nicely, thank you," was her somewhat chilly response.

He shrugged and watched as she got her buckskin ready to ride, thinking that Miranda Baldwin was certainly a competent young woman who went at a task directly and got it done with no waste motion or delay. When she had made sure her cinch was properly tightened, she led the mare out of the barn. Cimarron followed her, admiring the way her hips swiveled seductively as she walked slightly ahead of him. With those hips of hers, he thought with some amusement, she could grind a man down to dust in no time at all. And, oh, my, wouldn't that be a wonderful way to die!

"What are you smiling about?" she asked him, swinging into the saddle.

"I couldn't tell you that," he responded, "or we might not get to be friends, which I hope we will get to be."

"Were you thinking of me as you must think of those professional women you encounter from time to time here in the Territory?"

"I was thinking you're a real fine figure of a woman is what I was thinking and I heartily hope you won't misread my meaning or think I'm insulting you. You see, I'm a man who just can't help admiring beauty wherever he happens to find it."

"I thank you for the compliment, Cimarron," Miranda said as they left the house behind them. "But I must also give you a word of warning."

"What word did you have in mind?"

"I am a very independent woman. I have no need of anyone else in this world. I certainly have no need of a man. Our relationship is and will remain one that is properly professional and strictly businesslike. You are a lawman with a job to do. I've arranged for you to come here to do that job. That is the nature and extent of our relationship. Is that quite clear?"

"Oh, it's clear as spring water, Miss Baldwin. And about as disappointing as a broken dam during the spring melt."

"A woman more or less alone out here in this savage land," Miranda continued, "must think of her reputation.

33

She must be circumspect and discreet. It is all too easy for a woman in my position to slip ever so slowly into a slough of degradation here in a land where the niceties of civilization are, by and large, missing from one's daily life.''

"It seems to me that you've been doing a good job of staying clear of that slough of degradation and staying civilized, Miss Baldwin. I noticed you had a spinet in your parlor and lace doilies on your tables and chairs.''

"I do my best under what are decidedly adverse circumstances.'' Miranda threw Cimarron a sidelong glance before continuing. "I'm surprised you noticed such things as my spinet and lace doilies.''

"I'm a man who keeps his eyes open to the world around him. It pays off, living like that. You can spot things that are out of kilter that way long before they can cause you any trouble.''

"You and I, Cimarron, we're of two different worlds. Yours is a world, I dare say, of unbridled passions. Violence is no stranger to you, and neither, I suspect, are the still baser passions I referred to before when we first met. I, on the other hand, am a woman sensitive of soul and a stranger to the baser appetites that can so often spell the downfall of any unwary man or woman.''

"A whole lot of what you say is true,'' Cimarron agreed, "but I wonder why it is you seem so eager to build a big fence around yourself. Is it to keep men like me out—or you safe inside?''

"I think that is an absurd speculation,'' Miranda retorted with a faint edge of anger in her tone. "It is also rather rude. A gentleman does not pry into a lady's innermost thoughts and emotions.''

"I never have worn the brand of gentleman, and I reckon it's way too late for me to start trying to now.'' Cimarron paused briefly. "Maybe *I* ought to give *you* a word of warning. I've always been a man who just won't be stopped by fences or even forts. Not if I should find I have a hankering to climb over a fence or bust into a fort.''

"That sounds like a threat,'' Miranda remarked in a low tone without looking at Cimarron.

"That's not a threat, Miss Baldwin,'' he quickly assured her. "That's a promise,'' he added and gave her a grin.

But if she saw his grin, she gave no sign. She rode on with Cimarron at her side, her eyes aimed directly ahead of her, her face expressionless. They rode that way, Cimarron's silence matching Miranda's, until they came within sight of a half-dozen men scattered about in the distance.

"My brother," Miranda announced, pointing to a man with a rolled red bandanna tied around his forehead to serve as a sweatband. He was pitching hay into one of several wagons that stood in the midst of the men. "And his hired hands."

She and Cimarron rode up to Baldwin and dismounted. "Paul," Miranda said, "this man is a deputy marshal who has come here as a result of my visit to Marshal Upham in Fort Smith. He intends to apprehend the man who shot you. His name is Cimarron. Cimarron, may I present my brother, Paul."

Paul Baldwin shielded his eyes from the sun with one hand, staring hard at Cimarron for a long moment before he broke into a broad smile and held out his right hand.

Cimarron shook it, studying the man as he did so. Baldwin was a tall man, almost as tall as Cimarron himself, and he had the same kind of wiry body that suggested a lean strength. His eyes were a darker shade of brown than those of his sister, and Cimarron thought he detected a wariness in them that was missing from Miranda's. He had the same high forehead as his sister and the same full sensuous lips. His hair, damp now with sweat, was as black as Miranda's, and there was a dark stubble stippling his cheeks and chin.

"I hate to say this, Deputy," Baldwin began, "but I think you've wasted your time in coming here."

"You do? How come?"

"Because I want to put the matter that has brought you here at my sister's ill-advised request behind me once and for all."

"But, Paul," Miranda protested, "you can't do that!"

"Ah, but I can, my dear," Baldwin smoothly assured her. "And I most sincerely want to do just that."

"But it could happen again, and next time you might not be merely wounded. You might be—" Miranda left her sentence unfinished.

Baldwin turned to Cimarron and said, "I appreciate your

35

coming here. But, as far as I'm concerned, the matter is over and done with. There was no need for you to come here in the first place and no need for you to remain here now that you know how I feel.''

"It's my job,'' Cimarron said, "to look into matters like the one you were mixed up in. Whoever fired that shot at you broke the law, and it's up to me to see that he pays the price.''

"Should you apprehend the culprit,'' Baldwin said in a flat voice, "I will not press charges against him.''

"Paul!'' an obviously shocked Miranda exclaimed.

"Be that as it may,'' Cimarron said as flatly, "I'm here now, and I'd like to hear what you can tell me about what happened to you.''

"Then I have failed to persuade you to simply let the matter drop?'' Baldwin asked, and when Cimarron answered, "That's right, you have,'' he sighed and said, "Do you mind if I and my men finish the day's haying first?'' Without waiting for an answer, he continued, "Why don't you and Miranda go and sit in the shade under that tree over there? We'll wind things up here for today in under an hour, I promise you.''

"If you'll excuse me, Miss Baldwin,'' Cimarron said, "I'll lend a hand with the haying. That way it'll get done sooner, and I'll get to talk turkey with your brother sooner than I otherwise would.''

Miranda acknowledged Cimarron's decision with a nod before turning and heading for the shade afforded by a locust tree growing in the distance.

"You got an extra pitchfork, Baldwin?'' Cimarron asked.

"I'm afraid not. But I'll tell you what you can do if you're willing.''

Moments later, Cimarron had one of Baldwin's rakes in his hands and was raking out a tall pile of cut alfalfa and sweet clover, spreading it in a thin layer on the ground where the sun would dry it so it could be used as winter fodder. He was hard at work on a second pile some time later when Baldwin called his name and announced that it was time to call it a day. Cimarron stored his rake in one of the haywagons, and then, as Baldwin beckoned to Miranda and she rejoined the men, Cimarron swung into the saddle and rode beside the first of the loaded haywagons as it headed back to the ranch.

Once there, Baldwin gave instructions to his men to drive the wagons to the barn and store the gathered hay in the loft before they stopped work for the day.

"I'll get supper ready," Miranda volunteered. "You'll stay and have some with us, won't you, Cimarron?" Without waiting for his answer, she added, "And you are, of course, welcome to spend the night with us."

Baldwin frowned and then said to Cimarron, "I see Miranda is determined to aid and abet you in launching your investigation into the shooting. So be it, then." He laid a heavy hand on Cimarron's shoulder. "I hope you won't misinterpret the things I said out on the range earlier, Cimarron. I didn't mean to be hostile toward you. I do appreciate your interest in the matter and any efforts you may see fit to make on my behalf."

"Maybe I can make a small contribution to our supper," Cimarron said. "I shot a wild hog earlier today. A nice lean critter. I cooked and ate some of him, but I've got a goodly amount of sidemeat left, which you're welcome to."

"Thank you," Miranda said as Cimarron pulled the pork from his saddlebag and handed it to her.

Then, when she had gone to the barn, Baldwin held out his hand. "I'll take your horse and put him up for the night," he said. "You go inside and make yourself comfortable. You can wash up in the kitchen."

Cimarron got out of the saddle and handed his reins to Baldwin, who rode off, leading the dun. He was in the kitchen, stripped to the waist and vigorously washing his face and torso, when the back door opened and Miranda entered the kitchen.

"Oh!" she exclaimed in surprise when she saw that the room was occupied. She took a step toward the door leading to the front of the house but halted when Cimarron straightened and stood facing her, rivulets of water running down his chest and dripping from his chin. His eyes were on her; hers on his bare torso. She stood there, seemingly transfixed as she stared at him. Slowly her eyes rose until they locked with his. Her lips parted and Cimarron waited for what she was about to say. But, instead of speaking, she licked her lips and swallowed hard.

He took a towel from the rack above the sink and slowly began to dry himself, running the towel up one arm, across his chest, and down the other arm. Miranda watched him intently as though his languid movements had hypnotized her. He moved slowly toward her, and when she did not withdraw from him, he dropped the towel and took her in his arms. She seemed to flow into him, the curves of her body blending warmly with his own. Her hands were at her sides, her cheek pressed against his chest. He cupped her chin in his hand, raised her head, and kissed her on the lips.

She suddenly stiffened, gave him a startled stare, slapped his face, and ran from the room.

Three

That night at supper, Miranda was cool and composed, at times boldly meeting Cimarron's searching gaze as if nothing had happened between them in the kitchen.

The conversation during the main part of the meal concerned the ranch—the prices cattle were currently bringing at the railheads in Kansas, Baldwin's plans to finish haying in the next few days, his hope that rain wouldn't arrive to spoil his plans and possibly ruin the hay he had spread out to dry. Baldwin spoke of the ever-increasing cost of such necessary items as rock salt, which he intended to spread the next day for his cattle, of how such sharply rising prices cut into the profit to be earned on a ranch such as his own, and of the winter that was coming and how it might affect the stock.

Cimarron complimented Miranda on the meal. "I have to tell you, Miss Baldwin, the sauce on that blueberry pudding you served, it sure did satisfy my sweet tooth. What did you put in it to give it such a fine flavor?"

Miranda flushed and looked down at the food on her plate, which she had barely touched. "Sugar," she murmured, "and rose water and a touch of ground nutmeg."

"I don't know what I'd do without Miranda," Baldwin remarked expansively. "She brings the joys of civilization to this wilderness we're both mired in."

"What made the two of you come here?" Cimarron asked. "And where'd you come from, if you don't mind my asking?"

"New Orleans," Baldwin said, answering Cimarron's second question first. And then, "When Father died, he left Miranda and me a little money—he was in the real estate business in New Orleans—and after I'd been running his business alone for nearly a year I decided to pull up stakes and come up here to Indian Territory." Baldwin glanced at his sister, as if he expected her to say something.

She did. "Paul and I hope to make the money Father left us grow as our stock-raising business grows. Then we can return to civilization again and enjoy the fruits of our labors."

Cimarron caught the black glance Baldwin gave his sister as she concluded her remarks. "What about the shooting?" he asked Baldwin, but his eyes were on Miranda as she rose and began to clear the table.

Baldwin didn't answer the question until Miranda, her hands full of dishes, had left the dining room. Then, "I do wish we could simply forget about that matter, Cimarron. Pretend it didn't happen."

Cimarron, ignoring the remark, said, "Your sister seems sure that a Fox Indian by the name of Clyde Hunter threw down on you."

"Chances are he was the one," Baldwin agreed with evident reluctance.

"But neither you nor Miss Baldwin saw him do the deed, did you?"

"That's correct. No one, including my sister and me, actually saw Hunter fire the shot."

"How did it happen?" Cimarron asked. "Where'd it happen?"

"Out on the range," Baldwin replied. "I and several of my hands were rounding up some strays and bringing them in to our winter range. Miranda was there. She had driven the chuck wagon out to meet us. Someone fired from the brush and hit me. He got away without any of us catching so much as a glimpse of him."

Cimarron thoughtfully stroked his chin. "Maybe whoever it was that fired wasn't aiming at you," he suggested. "Did you ever think of that?"

"No," Baldwin responded quickly. "I never did. Because no one was near me at the time of the shooting. There could be no chance that anyone other than I myself was the gunman's intended target."

"You're sure of that, are you?"

Baldwin nodded. "Miranda was at the wagon a good hundred yards away from me. My men were off in the other

40

direction—at least fifty yards from where I was—bedding the cattle down for the night."

"Baldwin, did you ever stand up to Hunter and tell him you think he was the one who shot you?"

"No."

"How come?"

"Hunter has made himself scarce since the shooting. I haven't seen him since the incident occurred. This whole thing is most unfortunate for everyone concerned," Baldwin mused. "I'm sorry Hunter has no sympathy or understanding for my position as a white rancher here on Fox land, but such is apparently the case."

"Your sister," Cimarron said, "told me Hunter's against anybody other than Indians having anything to do with Indian land."

"That's true. And he is a veritable firebrand who avidly and frequently promulgates that point of view among his people."

Cimarron's gaze shifted from Baldwin to Miranda as she returned to the dining room carrying a coffee pot.

Miranda filled Cimarron's cup with steaming black coffee.

Baldwin said, "Hunter's an idealist, and his idealism, which may be the result of his education at Hampton Institute in Virginia, has changed of late, I'm afraid, into crass cynicism, a fate suffered by many idealists before him. I suppose one might venture to speculate that he drinks as heavily as he does because of his failure to so far make a better life for his people, the Fox."

"Some men I've known in my time," Cimarron said, "find a kind of fury in the bottom of a bottle, which makes them do some pretty hotheaded things."

Miranda, after filling her brother's cup with coffee, placed the coffee pot on a sideboard and resumed her seat at the table. "Hunter has made threats against my brother," she said. "And against other ranchers as well. I told you that."

"But they are, by and large, idle threats," Baldwin insisted. "I'm convinced of that because I have a legal permit to work my land. A permit obtained for me from the Indian Bureau by Abel Grath, who is the agent here on the Sac and Fox reservation."

"Your sister mentioned that to me. But I reckon you know

that Indians—some of them anyway—don't take too kindly to white folks living on what they and the government call their land."

"I must say I can, to a degree, understand their position," Baldwin remarked and lit a cigar.

"Well, I can't!" Miranda sat stiffly with her hands fisted in her lap. "They are most decidedly shortsighted, such Indians as Clyde Hunter. They don't know which side their bread is buttered on."

"Now, now, Miranda," Baldwin soothed. "Let's not be too harsh on Hunter, shall we?"

Miranda refused to meet his gaze and remained rigidly silent in her seat at the table.

Baldwin turned back to Cimarron. "These Fox Indians— they're genuine primitives—even supposedly educated ones like Clyde. At bottom, they can neither be trusted nor expected to make good in a world that is, in reality, no longer theirs. I mean no disrespect—"

Maybe you don't, Cimarron thought, but you sure do sound to me like you mean that Indians don't deserve anything but contempt.

"—but reservation life—the paternalism of the government— are the best things that could possibly happen to the Foxes," Baldwin continued glibly. "The Indians are, after all, only a few years away from a life of utter savagery. It seems to me that they should be grateful to the whites who are willing to confer—to *try* to confer—upon them the graces and amenities of civilization. "However," Baldwin sighed, "they apparently prefer to fly in the face of reason and reality and continue wallowing in the mire and mud of their rather bestial past."

"My sentiments exactly," volunteered Miranda.

Cimarron resisted the urge to argue with the Baldwins as pathetic images of once-proud Indians who were now living on reservations in often drunken and diseased squalor drifted through his mind. "Where might I be liable to find Hunter when I go looking for him?" he asked.

"In the nearest illegal saloon," Miranda snapped waspishly, then quickly added, "or hanging about some poisonous still out in the woods somewhere."

Baldwin shook his head in chagrin and said, "Pay no

attention to Miranda, Cimarron. She's upset, naturally enough, because of what happened to me, and so she tends to make inflammatory statements about Hunter. I'd suggest, to answer your question, that you try visiting the agency. Abel Garth, the Indian agent, ought to be able to tell you if Hunter is there. At one time, Hunter taught school at the agency, but I'm not sure if he continues to do so.''

"I'm obliged to you, Baldwin. I'll head up there first thing in the morning.''

"Very well. And now, Cimarron, may I suggest that you join me in the parlor, where I can offer you a fine French Chablis I brought here from New Orleans.''

Cimarron followed Baldwin into the parlor and accepted the glass of white wine the rancher poured for him. He was on his second Chablis when Miranda reappeared and, at her brother's suggestion, seated herself at the spinet in a corner of the room.

As she began to play, Cimarron leaned back in his chair, closed his eyes, and sighed softly with contentment. Miranda's music swirled through the room, and he found himself dreaming of a marble-floored and velvet-curtained ballroom that was crowded with dancers—scenes he had once viewed through a stereopticon with a woman named Marcy while both of them waited impatiently for Marcy's elderly aunt and watchful guardian to go to bed and leave them alone.

As Miranda played on, Cimarron dreamed on about Marcy and all that they had shared when the old aunt had finally gone creaking up the stairs to bed. A smile blossomed on his face. But it vanished when Miranda suddenly announced that she was tired and intended to retire. When she had left the room, he drained his glass, thanked his host for his hospitality, and made his way up the stairs to the bedroom Baldwin had shown him earlier.

He awoke some time later, not knowing how long he had been asleep, and lay listening to the faint *plink-plink-a-plink* of the spinet that drifted up to him from the floor below.

And then he listened with disbelief to the words he heard being sung in a hushed voice by a woman he was sure was Miranda.

Lie down by me lover
Lie down here real quick
I'm in need of some loving
And your great big dick.

He got up, not able to believe he had heard what he nevertheless knew he had just heard, and pulled on his jeans. He left his bedroom and made his way down the hall to the landing, then down the steps as Miranda, in the parlor below, hiccupped and then continued crooning in a sing-song voice.

Do it to me here and do it to me there
Where you do it to me I just don't care.

When he reached the entrance to the parlor he halted and stood staring. Miranda, her long black hair unbound, stood unsteadily in front of her spinet wearing a white cambric nightdress with an eyeletted blue ribbon tied in a bow at her neck. The coal oil lamp on the table beside the spinet sent shadows scurrying across the room and up the walls. Miranda, swaying unsteadily on her feet, raised the glass in her hand, drank from it, and then poured more brandy into it from the bottle resting on the table beside the lamp. She hiccupped, giggled, and then clapped a hand over her mouth. She turned toward the doorway and gasped when she saw Cimarron watching her. Swaying on her feet, she raised her left hand and placed her index finger on her lips.

"Ssshhhh!" she whispered sibilantly.

Cimarron couldn't help smiling as he crossed the room and stopped before her. "You're having a little party all by yourself down here, are you, Miss Baldwin?"

"Sshhhh!" she repeated. "My brother sleepsh like the dead, but I've heard tales about the dead walking when midnight strikes. And call me Miranda, if you don't mind."

Cimarron took the glass from her hand and placed it on the table beside the almost empty brandy bottle.

"Give me that!" Miranda demanded and reached for the glass.

He caught her hand and then, putting his arm around her and picking up the lamp, he began to lead her out of the parlor.

"You came too soon," she slurred as they reached the foot of the stairs.

He wondered what she meant.

44

"I was trying to get up the courage to come to your room," she explained.

"You were going to come to my room? After you went and slapped my face when we met in the kitchen earlier tonight?" That don't make sense to me, he thought. He studied her face, wondering if he would ever be able to understand the ways of women, while strongly suspecting that he would not.

"I was going to"—Miranda hiccupped—"sedush you."

Cimarron, deciding not to look a gift horse in the mouth, took her arm and guided her up the stairs. When they reached the landing, she pointed down the hall. "Thish way. My room's down thish way."

Cimarron led her in the opposite direction and was pleased to find that she offered no resistance to his guidance. Once he had her in his room, he closed the door and took her in his arms. He ran his hands over her body, feeling her warm flesh through the thin cloth of her nightdress.

"Don't!" she murmured and moved his left hand so that it covered her right breast.

"I won't," he promised, stiffening as he fondled her breast.

"You, sir, are a gentleman—*hic*—and a scholar."

"Plus one or two other things besides."

"A soldier and a statesman? Here, let me do that."

She completed what Cimarron had started and a moment later, the blue ribbon that was threaded through the eyelets at the neckline of her nightdress had been untied.

Cimarron drew a deep breath as Miranda slipped her night-dress over her head and stood naked and swaying before him.

"I—" he began.

But Miranda interrupted him with, "You shouldn't parade about in front of ladies half-naked the way you did earlier today."

He was about to speak, but his words died in his throat as Miranda began to unbutton his jeans. When they dropped down around his ankles, he stepped out of them.

Miranda reached out, seized his shaft and, holding tightly to it, led—practically dragged—him to the bed. "Hurry," she whispered, "before I sober up and remember how to behave like a lady."

In the lusty minutes that followed, Cimarron was delighted

to find that Miranda behaved in no way like a lady if that meant behaving modestly and with decorum. She flopped down on the bed and pulled him down on top of her. Her hands went everywhere upon him, and so were her lips as she twisted and turned under and on top of him. She was an avid explorer and he the map of a country she seemed determined to get to know intimately. Her hot hands caressed his face and body. He groaned as he thrust his hardened flesh into her and she, astride him as he lay flat on his back, began to twist her hips and utter little yelps of pure pleasure. The wet juncture of their joined bodies seemed to Cimarron to be the very center of the universe as he thrust upward into Miranda and she began to bounce up and down upon him. He deemed the rest of the world well lost as his pleasure grew steadily, kept increasing—and he exploded.

Miranda cried out as her own body suddenly convulsed in orgasm. She threw back her head and her long black hair cascaded down her back. She made a series of guttural gulping sounds, and then she rose and lay down on the bed. Pulling Cimarron over upon her, she nibbled his lower lip and then huskily asked, "Can you—again?"

"I reckon I can," he replied. "With a woman like you—yep, I'm pretty sure I can." And, to prove his point, he began to buck. Slowly. Gently. And then more rapidly.

Under him, her arms wrapped around his torso and her legs wrapped around his thighs, Miranda matched his eager rhythm, holding him as if she never intended to let him go.

It was some time before Cimarron felt himself beginning the ascent that would take him to another climax. He reveled in the sensations that were flooding through him. He let himself luxuriate in the hot flesh of Miranda's body as he began to soar. He erupted a second time and, Miranda too, as if in response to his orgasm, experienced another one of her own.

They lay there then, still locked together, both of them drained, still, and silent. It was Miranda who spoke first.

"I don't know what possessed me," she murmured.

Cimarron, grinning, thought: I possessed you.

"I have never behaved like this before—so wantonly, I mean." Miranda lowered her gaze.

"It must have been the brandy," Cimarron suggested.

"Yes, the brandy. I couldn't sleep for thinking about

you—for wanting you so badly. I told myself I would have one drink. A small one. To settle my nerves and help me sleep. But then I had another, and I could see you so plainly—it was as if you were right there in the parlor with me. I wanted you. I *needed* you! I decided I would go to your room. I would, that is, as soon as I worked up enough courage to do so. And then—I really don't remember what happened next.''

"You played the spinet and sang some songs."

Miranda gasped. "I remember now. You heard?"

"I thought you had a real nice singing voice."

Miranda smiled faintly and hugged him.

He hugged her back. "It was so good—great."

"Yes, it was, wasn't it? But Paul would probably thrash me if he found out what I did."

"What you did, it's none of your brother's business."

"I know you're right. But I've always felt—ever since Paul and I were children together—that I was somehow responsible to him. That I—oh, I don't know." Miranda paused a moment. "I felt as if life was a game that I had to play by Paul's rules. He's two years older than I am—but that can't be it. I think I—I was afraid of some of the feelings I had when I was a young girl. For boys, I mean. So I suppose I pretended to myself that Paul wouldn't approve of what I was thinking and certainly not of what I wanted to do with one or two of those boys.

"Then, when Father died, I found myself depending upon Paul in much the same way that I had depended upon Father when he was alive. I've never, it seems, been able to live my own life. It always seemed easier to me to do what other people wanted me to do—to be what they expected me to be. Until tonight. Who are you really, Cimarron? What did you do to me?"

"I don't know how to answer you, Miranda, and that's a fact. I'm just a man, and what I did to you—well, it's about the most natural thing in the world."

"I don't mean what you—we—did just now. I mean before— when we first met and later when I saw you shirtless in the kitchen."

Cimarron kissed her lightly on the lips. "It wasn't my doing so much, I reckon, as it was you deciding deep down

47

inside yourself to play the game of life by your own rules for a change instead of by your brother's."

"I don't know why I've always acted as if Paul were the stronger person. He isn't always." Miranda fell silent for a moment and then said, "There's something I should tell you about Paul and me. We didn't choose to pull up stakes and leave New Orleans as Paul told you earlier tonight. We had to leave—and we left in disgrace. One step ahead of the law, as a matter of fact. After Father died, Paul took over his real estate business. Now Father was a scrupulously honest businessman, but Paul, seeking greater and greater profits, began to develop several shady deals involving a number of investors in parcels of land both in and outside of New Orleans. What Paul did, I was very much upset to learn from him later, was swindle those investors out of their money and use it to buy up nearly worthless property in a badly run-down section of the city that he believed was ripe for development. As it turned out, that section simply continued to deteriorate, and Paul lost all of the money that had been paid him by the investors. When they began pressing him to turn over to them the parcels of real estate he was supposed to have purchased for them, Paul's house of cards collapsed. He had to flee."

"But you—you could have stayed. What happened, I take it, it wasn't in any way your fault."

"That's true. It wasn't my fault, and I could have stayed, I suppose. But Paul was distraught. He got drunk one night. He had a gun. That was the night he told me what he had done. I thought he was going to kill himself. I suggested that we go away somewhere together. He finally agreed. He suggested Indian Territory. He said it was a lawless place where none of the men he had swindled would ever find him. And—here we are."

"Miranda, what you just told me about your brother, it raises a question in my mind. Do you think maybe it could have been one of those real estate investors you say your brother swindled who took a shot at him?"

She shook her head. "I too considered that possibility immediately after the shooting. But none of those men knew where we went when we left New Orleans. We left like thieves in the night—with no warning and under cover of darkness."

"Word could have got back to New Orleans about your whereabouts."

"How?"

"In any one of a number of ways. Maybe somebody from New Orleans was passing through the Territory and happened to see your brother. When that somebody got back home, he might have mentioned seeing your brother. Word could have gotten around and into the ears of one or more of the men your brother swindled, who then tried to settle his score with your brother."

Miranda was thoughtful for a moment. And then, "No, I can't really give credence to that theory of yours. I think it's—please don't be offended, Cimarron—quite farfetched."

"Maybe it is. Maybe it's not."

"It was Clyde Hunter who tried to kill my brother," Miranda insisted. "I'm convinced that he was the one who wounded—nearly killed—Paul." She ran a finger over Cimarron's lips. "You'll catch him, won't you?"

"Hunter? I intend to try real hard to. In fact, I'll be heading out after him first thing in the morning."

Miranda kissed Cimarron's cheek. "Good," she said. "That's a truly comforting thought. But meanwhile—I mean morning is simply hours and hours away—"

Cimarron rolled over and entered her again, causing her to moan with pleasure.

Cimarron arrived at the Sac and Fox Agency on the southern bank of the Deep Fork of the Canadian River during midmorning of the following day. He dismounted in front of the largest of the frame buildings that were clustered together as if seeking protection from one another. He wrapped his reins around the hitchrail in front of the building and entered it to find no one in sight.

"Halloo!" he called out and, in response to his shout, a corpulent man wearing a frock coat over a brocade vest appeared from a side door and gave him a cool stare.

"I'm looking for the Indian agent," Cimarron declared. "Are you—"

"I am Abel Garth, sir, at your service."

He's a fat little fellow, Cimarron thought as he appraised Garth. Looks a little bit like a real pale Santa Claus, or a boulder on short legs topped by a smaller bald one. He waxes that skinny little mustache sprouting on his upper lip, and his eyes glitter like pyrites in the sun.

"What may I do for you, sir?" Garth inquired politely but with a touch of impatience in his tone.

"My name's Cimarron. I'm a deputy marshal here in Indian Territory, and at the moment I'm looking for a man named Clyde Hunter. Would you happen to know where I might find him?"

"Ah, Clyde Hunter." Garth folded his hands over his protruding stomach and, with a nod of his head, indicated that Cimarron was to seat himself.

When Cimarron had done so, Garth sat down opposite him and crossed his legs. "Clyde is not here, Deputy. He's here sometimes but not now. I don't know where he is and I suspect, if he's as drunk as he usually is, even he doesn't know where he is. What business have you with Clyde Hunter, if you don't mind my asking? I hasten to add that I ask only because I am concerned about all my charges here on the reservation, Clyde Hunter included. Especially when one of them has aroused the interest of the law, as Clyde has apparently done. I'm sure you understand my position and will take no offense at what might, under other circumstances, be deemed prying on my part."

"Somebody took a shot at a cattle rancher name of Paul Baldwin, and Baldwin's sister, she thinks it might have been this Hunter fellow."

"Ah, so that's it, is it? I suspected that might be what brought you to the reservation, Deputy. A sorry affair, that. Baldwin was almost killed in cold blood."

"What do you know about what happened, Garth?"

"Nothing much other than what is, I gather, general knowledge. Someone shot at Baldwin for reason or reasons unknown, and Baldwin was wounded in the incident but he recovered."

"Do you have any idea who might have done it?"

"I have some ideas, but I caution you they are only that—ideas. Perhaps theories would be a better word. I have no proof. I wasn't there. I—"

"Let's hear your ideas—or theories as you call them."

"Clyde could have done it. He had reason to—at least in his own mind he did."

"He didn't take too kindly to white folks leasing Fox land, I've heard."

"That's correct. Clyde has at times spoken out very ardently—even ferociously—against the practice and has tried to incite his fellow Foxes to take action against the lease holders."

"Action? What kind of action was Hunter after?"

"He wanted to form a posse and run the ranchers off their leased land. In his cups, Clyde Hunter is a violent man, I'm afraid."

"Did he get anybody to throw in with him?"

"No, not that I know of. Most of my charges are passive people. They are resigned to the fortune that fate has meted out to them. Are you at all familiar with the history of the Sac and Fox tribes, Cimarron?"

"I know a little bit about them, not a whole lot. I know they've been driven from pillar to post for a pretty long time."

"That is, if anything, an understatement of the Indians' plight. They have been forced to cede parcels of their land in Iowa, Wisconsin, and Illinois over the last seventy-five years until they now have nothing left but this reservation here in Indian Territory. Most of them were removed to this reservation in 'sixty-seven and to one even smaller parcel of land— the Osage River Reservation in Kansas. A few Indians remain in Iowa, and they have steadfastly battled each cession of Indian land. To this day they continue to resent the loss of their landholdings and the government's attempts at acculturation."

"Can't say as I blame them much if that means, as it mostly does in cases like this, putting a hoe in a hunting man's hands. That don't make him a farmer or happy trying to be one which by his nature, he's not and never has been."

"A few of the Fox Indians here and on the Osage River Reservation in Kansas vow to return to Iowa. Some have already and they've been met by severe hostility from the whites in Iowa. And the proper division of annuity payments among the Iowa, Kansas, and Indian Territory factions of the tribe is a continual source of friction among the Indians, between these factions and this agency, and also between them and the federal government as represented by both Congress and the Indian Bureau in Washington."

"We seem to be straying far afield here, Garth," Cimarron pointed out. "Or are you sort of suggesting to me that this political friction among the Foxes might have spurred some one of them to take a pot shot at Paul Baldwin?"

"Which seems, doesn't it, to bring us back again to Clyde Hunter?" Garth said. "He is, I must tell you, a firebrand of one of the more radical Indian factions, a group that wants all 'intruders,' as they are pleased to call them, off Indian land. Fortunately for all of us in this tense and difficult situation, voices of moderation are occasionally raised among the more progressive elements on the reservation. But those who would walk the white man's road are bitterly and sometimes violently opposed by men like Clyde Hunter, who seem to be urging the Foxes to return to the good old days when the Great Spirit smiled on his red children, and the prairies and woods—free of the hated white men—teemed with buffalo, deer, and other game."

"It sounds to me like you've got your hands full running this outfit, Garth."

"My job can be trying, I'll admit. But I want to do all I can for my charges while I can. After all, how's a man's life to be measured if not by how much he can contribute to the well-being of other people who share this vale of tears with him?"

Cimarron was about to respond when the outer door opened and a tall man wearing worn work clothes lunged into the room. "Garth, I got to talk to you!"

"Hello, Earl," Garth said as the man's eyes fell on Cimarron. "May I introduce Deputy Marshal Cimarron. Cimarron, this is my colleague and good right arm, Earl Briggs, without whom I would never be able to manage this agency."

Briggs stood in the middle of the room, his sharp black eyes on Cimarron. "What's the law want here?"

"Cimarron is looking into the shooting of Paul Baldwin," Garth replied.

"Looking into it? What's to look into? Everybody knows it was Clyde Hunter who shot Baldwin."

52

"How'd everybody find out that fact, Briggs?" Cimarron asked in a level voice.

"Well," Briggs drawled, "it's common knowledge is what I meant. Folks talk."

"And you listen, do you?"

"Well, sure I do. Everybody knows that Hunter's one real bad Indian. The man can't handle his liquor."

"No one saw Hunter do the shooting, Earl," Garth pointed out. He went on to lecture Briggs on charity and the presumption of innocence until guilt was proven.

As Garth talked on in his smooth voice, Cimarron silently appraised Earl Briggs. The man looks like he could use a bath, he thought. Not to mention a shave and a change into some clean clothes. He noted the patches of red dust on Briggs's clothes and the thick film of the same red dust that covered his badly scarred boots. He didn't like the look of Briggs. But he wasn't sure why. Maybe it's the way the man slouches instead of standing up straight, he thought. Maybe it's the way he is so quick to pounce on Clyde Hunter and accuse him of shooting Paul Baldwin. Or maybe it's just the way the man seems to snarl his words rather than speak them. Whatever it is, he thought, the man rubs me wrong.

"Have you seen Hunter recently?" Garth asked Briggs.

"I seen him, sure I did."

"Where?" Garth and Cimarron asked Briggs in unison.

"Out in back of the agency school," Briggs answered.

"Was he sober?" Garth asked.

"No," Briggs said, "he sure as hell wasn't. He was drunk as usual."

Garth glanced at the banjo clock on the wall. "Thank heaven the children have all gone home for the day."

Cimarron rose. "Can you gentlemen point me in the direction of the agency school?"

It was Garth, in the face of Briggs's almost sullen silence, who gave Cimarron the directions he had requested.

"I'm obliged to you," Cimarron told the agent and left the building.

Leading his horse, he strode down the dusty path that led away from the agency's headquarters, heading for the school. As he approached it, he saw a young woman hurrying toward it from the opposite direction. As she rounded one side of the

53

schoolhouse, he rounded the other, and they met in the rear of the building.

"Have you seen Mr. Hunter?" she asked Cimarron.

"Nope. But I was looking for him like it seems you are."

"He's gone," she remarked forlornly. "I've come too late."

"Did you have some business to conduct with him?" Cimarron asked her.

"Oh, I wish I were a man!" she exclaimed.

Cimarron knew he didn't share her wish. If she were to turn into a man, he thought—it hurts me just to think about all the loveliness that'd be lost to the world in such an awful event.

"If I were a man," the young woman continued angrily, "I'd thrash that Clyde Hunter for the way he's been ruining his life." The woman frowned. "Who, sir, if I may inquire, are you?"

He introduced himself and showed her his badge.

"Aha!" she cried, wagging a finger at him. "You've come to arrest Clyde for shooting Paul Baldwin!" she accused.

"I—"

"Well, I'm warning you, Deputy. Don't you dare arrest him. If you do, you'll have me to reckon with!"

Cimarron thumbed his hat back on his head and stood with both thumbs hooked in his cartridge belt as he watched the young woman walk briskly away from him, her head held high, her bustle flouncing, and her skirt swirling to reveal her trim ankles.

Four

"Wait!" Cimarron called out and went running after the woman. "I didn't get your name," he said when he caught up with her.

"That's because I didn't give it to you," she replied, and kept on walking.

"Mine's Cimarron." When the woman made no response, he continued, "What made you think I was out to arrest Clyde Hunter?"

"That's easy to answer. Everyone in town has heard that Miranda Baldwin went to Fort Smith to lodge a complaint against Clyde, and everyone also knows that she insists that Clyde was the one who fired on her brother—and all of these accusations of hers are made without a single shred of proof!"

"Well, I'm not going to arrest Clyde Hunter," Cimarron announced.

When the woman suddenly halted, so did Cimarron. As she stared quizzically at him, he added, "Not unless Hunter's guilty of the crime he's accused of, I'm not. But if he is the one who tried to ventilate Baldwin—well, that's a horse of a different color."

The woman's face had assumed a hopeful expression, but at Cimarron's last words it fell. As she turned to leave, Cimarron grabbed her arm.

"Let me go!" she cried indignantly.

He held her tightly. "I reckon you must have heard, the same as I did, that Hunter was making a ruckus at the school. Like me, you came looking for him. I had my reason to try to find him. What was yours?"

When the woman's lips set themselves in a tight little line,

Cimarron sighed, and said, "You seem to think Hunter's innocent of the crime he's been accused of. So didn't it ever occur to you that you ought to tell a lawman like me why you think he's innocent so I can turn my attention from him to the truly guilty one?"

The woman's lips began to quiver. She blinked back tears. "But I don't know if Clyde is innocent or not," she cried. "He told me he is and I believe him, but I can't prove it. He can't either because he was on a bender at the time of the shooting and has no idea where he was or what he was doing. So he has no alibi for the time in question."

"Maybe he was out on the range with Baldwin in his gun's sights."

"He wasn't!" the woman insisted. "Clyde is not a killer!"

"Maybe he wasn't aiming to kill. Maybe he was bent on throwing a scare into Baldwin, hoping to run him off the land he's grazing his beeves on."

The woman shook her head. "I know Clyde is not capable of doing a thing like that. Oh, he's a hot-tongued talker, all right. There's no doubt about that. And he doesn't like the idea of Abel Garth leasing Fox land to white men for any purpose. But a killer he is not! I'd stake my life on that."

"You sound like you're fairly well acquainted with Hunter."

"We work together from time to time. When he's sober. I run a Christian mission school for Indian children, and sometimes Clyde would come and teach our children. Mostly, he taught them the history of the Foxes. But he also taught them wonderful things like pride and dignity and self-respect. The children loved him."

"You still haven't told me your name."

"It's Bonner. Isabel Bonner."

"Miss or Mrs.?"

"Miss Isabel Bonner."

"What did you have in mind to do if you caught up with Hunter down there behind the schoolhouse?"

"Take him to the mission and try to sober him up. Try to talk some sense into him. I've done it before when he's gone on one of his benders."

"If you'd like, I'll walk you back to your mission."

After Isabel had acknowledged Cimarron's offer with a brief nod, the two of them made their way between two buildings, across the wide dirt path that paralleled them, and into a two-story building on the far side of the path.

"This is the mission," Isabel announced as they stood in the shadowy hallway just inside the front door. In there is our schoolroom and over here is the parlor. Will you come in and sit down, Cimarron?"

He did and then accepted Isabel's offer of a cup of coffee. When she brought it to him, he took a sip and said, "It's an interesting thing."

"What is?" Isabel asked as she seated herself across from him.

"Here on the one hand is a woman—you—ready to stand up and fight for Hunter, and on the other hand there's another woman—Miranda Baldwin—who seems bound and determined to see the same man jailed. This Hunter, he must be quite some kind of fellow to get two such lovely ladies all hot under the collar where he's concerned. One for him and one against him."

And the two women were lovely, Cimarron thought. Miranda in a dark and somewhat sultry way. Isabel Bonner in a bright sunlit way with her blonde hair, pale skin, pink lips, and lake-blue eyes. They're as different-looking as night and day, he thought. But both of them are pretty as pictures, each one in her own way.

"Clyde is a passionate man," Isabel stated. "Such a man tends to arouse the passions of women. Either for or against him."

"Miss Baldwin seems sure that it was Hunter who fired on her brother on account of, I'm told, Hunter liked to talk trouble against white ranchers like Baldwin who've been leasing Fox land."

"Clyde did speak out against the practice, yes. Many times. But he would never resort to violence to accomplish his ends."

"By his ends I take it you mean ridding the reservation of white ranchers."

"Yes. Clyde wanted the tribal council to offer the legal residents of the reservation—the Foxes—a referendum so that they could make their wishes on the matter known. He was confident that the vote would go against the leasing of land to whites. As a white woman, I tried at first to persuade him to

57

live and let live. However, in the end, it was Clyde who convinced me of the validity of his position.

"He insisted that each encroachment of Fox land by whites, however small in and of itself, spelled ultimate doom for the Foxes as a cohesive people joined together by both their shared history and their commonly owned land. Clyde was fond of saying that if you take a man's home from him you have also taken his heart without which he cannot live. The Foxes have had their land taken from them before—many times. Clyde was keenly aware of that and determined not to let history repeat itself here. He was, you see, involved in what was essentially a political battle on one level, an economic problem on another, and a struggle for the survival of an ancient people and their equally ancient ways on still another level.''

"This political battle you speak of," Cimarron said, "is between the conservative and the progressive factions of the tribe, am I right?"

"Yes. And the economic struggle is one of attempted self-sufficiency on the one hand and government handouts on the other—whether those handouts take the form of money returned to the Foxes from the land leases or from the government's annuity payments.''

"And the struggle for survival you mentioned, by that you mean, I reckon, keeping the old Indian ways alive in the face of the white world trying hard to push them aside.''

"Not just push them aside, but in many cases, stamp them out by degrading their practitioners. By selling whiskey to the Indians, for example. By encouraging them to gamble. By paying them for the use of their land and thus automatically forcing many of them into lives of idleness where they become content to depend on the income from their leases and have little or no interest in trying to better themselves or their families.''

Before Cimarron could reply there was a knock on the front door, and Isabel rose to answer it. When she returned to the parlor there was an elderly Indian with her.

"Cimarron, may I present Mokohoko, Clyde Hunter's uncle. Mokohoko, this is the deputy marshal I just mentioned to you.''

Cimarron rose and shook hands with the old man.

58

"You have come to take my nephew to jail?" Mokohoko asked in a quavering voice.

"Nope, I've not," Cimarron answered and the old man, who was barely five feet tall with a seamed brown face and shining black eyes, expelled his breath, making a faint hissing sound. "Not unless it turns out your nephew's guilty of a crime."

"My nephew did not shoot Paul Baldwin," Mokohoko stated.

"I told him that," Isabel said to the old man. And then, to Cimarron, "Mokohoko has come here to the mission, he told me, because he heard that Clyde was causing a disturbance at the schoolhouse. When he didn't find Clyde there, he came here, knowing that I sometimes bring Clyde here to try to help him when he's drunk."

"My nephew does not know if he is a red man or a white man," Mokohoko murmured, sadly shaking his head. "His mother should not have married a white man. My nephew is a man torn in two by his mixed blood."

"Halfbloods, I grant you, can have trouble on account of who they are," Cimarron said to the old man. "I've seen it happen. But it seems to me that being a halfblood by itself, that's not enough to lead a man down the road to rack and ruin. More likely, it's the way a halfblood looks at himself. The way he thinks about himself. If he lets himself get all mixed up about who and how he ought to be—"

"I sent him to the white man's school because I wanted him to learn to live in the white man's world," Mokohoko said and sighed. "I thought it was the right thing to do. There is no room left in this world for the red man. The whites fill it now. They squeeze us out." Mokohoko turned and headed for the front door.

Isabel gave Cimarron a worried glance and then hurried after the old man. She returned minutes later and announced, "Mokohoko blames himself for Clyde's behavior. I've tried to tell him it isn't his fault. Clyde is a grown man and must assume responsibility for himself and for what he does. But poor old Mokohoko won't listen to me. I think he feels so badly because he had such high hopes for Clyde. And the ironic thing about all this is the fact that Mokohoko put Clyde through Hampton Institute in Virginia with the funds he obtained by leasing almost all of the acreage he once farmed. He lived during those years from hand to mouth. But he didn't care a fig about himself, only about Clyde. His friends and neighbors helped him scrape through, and of course he received his annuity payments. But they were hard years for him nonetheless.''

"And now the old fellow sees all his efforts slipping down the drain on account of the way his nephew's turned out.''

"Yes, that about sums it up, I suppose.''

"It was a pleasure talking to you, Miss Bonner,'' Cimarron said.

"Please call me Isabel. I hope we'll be friends.''

"I hope we will be too, Isabel. Now, if you'll excuse me, I think I'll mosey around and see if I can't get a line on Hunter—find out where he's gone to ground.''

Isabel accompanied Cimarron to the front door. When they were standing on the front porch of the mission, she asked, "Are you coming to the mission fair this afternoon?''

"The mission fair? This is the first I've heard there was to be one.''

"The annuity payments are to be made beginning at noon, and right afterward the mission is having a fair. We sell cakes and pies and our children's handicrafts and try in other ways to raise money at the fair for our charitable work. I do hope you'll come.''

"I'll be there, you can count on it,'' Cimarron assured Isabel and thought, I'll be there for two real good reasons. On account of a pretty lady like yourself'll be at the mission fair and because maybe Clyde Hunter'll show up at it too.

The noonday sun streamed down upon Cimarron as he leaned against the front of the agency building. He watched the Indians in the long line that snaked away from the desk on the building's porch, behind which Abel Garth and Earl Briggs sat.

Each Indian, as he approached the desk, spoke his name. Garth checked it against a list of names that were on a paper in front of him, and he told Briggs how much the man was to be paid. Briggs then counted out the money due and handed it to the Indian, who then made way for the next man in line.

In the distance, someone let out a war whoop. It was followed by the sound of music—a fiddle and a drum.

Peering through the hazy air, Cimarron made out the figures of several dancing men, all Indians. Women stood to one side watching the dancers, some with babies, most with happy smiles on their dusky faces. Cimarron turned his attention in the opposite direction and saw the cluster of tables that had been set up in and around the mission building to display pies and cakes, sealed jars of preserves and pickles, and handicrafts of many kinds. Behind the tables were women, both Indian and white, of all ages. Moving among them, apparently giving them last-minute instructions, was Isabel Bonner. Cimarron's eyes followed her, roaming over her shapely body and coming to rest on her face. As she turned in his direction and caught sight of him, she smiled faintly.

A young Indian boy wearing jeans, a cotton shirt, and clodhoppers came running up to Cimarron. "I saw him!" the boy cried, glancing back over his shoulder. "He's over there!" The boy pointed to a crowd that had gathered in front of a squat Indian standing on a wooden crate and speaking earnestly to his listeners.

"Which one is he?" Cimarron asked the boy.

"Clyde Hunter's the one without a hat," the boy answered and then held out his hand.

Cimarron rummaged about in a pocket of his jeans and came up with the twenty-five cents he had promised to pay the boy if he pointed out Clyde Hunter. As the boy went scurrying away, Cimarron made his way toward the crowd that the orator was so enthusiastically haranguing.

"—and so I say to you *rebel!*" roared the man standing on the crate as Cimarron joined the crowd, taking up a position to the right of the man identified as Clyde Hunter. "Close your ears to those who tell you to take your children out of the mission school so that you will not hear the wicked words they speak. Close your eyes to them when they beckon to you and say, 'Come back with me to Iowa where life will again be good for the Mesquakie.' "

"What's he talking about?" Cimarron asked Hunter. "I mean who or what are the Mesquakie?"

Hunter gave Cimarron a scornful glance and responded sharply. "I would not expect a white man to know the answer

61

to that question. What white man knows anything of Mesquakie history?''

"I asked you in good faith," Cimarron responded calmly. "I don't know why you've got your back up. I sure didn't mean to get you riled up."

Hunter's black eyes, which had been blazing as he listened to the speaker, softened. "Sorry, friend," he said in a more temperate tone. "It's just that know-nothing Indians like Hardfish up there get under my skin. Mesquakie is the correct name for what you whites call the Foxes."

As Hardfish pleaded with the crowd to 'embrace the white world and its ways,' as he put it, Cimarron spoke to Hunter. "I never heard the name Mesquakie before. But then folks say there's a first time for everything, and I reckon they're right on that score."

"The misnomer first occurred in the seventeenth century when a Frenchman questioned one of the Mesquakie about who he was, and the man identified himself by clan rather than tribe, as was our custom then. He called himself a Fox, which was the name of his clan, so the Frenchman began calling us all Foxes. The name has persisted to this day since the American authorities in the Central Superintendency of the Indian Bureau also insist on calling us Foxes and not by our true name, Mesquakie—which, by the way, means 'People of the Red Earth.' The name comes from the fact that we believe we were created from the Red Earth."

"I'm obliged to you for taking the time and trouble to straighten me out on the matter. I don't much relish being as ignorant as I am about some things."

Hunter's expression, which had been stiff and unyielding, relaxed. He almost smiled at Cimarron. "This is the first time I ever heard a white man admit he was ignorant of some aspect of Indian history. Or, more importantly, express a desire to learn the truth about any particular Indian matter."

As Cimarron once again turned his attention to Hardfish, the man exclaimed, "Lift up your spirits, my brothers and sisters! A new day dawns and a new spirit is abroad in the land!"

Out of the corner of his eye, Cimarron saw Hunter take a surreptitious swig from a bottle he took from his hip pocket. After corking the bottle and returning it to his pocket, he shouted, "Hardfish, just what is this new spirit that you claim is abroad in the land?"

Hardfish tried to ignore Hunter's heckling but Hunter persisted. "Do you refer to the earth that is a spirit—and our grandmother? But that cannot be, since the earth is an ancient and not a new spirit."

"Send your children to the mission school—"

Hunter laughed derisively and without humor. "Don't change the subject, Hardfish! Tell us about spirits. Do you speak of the snow and the trees, which are, as we Mesquakies know, also spirits who guide and protect us? Or do you speak of the moon, the spirit of the wolf? Of the sun perhaps, which is also a spirit and our grandfather?"

"Pay no attention to the halfblood!" Hardfish shouted, trying to silence Hunter. "Listen not to his talk of the old days. The days that are dead—"

"They need not be dead!" Hunter shouted at the top of his voice. "We—you, me, all of us—can keep them alive. We *must* keep them alive!"

"Why do you turn away from the new day, Hunter?" Hardfish asked. "You of all people, who are as much a white man as a red one—"

Cimarron made a grab for Hunter but missed, as Hunter went plunging angrily through the crowd toward Hardfish.

By the time Cimarron had forced his way through the thick crowd and caught up with his quarry, Hunter had dragged Hardfish down from his makeshift platform and was pummeling him with his fists. Cimarron reached out to seize Hunter, but he was grabbed from behind by two Indians who held him prisoner, his arms pinioned behind him. The crowd split into opposing factions, each of them cheering on their own champion, some backing Hardfish, others Hunter. Cimarron tried to fight free of his captors but, despite his strenuous efforts, failed.

As both men fell to the ground, Hardfish suddenly gained the advantage. Straddling Hunter, he struck the man's face twice with his fists, and blood began to flow from Hunter's nose. Then Hunter managed to land a sharp punch that hit Hardfish in the ribs, knocking the wind from the man. Seizing his opportunity, Hunter managed to topple Hardfish. He sprang to his feet and, to the encouraging cheers of his supporters in the crowd, hauled Hardfish to his feet and landed a series of hard-flung jabs on his opponent's body.

"Get him!" Hardfish gasped, his words barely audible. But some of the men in the crowd heard Hardfish and sprang to his defense. Hunter was quickly bowled over by them. As one of Hardfish's defenders was about to kick the downed Hunter in the head, Cimarron kicked backward and his boot struck the shin of one of his two captors. The man howled in pain and loosened his grip, enabling Cimarron to break free and grab the Indian who was about to kick Hunter. Holding the man by the scruff of the neck, he reached out with his free hand and grabbed another Indian. In one fast and fluid motion, he cracked the skulls of the two men together and then let them fall unconscious to the ground.

Someone behind them let out a wordless yell and slammed a fist into the side of his head. Cimarron spun around and delivered a well-aimed uppercut that almost broke his assailant's jaw.

Hunter got to his feet, and standing shoulder to shoulder with Cimarron, slugged it out with the supporters of Hardfish. Both men managed to hold their own while taking a number of punishing blows on their heads and bodies. They were aided by several other men in the melee who apparently were in sympathy with Hunter's position.

Dust rose in waves around the fighting men, choking and blinding them. Cimarron dodged a badly thrown right cross and dropped the Indian who had thrown it with a left uppercut.

A shot rang out.

Cimarron, blinking and with his eyes watering due to the thick dust, was barely able to make out the figures of several Indian men, all of them armed, standing on the edge of the battling mob.

"Police!" one of them shouted and fired a shot into the air.

"Come on!" Cimarron yelled to Hunter who was pounding a sagging man with both of his fists. When Hunter did not respond, Cimarron reached out and pulled the man to one side. "Let's go!" he muttered. "The Lighthorse police'll have both of us in jail if we don't get the hell out of here fast!"

Hunter gave a curt nod, and he and Cimarron shouldered

their way through the crowd away from the Lighthorsemen. Then they were running, Cimarron in the lead, toward the mission. Cimarron glanced over his shoulder and pointed. Hunter nodded and followed him through the maze of tables and the women staffing them and around the far side of the building, the startled cries of the women a noisy wave in their wake.

When Cimarron halted at the rear of the building, so did Hunter, who smiled and then wiped the blood from his upper lip with the back of his hand. Panting, he said, "I thank you for coming to my aid. Without your help back there Hardfish and his boys probably would have turned me into mincemeat."

"Do you always try settling your quarrels in such a knuckle-and-skull fashion?"

"Not always," Hunter replied somewhat ruefully. "But this time—well, I just got fed up with listening to Hardfish spout his so-called progressive views, which to my mind, will lead to the death of the traditional Mesquakie way of life." Hunter pointed at a group of men in the distance. "That's what comes from embracing the way of the white man."

Cimarron watched in silence as the men Hunter had pointed out passed an uncorked bottle from hand to hand, each of them drinking heartily from it amid much laughter and general merriment.

"Whiskey peddlers," Hunter muttered angrily. "They descend on the agency every annuity day like a plague of locusts."

As Hunter started for the front of the mission, Cimarron grabbed his arm and said, "Wait here. Let me see if the coast is clear or if those boys are still waging war on each other out there." When he had checked and found that the fight had apparently ended, and the fighters had dispersed, he beckoned to Hunter. As the pair moved among the maze of tables which were surrounded by women, Hunter muttered an oath, causing a woman standing next to him to blush and turn away.

"Who might you be damning?" Cimarron asked him.

By way of reply, Hunter pointed to a group of Indians who were seated on the ground not far away. "They will gamble like that all day," he remarked bitterly. "By the time the sun sets—possibly long before then—many of those Mesquakies will have lost their entire annuity payments.

"And by the time the game is finished," Hunter continued, as he and Cimarron came abreast of the group of gamblers, "many of these men will have lost not only their annuity payments but many of their possessions as well."

Cimarron stopped when Hunter did and stared down at the two-sided dice that rested in a wooden bowl in front of one of the Indians. They were made of horn with one side intricately carved, the other painted red. After a guttural exchange of words among the players, the Indian seated in front of the bowl picked it up, tossed the dice into the air, and let them fall on a blanket spread on the ground.

The man who had tossed the dice wore no expression as he looked up, pointed to one of the watching women, and then to the Indian seated opposite him.

Hunter swore under his breath.

Cimarron gave him a sidelong glance as the woman moved to stand beside the Indian the gambler had indicated.

"That man," Hunter said when he noticed Cimarron staring at him, "has just lost his wife to that other player."

Cimarron turned his head and studied the woman and then the two men who had wagered for possession of her. All three of their faces were totally devoid of expression.

"These men should be at work—engaged in something useful, something productive," Hunter declared angrily. "But here they sit idly gaming and wasting their time. And yet why should they bother with productive labor when they can live quite comfortably on the annuities they receive as wards of the American government? They receive more from the government than most—perhaps all—of them could earn on their own. But the whole process of reservation life and annuity payments is like an insidious wasting disease. It saps not only a man's strength but his dignity, his pride, his self-respect."

Hunter had turned away from the gamblers in disgust, when a woman called his name. Cimarron saw Isabel Bonner weaving her way among the tables in front of the mission as she hurried toward Hunter.

"Clyde," she cried as she approached him. "I was so worried about you. I heard that you were causing a rumpus at the schoolhouse but when I went there—" She stepped closer to Hunter. "Are you quite all right, Clyde?"

"If you mean am I sober, the answer is no. But then neither am I drunk. I am somewhere in a limbo that can be called neither complete sobriety nor total drunkenness. Oh, Isabel, Isabel," he concluded sadly, shaking his head.

"What is it, Clyde? What's wrong?"

"Don't you know enough about me by now to know that you are being foolish in wasting your time trying to save me from demon rum?"

"I am trying to save you from yourself," Isabel responded. "I've told you many times, Clyde. You are your own worst enemy."

Hunter shrugged and took the bottle from his pocket. Before he could put it to his lips, Isabel slapped his hand and the bottle fell to the ground, struck a stone and smashed.

"Damn you!" Hunter cried.

Hunter raised his hand, but Cimarron seized it in a firm grip before the halfblood could strike Isabel, who stood unflinching before the threat. "That's no way to treat a lady, Hunter!"

Hunter's face seemed to collapse. He made a noise deep in his throat that was half-snarl, half-sigh. "Isabel, I'm sorry," he murmured shamefacedly, his head lowered. "I didn't think. I—"

"Let him go," Isabel said to Cimarron and, when Cimarron had done so, she asked, "Have you arrested him?"

Hunter's head snapped up and he stared hard at Cimarron. "Arrest me?" he snapped, his black eyes blazing. "Who are you?" he asked Cimarron.

"He's a deputy marshal, Clyde," Isabel said. "His name is Cimarron and he's here to—"

"Arrest me," Hunter said, the two words sounding like dropped stones. "For shooting Paul Baldwin."

"I'm not here to arrest you, Hunter. You're too quick to jump to the wrong conclusions. I'm here to find out who shot and wounded Paul Baldwin."

"Then am I to understand that you don't believe the accusations that have been made against me?" Hunter asked warily.

67

"I don't believe or disbelieve them. I told you. I'm here to find out what happened."

"I didn't do it."

"Miranda Baldwin thinks you did," Cimarron countered. "Her brother thinks pretty much the same thing."

"They've no proof that I did it," Hunter snapped. "So it amounts to their word against mine."

"That's true, isn't it, Cimarron?" Isabel asked, hope bright in her eyes.

He nodded.

Hunter muttered something unintelligible and followed it up with, "If you're interested in apprehending criminals here on the reservation, Deputy—"

"Call me Cimarron. It sounds friendlier. You know, a lot less official."

Hunter hesitated a moment and then, "He's the one you ought to arrest, Cimarron."

Cimarron turned and looked in the direction Hunter had pointed. "You mean Abel Garth or Earl Briggs?" he asked as he watched the two men rise from their table and enter the agency building.

"I was speaking of Garth," Hunter answered, "but Briggs is in on it too."

"In on what?" Cimarron asked, turning back to face Hunter.

"Garth charges fees for the land leases he grants. He also collects monthly fees from the whites he leases Mesquakie land to. And he pockets that money except for a percentage he pays to someone in the Central Superintendency of the Indian Bureau who provides him the land leases. Garth's scheme is making him a rich man."

"You're about as eager to make accusations as Miranda Baldwin is, Hunter. You got any more proof of your charges against Garth and Briggs than she has of hers against you?"

"I had proof," Hunter stated defensively. "There was a man—a rancher—he told me when he was in his cups one day about the arrangement he had with Garth and Garth has with his contact in the Indian Bureau."

"You say you had proof? You don't have it now?"

Isabel said, "Mr. Loomis—the man Clyde just referred to—disappeared some time ago."

"What happened?" Cimarron asked.

Hunter shook his head. "No one really knows. One day Loomis was there on his ranch, and the next day he had vanished."

"No one has seen him since," Isabel volunteered. "Not his family. Not anyone."

"What about the other holders of leased land?" Cimarron asked Hunter. "Did you ask any of them about this setup you just told me Loomis told you about?"

"I did," Hunter replied, "but they all vehemently denied any knowledge of such a scheme."

"You couldn't find anybody else to back you up?"

"There are two Mesquakie men, friends of mine, named Neapope and Poweshiek. There's another man, a former Lighthorseman who rode for Garth, by the name of Pushetone-qua but—well, let's just say that he and I haven't been able to come to an agreement concerning his testimony against Garth and his cohorts."

"Clyde is telling you the truth, Cimarron," Isabel interjected.

Cimarron didn't know whether he could believe Hunter or not. If anybody's got a reason to hold a grudge against Garth, he thought, it's Hunter, with his dreams of turning his tribe back into what it once was instead of letting them stay a bunch of gambling whiskey-guzzlers living on government grants from the hand of Abel Garth.

"What are you going to do about Clyde's charges against Mr. Garth, Cimarron?" Isabel challenged.

"Do about them?" he repeated mildly. "Well, I reckon I'll look into them. Might as well as long as I'm here."

"They might have something to do with the shooting of Mr. Baldwin," Isabel suggested.

"They might at that," Cimarron agreed, his words almost drowned out by the sound of a fiddle tuning up in a nearby building.

"Oh, the dancing!" Isabel cried happily. "It's about to begin over in the Meeting Hall." She turned to Cimarron. "Do you think we can put all this unpleasantness behind us for awhile and just enjoy ourselves?"

Cimarron offered Isabel his arm. So did Hunter. She took the arms of both men and let them lead her into the Meeting Hall, where a large crowd had gathered.

Five

They arrived in the Meeting Hall as a square dance was about to begin.

"Oh, hurry, or we'll be left out!" Isabel cried, her eyes shining. She led Cimarron and Clyde into the midst of the dancers, and all three took up positions in a group totaling eight dancers, some of them Indians, some whites.

On a raised platform at one end of the Meeting Hall, the fiddler ran his bow across his fiddle, making a screeching sound to gain the attention of the dancers. He was joined on the platform by a caller who shouted, "A flourish!" Then he launched into the patter accompanying the square dance's opening figure.

Everybody in your places,
Straighten up your faces,

Cimarron bowed to Isabel, who was to be his partner.

Loosen up your belly-bands,

Isabel blushed but couldn't hide her smile.

Tighten up your traces,
For another long pull.

Cimarron bowed to the other ladies in the set, and then all eight dancers joined hands and circled to the left until the caller shouted, "Break!"

Cimarron, Isabel, and the others—the men's arms around their ladies' waists, the ladies' right hands supported by the men's left hands, and the ladies' left hands resting on the men's shoulders—pivoted twice to the right and them promenaded with hands clasped, left in left, and right in right, back to their original positions.

Swing on the corner
Like swinging on the gate,
And now your own
If you're not too late.
Cimarron swung Isabel, and the caller continued:
Now allemande left
With your left hand
And right to your partner
And right and left grand.
And promenade eight
When you come straight.

When the dance ended, Isabel was flushed and smiling, and both she and Hunter accepted Cimarron's invitation to have a cup of coffee with him. They made their way to a table in one corner of the hall where Cimarron ordered three cups of coffee. They stood drinking from their cups and watching as the dancing continued until the caller announced a game of drop-the-handkerchief.

"Those of you fillies and colts," he shouted, "who are of a mind to join in the game, form a circle!"

"Oh, let's play!" Isabel suggested, setting down her cup. "Shall we, Clyde? Cimarron?"

"You two go ahead," Cimarron suggested. "I'll see you later." He emptied his cup as Isabel took Hunter's hand and led him to where people were forming a circle in the middle of the floor.

"Join hands, everybody!" the caller ordered.

Cimarron put down his empty cup when he saw Miranda and Paul Baldwin enter the Meeting Hall. He started toward them, his eyes on Miranda. But, before he could reach them, Miranda said something to her brother, and they took up places in the circle of players.

"We need somebody to volunteer to be 'it,' " the caller cried.

"I'll be 'it,' " Hunter volunteered. He stepped out of the circle and took the bright red bandanna the caller handed him.

Cimarron, watching Miranda with admiring eyes, suddenly decided to join the game. He hurriedly took Hunter's place in the circle.

"Oh, you've changed your mind about playing, I see,"

Isabel said and took his left hand as his right closed on the left hand of the woman on his other side.

"On your mark," the caller cried, "get set, *go!*"

As Hunter made his way slowly around the outside of the circle, Cimarron saw Isabel's head turn to watch his progress. He saw her face fall when Hunter, long before he reached her, stopped behind Miranda Baldwin just as Miranda happened to notice Cimarron's presence. Hunter dropped the bandanna behind Miranda and began to run around the perimeter of the circle formed by the players. Miranda glanced over her shoulder at Hunter, and then, instead of obeying the rules of the game and chasing him, she remained in her place, standing still and looking neither right nor left. When Hunter realized she was not pursuing him, he slowed and shamefacedly turned and walked out of the Meeting Hall.

"That was a terrible thing for her to do!" Isabel exclaimed, addressing Cimarron. "That Baldwin woman was deliberately trying to insult Clyde by not chasing after him."

"It might also have been a foolish thing for *him* to do," Cimarron suggested, "since she thinks he tried to kill her brother."

"Yes," Isabel declared sadly. "He was foolish. There are plenty of other women playing the game who would have been delighted to have him drop that bandanna behind them."

And you're one of them, Cimarron thought, noting the disappointed look on Isabel's face. I wonder why Hunter can't see the fire he's kindled in her eyes. Maybe he can, but he's got Miranda on his mind.

The caller clapped his hands for attention. "It looks from here like the gentleman who was 'it' has declined the honor and retired from the lists, so to speak. Who'll volunteer to take his place?"

Cimarron was surprised—and pleased—to see Miranda's hand shoot up into the air. He watched her make her deliberate way around the circle, the red bandanna that Hunter had dropped behind her in her hand. He almost held his breath as she neared him, and then he broke into a big grin when she dropped the bandanna directly behind him.

He turned quickly, scooped it up, and went racing after her as she sped around the outside of the circle. He soon overtook her and holding her tightly against him, said, "Where I come

72

from down in central Texas, when a fellow catches a girl like this before she can get more than halfway around the circle, it means she's not only still 'it' but he can call into play another rule of this game we called "catch-a-kiss-or-candy. You got any candy to give me, Miranda?"

She coyly shook her head.

So he kissed her on the lips to the cheers of the men in the hall and the bashful titters of most of the woman. Then he left her and returned to his place in the circle beside Isabel.

Later, when the game ended, Isabel said, "Excuse me, Cimarron. I'm going to look for Clyde."

"I'll go with you if you don't mind."

Together, they made their way out of the Meeting Hall. They found Hunter standing outside the building's entrance amid a group of Indians who were passing a jug among themselves.

"Oh, dear," Isabel murmured and halted.

Cimarron left her side, strode up to Hunter, and said, "It's my opinion that Isabel wouldn't mind one bit if you were to see her home."

Hunter glared at Cimarron. "Did you see her, what she did to me, the high and mighty Miss Miranda Baldwin?"

"You're an educated man, Hunter. Did you ever happen to read the memoirs of that old-time fellow, Casanova?"

"What's Casanova got to do with this?"

"I'm willing to wager that even he didn't succeed with every single lady he ever went after. I reckon the ones that got away from him he just didn't bother to mention in those memoirs of his. And, if I'm right, you've got nothing to look so down-in-the-mouth about—especially considering that Isabel Bonner has, I've noticed, a fond eye for you."

Hunter glanced at Isabel and then waved away the bottle one of the other Indians offered him.

"I'm close to a hundred per cent convinced that not even Casanova could have rolled around in the hay with every single woman he set his sights on," Cimarron said.

Hunter smiled faintly.

Together the two men rejoined Isabel. They had no sooner done so when Miranda and Paul Baldwin emerged from the Meeting Hall. Both brother and sister stopped in their tracks when they saw the trio standing just outside the door. They

73

exchanged glances, and then Miranda's icy eyes fell on Cimarron.

"It seems quite obvious to me that Marshal Upham has sent the wrong man to investigate the assault on my brother," she remarked angrily. "I didn't ask that the marshal send someone to *befriend* the would-be murderer. I asked that they send someone to *arrest* the felon before he could do any further harm to anyone."

Cimarron removed his arm from Hunter's shoulder. "Miranda, Hunter here tells me he didn't shoot your brother."

"And you, I suppose, believe him!"

"I didn't say I believed him."

"But neither, I notice, have you said that you disbelieve him!" Miranda snapped.

I wasn't the one who shot at you, Baldwin!" Hunter interjected. "And I don't like the way you and your sister have been going around telling everyone I was."

"Can you prove you didn't do it?" Baldwin asked angrily.

"Hold on there," Cimarron said. "It's not up to Hunter here to prove he's innocent. It's up to anybody who can to prove he's guilty."

"That's right!" Isabel said firmly. "It's time you two stopped persecuting, Mr. Hunter."

"So!" exclaimed Miranda with a theatrical gesture that encompassed Cimarron, Isabel, and Hunter. "The villain has not one but two defenders!"

"Mr. Hunter is deserving of a vigorous defense," Isabel stormed, "when he is faced with such wild and wholly unjustified accusations, which are injurious to his good name and reputation!"

"Good name?" Baldwin asked, his eyebrows rising. "Reputation?" He laughed scornfully. "That Indian has a reputation for being a drunken bum and a rabble-rouser, and if he ever had a good name it's long since been drowned in all those bottles he's emptied lately."

"When you talk me down, Baldwin," Hunter said in a tense voice, "it's a clear-cut case of the pot calling the kettle black. I may drink too much at times, but at least I'm not involved in a corrupt scheme to exploit Mesquakie land for my own personal gain."

"Are you accusing me of—"

"I'm accusing you of being in collusion with Abel Garth—and maybe Earl Briggs too—as you, and other ranchers as well, go about the insidious process of expropriating Mesquakie land."

Baldwin's response was merely another scornful laugh.

But Miranda, her face flushing, reacted far more strongly. "Paul, are you going to take that from him? Aren't you going to fight back?"

"My dear Miranda, one does not allow oneself to be troubled by drunken Indians."

"You're claiming what Hunter said about you and the Indian agent's being in cahoots is not true?" Cimarron asked Baldwin.

"Of course the charge is false," Baldwin answered. "In fact, it's ridiculous. I am not expropriating Indian land. I am merely leasing a relatively small portion of it."

"I think I'd best have me a talk with Garth and Briggs about the matter," Cimarron said. "See if there's any fire where Hunter claims he sees smoke."

"I'm surprised," said Miranda in a chilly tone, "that Marshal Upham would send a deputy who is apparently more interested in taking sides with an Indian of ill repute than in standing shoulder to shoulder with one of his own kind against slanderous charges that have no basis whatsoever in fact."

"What proof do you have that Mr. Hunter's charges against your brother are in any way slanderous, Miss Baldwin?" Isabel asked bluntly.

But before Miranda could answer Isabel's question a man rode up to them and drew rein.

"Mr. Baldwin," the rider said breathlessly, "we went by the ranch and the boys there said you were here. I'm afraid I've got some pretty bad news to give you."

"What's wrong, Bates?" Baldwin asked.

"Me and two of your other hands rode out to where we left some of your cattle last night on the south bank of Bear Creek, and when we got there we found a bunch of them dead and another bunch dying."

"What happened to them?" Baldwin asked sharply.

"I don't rightly know, Mr. Baldwin. There weren't no wounds on any of them that either me or any of the other boys could see. My guess is somebody poisoned them some-how or other."

Baldwin turned on Hunter. "You killed my stock!" he accused.

"You're crazy, Baldwin!" Hunter protested. "I've been nowhere near your stock!"

"Who else would want to kill my cattle?" Baldwin countered. "Only someone who wants to run me off my land, and for my money, Hunter, that someone is you and nobody else."

Before Hunter could respond to the charge, Cimarron spoke to Baldwin's rider. "When was the last time you checked the stock out at Bear Creek?"

"We checked them last night and again when we got there first thing this morning. Then we rode east to round up a few strays. When we got back with the strays—it was just after we'd made our nooning—we found most of the beeves dead or dying."

"Baldwin," Cimarron said, "you're accusing the wrong man of the crime of killing your stock. I happen to know Hunter was here at the agency for the past two, three hours. There's just no way he could have poisoned your cattle and been here at the same time."

"A confederate," Miranda suggested waspishly. "He hired someone to do the dastardly deed for him!"

"Miranda," Hunter said with a sigh, "you are most defi-nitely bound and determined to do me in, one way or the other, aren't you?"

She ignored him. When her brother announced that he was riding out to inspect his cattle, she declared that she would go with him.

Cimarron stood with Hunter and Isabel and watched them board their horses and ride out.

"If lightning struck the Baldwin ranch," Hunter muttered under his breath, "Baldwin and his sister would swear I somehow made it happen."

"Pay no attention to them, Clyde," Isabel whispered. "They're just looking for a scapegoat to blame for what has happened, and obviously they have chosen you."

"I think it's time I started wearing a gun," Hunter said.

"In case Baldwin or his riders take it into their heads to mete out justice, vigilante-style."

"If a man takes to carrying a gun," Cimarron said, "he'd best know how to use it."

"I can use a gun," Hunter boasted. "Well enough at least to defend myself with it."

"To some men, the sight of another man with a gun on his hip is like an invitation to a lead-slinging party—especially if there's bad blood between them. Baldwin, I notice, don't tote a gun."

"What Baldwin does is his business," Hunter said. "What I do is my business."

"I wish you wouldn't, Clyde," Isabel said.

"Wouldn't carry a gun?" he asked.

She nodded.

"A man has to do what he can to protect himself."

"It's time I was moseying on," Cimarron told them. "I think I'll wander on out to Bear Creek and see if I can maybe find out what happened to Baldwin's stock. Be seeing you two."

Cimarron made his way to the main agency building, where he had left his horse. He was in the process of freeing its reins that were wrapped around the hitchrail in front of the building when he happened to notice Abel Garth and Earl Briggs surreptitiously watching him from behind the calico curtain hanging in one of the building's front windows. The pair of them look like two Peeping Toms, he thought with some amusement. Not to mention that they don't have exactly friendly expressions on their faces. Maybe, like a whole lot of other people I've run into in my time, they don't have any particular fondness for lawmen like me. He swung into the saddle and rode away from the building, thinking that people who spied on lawmen were either nosey or else they wanted to keep tabs on any lawman in their vicinity who tended to make them nervous. If I make Garth and Briggs nervous, he thought as he left the agency behind him, I wonder how come I do. He shrugged. Maybe those boys are just nosey parkers, he thought. But he doubted that.

When he caught up with the Baldwins and their hired hand he explained that, since he was a lawman and was in the area, he thought he might just as well look into the killing of their cattle. "Maybe I can catch the culprit who did it for you," he concluded.

"I rather doubt that you can," Miranda remarked, "since you seem unable—or unwilling—to catch Clyde Hunter."

"I've not caught Hunter on account of I'm not chasing him," Cimarron declared mildly. "At least, at the moment I'm not."

"So we see," said Baldwin in a tone that was almost as sarcastic as his sister's.

As they rode on Baldwin and his hired hand pulled ahead. Finding himself alone with Miranda, Cimarron moved his dun closer to her buckskin mare and said, "I got to tell you I was tickled to death you picked me in that game of drop-the-handkerchief back at the Meeting Hall."

"I hasten to assure you that I never would have done so had I known beforehand that you had become such good friends with Clyde Hunter."

"Speaking of Hunter," Cimarron said, "he picked you, I noticed. Now how come he did a thing like that, do you reckon?"

"I haven't the slightest idea. But whatever his reason, I should think he would have known better."

"You mean on account of you think he's the one who tried to do in your brother."

"That and because he should have known I would not consort with an Indian. Paul and I have quite similar feelings where Indians are concerned. We both treat them civilly and we do them no harm, but neither of us would ever think of becoming—intimate with one of them."

"Playing a game with Hunter, that don't strike me as becoming particularly intimate with him."

Miranda turned her head to stare coldly at Cimarron. "If you had been an Indian what happened between us at the house—I never would have allowed it to happen. Not in a million years!"

"Well, all I can say on that score is I'm mighty glad the good Lord didn't see fit to have me a born a redskin. On the other hand, I don't think my being born an Indian would have been a total loss. Some Indians I've known in my time were better men than I can ever hope to be. They were a whole lot braver than I am, and they had more guts than you could hang on a fence.''

"I really would rather not continue this discussion, if you don't mind. I find it tiring.''

"Well, I sure don't want to tire you out, so I'll hold my tongue.''

But he soon found, as he continued riding along beside Miranda, that he couldn't keep the promise he had made her. He asked her about her life in New Orleans. He asked her if she had a beau. He asked her if she thought the two of them could get together again some time soon.

Miranda's answers were short and sharp and told Cimarron little. She phrased them in such a way that he realized he knew as little about her after she had answered his questions as he did before he asked them.

"There they are!'' Baldwin's rider called out and pointed west to where two men stood smoking cigarettes. "Over yonder.''

Baldwin stood up in his stirrups and peered into the distance. Then, sitting his saddle again, he put heels to his horse and went galloping toward his other two ranch hands and his decimated herd of cattle.

When Cimarron and Miranda caught up with him, Baldwin had dismounted and was kneeling on the ground beside one of the dead animals and examining it closely.

Cimarron sat his saddle and watched the red-eyed cowbirds that fluttered nervously here and there among the living and dead cattle as if, in their bronzish-black plumage they were distraught mourners where Death held dominion.

Cimarron's eyes roamed the surrounding land, and at first he saw nothing unusual. But then his attention was claimed by a barely visible pile of vegetation resting on an otherwise barren patch of ground about a half mile to the north of his position.

"They've been poisoned all right,'' Baldwin muttered and got to his feet.

"But how, Paul?'' Miranda asked as she dismounted, a puzzled frown on her face.

"I'll be damned if I know,'' Baldwin replied and then, "Sorry for the bad language, Miranda.''

Cimarron left the others and rode north, barely aware of

Miranda asking "Where does he think he's going?" as he concentrated on the patch of ground that had claimed his attention moments before. When he reached it, he dismounted, hunkered down, and stared at the vegetation piled on the ground. He picked up one of the three-foot-long plants, noting its spotted stems, and then dropped it. He got to his feet and shouted for the others to join him.

When they did, Cimarron pointed to the uprooted vegetation that had begun to wither. "That's what done your beeves in," he told Baldwin.

"What is it?" Miranda asked.

"Cowbane," Cimarron answered. "Some ranchers, they call it rosin weed. Its real name, though, is water hemlock."

"But we cleared our range of rosin weed back in September before we brought the stock down from the high country," one of Baldwin's ranch hands pointed out.

"It looks like somebody uprooted that poisonous stuff," Baldwin stated solemnly, "and then hauled it out here and dumped it right where there was a good chance of my cattle finding and feeding on it."

"You'd best get your surviving cattle clear of this spot quick, Baldwin," Cimarron advised. "And were I you, I'd send some of my men out on the scout. Whoever dumped this cowbane here might very well have done the same thing in other places on your range."

Baldwin nodded and then ordered his three men to drive the surviving cattle back to the ranch. "Once they're safe," he told his men, "you boys had better ride out and look for more of that stuff." He pointed to the poisonous plants. "Keep tightening your circle as you ride so you don't miss any spots."

"Yes, sir, Mr. Baldwin, I'll do that soon as we get back to the ranch," Bates, the rider who had brought the bad news to Baldwin, assured his employer.

Ten minutes later, they all moved out, heading east and driving less than a score of surviving cattle before them. They had gone no more than a few miles when two of the cattle dropped to the ground. They lost another one just as they reached a fence that encircled what Cimarron estimated to be close to an acre of empty land.

"What's that fence for?" Baldwin asked.

"We found out there's quicksand in that sink there, so we fenced it off for safety's sake," replied one of his men. "There's good solid ground off to the east of it."

Cimarron helped Baldwin's men keep the cattle bunched as the drive continued. He rode drag with Baldwin and Bates while the other two ranch hands rode point at the head of the herd and Miranda rode on the herd's right flank.

Suddenly, one of the two men riding point let out a startled yell, immediately followed by a dreaded word shouted at the top of his voice: "*Quicksand!*"

Miranda gave a shrill cry and tried to turn her horse, but before she could the animal broke through the dried crust of earth covering the swirling sands beneath it, and horse and rider began to descend into a deadly sink.

"Get back!" Cimarron yelled to Baldwin and Bates.

"Miranda!" Baldwin cried, as sand that seemed to be billowing crept up along her horse's ribs and her thighs.

"Paul, help me!" she screamed.

"I'm coming, Miranda!" he cried and lashed his horse with his reins as Bates managed to turn his horse and ride out of the sink before it trapped him.

Cimarron quickly seized the coiled lariat that hung from his saddle horn and used it to strike Baldwin squarely in the face, forcing the obviously distraught man to retreat to solid ground.

"Paul!" Miranda shrieked as she saw her brother riding away from her as a result of Cimarron's action.

The cattle, caught in the sucking quicksand, bawled and rolled their terror-stricken eyes. Air bubbles rose around their trapped bodies and burst with soft plopping sounds, throwing brownish water into the animal's faces and contributing to their panic.

"Help!" screamed one of the point men.

Cimarron saw the man throw up his arms, and he heard him scream again as his horse disappeared from sight into the deadly sink. The man's scream died when he went the way of his horse.

Near the spot where horse and rider had just disappeared, the other point rider suddenly threw himself from his sinking horse as Cimarron dug spurs into the flanks of his dun and forced the terrified animal to move out into the field of death toward Miranda. Out of the corner of his eye he saw the second point rider desperately trying to claw his way across the sea of sand to the safety of solid ground in the distance. Just before he reached Miranda, he saw the man go under, rise up momentarily, and then sink down into the sand, where an awful suffocating death awaited him.

"*Cimarron!*" Miranda screamed and thrust out her arms toward him. He hung his lariat on his saddle horn and moved his sinking dun closer to her. Her hands clawed desperately at him, and she sobbed in terror as both of their mounts slowly disappeared into the sand and the ooze rose to the level of their chests.

He batted Miranda's frantic hands away from his face. "Put your arms around my neck and hang on to me!" he ordered her.

"We're going to die!" she screamed. "*Oh, dear Lord, I don't want to die!*"

Cimarron, as the quicksand's severe pressure on his legs increased, and Miranda's arms encircled his neck, managed to climb up onto his submerged saddle. "Hold tight!" he told her as she whimpered piteously.

He felt his dun sinking deeper beneath him and knew he had no time to hesitate. As the few cattle whose heads still remained above the shifting sands bawled their fright, Cimarron did the only thing he could—he jumped.

But he missed the steer that had been his target and fell, Miranda clinging tightly to him, into the deadly quicksand.

Six

Spluttering and spitting, Cimarron, with Miranda still clinging tightly to him, rose above the roiling surface of the quicksand and made a grab for the steer. This time his hands closed on its horns.

Gripping them firmly, he fought his way up out of the sand that was ruthlessly sucking him and Miranda down into its depths. He finally succeeded in climbing onto the back of the steer, which bellowed its alarm as it sank deeper into the sand. Its head rose high into the air at a right angle to its body as it fought desperately against the death about to claim it.

"Stand up!" Cimarron ordered Miranda and then helped her stand on the back of the unsteady steer. "Let go of me!" he demanded, and when she did, he scooped her up in both arms. Then, to the encouraging shouts of Baldwin and Bates, who were standing on solid ground, he hopped, skipped, and jumped in a precarious journey from one doomed animal to the next. As he landed on the back of one cow, he lost his balance. Believing he was about to fall, he hurled Miranda in the direction of the two men standing safely beyond the sink.

The men caught her and eased her to the ground. Cimarron, his balance regained but still precarious, made a mighty leap to the back of a steer that was close to the edge of the quicksand. Another leap landed him on solid ground, where he dropped to his knees, his head lowered, his arms hanging limply at his sides, his chest heaving.

He looked up as Baldwin hunkered down in front of him, put a hand on his shoulder, and asked, "Are you all right?"

He nodded. "Miranda—is she—"

"She's shaken up. But she'll be fine once the shock of what happened to her wears off."

Cimarron drew a deep breath, then another.

"I'm grateful to you, Cimarron," Baldwin said. "More than that. I'm in your debt for saving my sister's life."

Cimarron made a dismissive gesture.

"I mean it," Baldwin insisted. "Without your help, Miranda would be as dead as those two men of mine who went down into the sink along with their horses. Cimarron, if there's ever anything I can do for you—anything at all— you just name it."

"There is something you can do for me, Baldwin," Cimarron said with a wry smile. "My knees feel kind of rubbery. Would you give me a hand up so I can see if they'll hold me?"

Baldwin, returning Cimarron's smile, did so; then both men made their way to where Miranda was sitting on the ground, Bates standing stiffly beside her.

As Baldwin helped his sister to her feet, Miranda said to Cimarron, "Thank you for saving my life."

He acknowledged her gratitude with a nod, then turned to look out over the shifting surface of the sink. He saw no sign of any of the cattle nor of the two men and their horses claimed by the silent sands. A chill seized him and he shivered. He looked down at his filthy clothes. Then his gaze shifted to the circular fence in the distance.

"Somebody moved it," volunteered Bates when he noticed what Cimarron was looking at. "I sure do wish I'd noticed that fact sooner only the sad truth is I didn't. If I had . . ." He fell silent, dropping his eyes.

"Clyde Hunter," Baldwin muttered, the name a curse slipping from between his lips.

Cimarron was about to protest Baldwin's snap judgment, but a crushing weariness overcame him and he said instead, "We'd best head back to the ranch where we can clean up, maybe grab some sleep. I for one am tuckered."

"You're welcome to use my mount," Bates told Cimarron. "Mr. Baldwin, he can send some of the boys out to help me put that fence back where it belongs, and they can bring my horse back here to me."

"Much obliged," Cimarron told the man. Minutes later, he rode out with Baldwin and Miranda, heading for the ranch.

After having slept for a total of ten hours straight, Cimarron awoke the next morning to find that the filthy clothes he had tossed on a chair before retiring the night before were now clean. His jeans, shirt, bandanna, and socks had been washed, his buckskin jacket and hat had been brushed so that no trace of dried quicksand could be seen on them, and his boots had been blackened. He dressed and went downstairs, where he found Miranda in the kitchen.

"Was it you who cleaned my clothes for me?" he asked her.

She nodded.

"I'm obliged to you."

"Would you like some breakfast?" she asked him and, when he gave her an affirmative answer, she proceeded to set before him a hearty breakfast of fried steak, baked potatoes, and boiled turnip greens.

"You feeling better?" he asked her as he ate eagerly to appease his growling hunger.

"Physically, yes, I am. But I'm still very much upset to think of the lengths—perhaps I should say the depths—to which Clyde Hunter is apparently prepared to go in his campaign to run my brother and me off this land."

"I don't suppose it would do a mite of good were I to point out to you, Miranda, that once again you've not got a stitch of proof that Hunter had anything at all to do with moving that fence out on the range yesterday."

"Who else would have been motivated to do such a truly terrible thing?"

Cimarron shrugged, forking greens into his mouth. He chewed, swallowed, looked up at Miranda, and said, "Beats me, I got to admit. Somebody did it, only I don't think it was Hunter."

"I suppose I should not be surprised at your support for the man. But it does disappoint me. All of us could have been killed yesterday."

Cimarron mashed a potato with his fork and ate it, skin and all. "Yes, we could have, so I intend to try hard to find out

85

who was it moved that fence. Maybe whoever moved it also took that shot at your brother. By the way, where is he?"

"Paul went out to make sure the fence has been put back around the sink. He left early this morning."

Cimarron drank the remains of his coffee and stood up. He went to Miranda and put his arms around her. "I do thank you kindly for that fine breakfast. It's made me fit to face the day." He buried his face against her neck.

She shuddered then as he kissed her.

He drew back and studied her. "You didn't want me to do that?"

"I'm sorry, Cimarron. I'm not myself today. I feel so—so on edge about everything. Actually, I feel frightened. Now more than ever, because of what happened yesterday. I'm afraid for Paul, of course, but now I'm also afraid for myself. If Clyde Hunter"—she caught the glint in Cimarron's eye that signaled his annoyance at her mention of the name—"or whoever it was who moved that fence should try again—my God, what will he do next time?"

Cimarron didn't try to answer her question. As he headed for the door, Miranda softly spoke his name. He turned back to her.

"When I brought your clothes to your room—"

"My thanks for seeing to them for me."

"I stood there looking down at you. You had thrown the covers off and you were—your body was—but I couldn't. I suppose fear can drive desire right out of a person."

"It can, I reckon. So what's got to be done if you and me're to get together again the way we were is for me to find a way to rid you of your fear. Which means get my hands on the jasper who's out to hurt your brother."

"The jasper, as you call him," Miranda murmured, "who doesn't care if he has to kill others in the process."

Cimarron nodded grimly. "Do you think your brother would mind if I borrowed one of his horses?"

"Oh, I forgot to tell you. Paul asked me to tell you to take the big black. You'll find him in the barn. Paul left gear for you to use as well."

This big brisketed horse'll most likely turn any man bow-legged for sure if he keeps straddling him, Cimarron thought as he rode the powerful black north, heading for the Sac and Fox Agency.

He was less than halfway to his destination when he saw riders coming toward him in the distance. He recognized Baldwin in the lead, and when he reached the men, he drew rein as they did and said, "Morning, Baldwin," noting that the rancher was now wearing a holstered sidearm.

"Where are you headed?" Baldwin inquired.

"Up to the agency to have me a talk with Abel Garth and his sidekick, Earl Briggs. But I've just now been thinking I ought to also have a word or two with Hunter's uncle, old Mokohoko. If you can point me in his direction, I'll put Garth and Briggs down at the bottom of my list of folks to talk to."

"Mokohoko has a wickiup over that way," Baldwin said, pointing. "It's about a mile southwest of the agency. You have business with the old man?"

"I want to hear what he has to say about his nephew. And I figure he might be able to tell me about any other Foxes who think the same as Hunter does about white intruders on reservation land."

Baldwin frowned and was about to say something, but before he could Cimarron said, "I'm obliged to you for this horse I have under me, Baldwin, and for the gear I put on him."

"I trust he and it are satisfactory."

"This black's got stronger wind, it seems to me, than a Texas Blue Norther, and as for the gear—well, I just about grew up on a Texas saddle like this one." Cimarron patted his double-rigged and square-skirted saddle. "Be seeing you, Baldwin."

He rode away and a little more than fifteen minutes later arrived at the wickiup, where he found the elderly Mokohoko standing and watching him approach.

He drew rein in front of the old man. "I see you grew tobacco over there this past summer," he remarked, indicating with a nod the bare field that was littered in places with the dessicated remains of tobacco plants. Now, if I were one of the Red Earth People, I could take me some tobacco and toss it in a fire and that way get to talk to the spirits. Then I might be able to find out exactly what it is that's going on around here between the People of the Red Earth and the white men who've been living on their land. It would sure save me a lot of time and trouble in getting to the bottom of who was it shot Paul Baldwin and why.''

For a long moment, Mokohoko merely stared silently at Cimarron, and Cimarron began to believe that his attempt to make friends with the old man had failed. But then Mohohoko indicated the round canvas-covered wickiup. "You are welcome to my home.''

Mokohoko turned and ducked to enter his wickiup. Cimarron dismounted and, leaving the black ground-hitched, followed the old man. Inside he found a small wood-burning stove in the center of the dirt floor and wooden sleeping platforms on two sides of the one large room. The stove had no stovepipe, but there was a smoke hole at the top of the wickiup. Mokohoko sat down on a hand-carved chair, and Cimarron seated himself on a similar one not far from the old man.

"Not many white men know who we are,'' Mokohoko stated. "They do not know that we were the first people to be created by the Great Spirit. They do not know that the Mesquakies were created out of the red earth. How is it then that you know this?''

"Your nephew told me.''

"He it was who told you how to use tobacco to talk to the spirits?''

Cimarron shook his head. "I knew another man once who was also one of the Red Earth People. A member of the Eagle clan. It was him told me things about his people.'' Cimarron pointed to the rawhide bundle that hung on a nail high above their heads. "He told me about things like that sacred medicine bundle there.''

Mokohoko looked up at it. "It loses its power. The white man's book makes it weak.''

"You mean the Bible?''

Mokohoko nodded, his eyes once again drilling into Cimarron. "Why came you here? I think it was not to talk to spirits. I think it was not to talk of sacred medicine bundles. I think it was to talk about whether my nephew was the one who tried to kill Mr. Baldwin.''

The old boy sure don't mince words, Cimarron thought

with admiration. He replied, "You're right. I'm here to talk about your nephew."

"Many people think Clyde tried to kill Mr. Baldwin."

"Many people once thought that this old earth of ours was as flat as a pancake. Every last one of them, as it turned out, were wrong."

Something that might have been amusement flickered briefly in Mokohoko's eyes. Then he said soberly, "When we met at the mission, I told you I believe my nephew did not shoot Mr. Baldwin."

"I remember you did. I also remember some other things you told me that time. You said, as I recall, that you sent Hunter to a white man's school so he could learn to live in the white's man's world."

"He learned many bad things there. How to get drunk. How to make trouble for other people."

"He could have learned both of those things even if he had stayed right here on the reservation. Mokohoko, it strikes me that Hunter's just having some trouble sorting out who and what he is. But from my talks with him, he seems to me to be leaning in the direction of becoming more Mesquakie than most Mesquakies. Which is why he don't take at all kindly to white men grazing their cattle on the land that belongs to the Red Earth People."

Mokohoko snorted. "The money I earned from leasing my land to whites was what paid for his education in the East. A funny thing, yes?"

"A funny thing, no, Mokohoko. But let's stick to the point."

"The point?"

"I've been given to understand that Hunter's been talking up the idea of running whites off Mesquakie land. Now, what I came here to talk to you about is do you know of any other Mesquakies who happen to be sailing in the same boat as your nephew?"

Mokohoko said nothing for a moment as he stared thoughtfully into space. Then, "You think one of the others who think as Clyde does might have been the one who shot Mr. Baldwin."

"Yep, I think that's possible. From what you say, I take it there are others."

"Yes, there are others. Young men, most of them. Two that I know of. My nephew shares their wickiup with them."

"Their names?"

"Neapope. Poweshiek."

"Your nephew mentioned them to me awhile ago. I take it those friends of his bought the bill of goods he was selling."

"No. They were the ones who spoke to my nephew about what they believe to be the evils of white intruders leasing Mesquakie land. Those two, they did not follow in my nephew's footsteps. It was he who walked in their moccasins."

"Where might I find those fellows? I'd like to have a talk with them."

"You will not find them."

"I won't? How come I won't?"

"They have disappeared."

"You mean they've left the reservation?"

"I mean they have disappeared. No one has seen them in the past two days. Some of the people say it is a good thing that they are here no more because they wanted us all to fight the whites."

"Maybe somebody got their hands on Neapope and Poweshiek. Maybe there's those bent on fighting back against boys like your nephew and anybody who happens to think the way he does," Cimarron suggested. "White men, I mean," he added.

Mokohoko nodded. "I am an old man, but my ears are good still. I hear the war drums beating, and the sound comes closer day by day."

Cimarron rose. "I thank you for taking the time to talk to me, Mokohoko. I've got but one last question for you before I have to be moseying on. Did you by any chance—or anybody you know—happen to see any strangers on the reservation lately—since about the time Baldwin showed up here and started ranching?"

"White men or red men?"

"White men. Dudes, maybe. City slickers."

When Mokohoko shook his head, Cimarron turned and left the wickiup.

Later, as he rode north toward the agency, he went over in his mind the conversation he had just had with Mokohoko. So Hunter's not the only hotblood who'd like to see white men

90

run off the reservation. There's at least two others—Neapope and Poweshiek. Only they've pulled out of the fight. Or were pulled out of it by somebody. Maybe there is a war going on here as Mokohoko seems to think, only it's not out in the open. Not yet anyway, unless you count the shooting of Baldwin. He mulled over Mokohoko's negative answer to his question about the presence of unfamiliar white city slickers on the reservation. The fact that Mokohoko didn't see any don't necessarily mean there aren't any here gunning for Baldwin to get even for the swindle Baldwin pulled on them.

Mokohoko's sure down on Hunter, he thought as he rode on, but at the same time he seems to care a lot about him. Then he thought about what Isabel Bonner had told him earlier concerning the sacrifices Mokohoko had made in order to send Hunter to Hampton Institute. The old man had only the best in mind for Hunter, he thought, and his thought prodded buried memories in his mind that began, as they always did once they were aroused, to haunt and torment him.

Once again he was a boy, and once again his pa's wide leather belt was striking the bare flesh of his buttocks, and once again the battle was joined between him and his pa. As his pa's belt reddened his flesh he obstinately refused to repent, and his pa as obstinately refused to countenance his son's behavior. Whether it was smoking dried cornsilk behind the barn or cursing a piece of cordwood that refused to split or playing "you-show-me-yours-and-I'll-show-you-mine" with a girl named Rae Ellen Smith in the hayloft, he was, in his father's words, "the spawn of Satan" and an "evil creature steeped in sin."

They fought, he and his pa, battle after battle in the never-ending war in which there were neither victors nor victories. There were only wounds they both suffered, some as visible as the welts his pa's belt made on his bared buttocks, and some as invisible as the scars left on two stubborn hearts by the mutual love they had for each other that remained unacknowledged and unspoken.

He would not repent. His pa would not forgive.

And so between them a gulf grew. And each year it widened. In time, as they stood on opposite sides of it, glaring at each other in anger and with an awful sense of something important forever lost, they became first strangers, and, finally, enemies.

And his pa would scream in a fury-filled voice, "The face of the Lord is against them that do evil . . ."

And he would roar, pretending not to see the tears in his pa's hurt eyes, "What Rae Ellen and me did up in the hayloft's not evil or wrong—it's as natural and as right as—as rain!"

" 'The words of his mouth are iniquity and deceit: he hath left off to be wise, and to do good!' "

And then to hide the hot and humiliating tears in his own eyes, he would turn away. Taking refuge in rage, he would pull up his pants and swear to himself that this time was the end, that he must go, that he would leave . . .

And one night he finally did leave under cover of darkness, taking nothing more than the clothes on his back, refusing to admit the regret he felt or to face the harvest of hate that had grown from the seeds of his own rebelliousness.

He became a swamper in a Saint Louis saloon. An errand boy for a brothel's women in a Black Hills mining camp. A riverboat gambler on the Mississippi. The lives he lived were like shadows flickering on the walls of his mind as he moved restlessly through time searching for something that had no name and that he could never find.

He did find women. They were the soft harbors and warm havens he sought when he wanted to escape from the way of the world or simply to pretend to himself that someone really loved him and that the nameless thing he sought had at last been found and its secret name was Paradise.

But, though the women were real, the dreams he secretly dreamed when with them were not. They were merely dreams, and he was always, afterward, a man alone.

And then—Texas. That one sunny day. The bank. He was kneeling in front of the open iron safe while the owlhoots with whom he had been riding through the panhandle were holding the terrified bank patrons and tellers at bay. He was scooping folding money into the sack in his hand when one of his companions yelled something about the law. He quickly turned and—a tall man was standing silhouetted in the doorway of the bank, his face hidden from sight as he went for his gun.

He fired. One shot. He ran. He was almost out of the bank, almost past the man he had killed who was lying on the floor, when he saw . . .

He halted. Looked down. His blood froze. His heart stopped. He hurled questions at the paralyzed patrons of the bank. They gave him hushed and nervous answers.

The sheriff, they said . . .

He stood staring down at the brass star pinned to the man's shirt—the star he had not seen when the man had stood with the light behind him in the bank's dark doorway.

. . . came to their town after the death of his wife . . .

Ma, he silently cried.

. . . a good man he was, and they asked him to be their sheriff, and he had agreed . . .

He was running then, out of the bank, and tossing the sack full of money to one of his confederates. He rode away alone, and alone he had been ever since, even when in a crowded room or in bed with a woman—alone except for the specter that dogged his backtrail crying out the name he had abandoned following the killing, calling out to his son who would not—did not dare—turn around to confront his ghostly accuser, the father he had shot to death and who now asked the awful and unanswerable question, "Why?"

He was never sure what the question meant. Did it mean why had he and his pa never been able to say how much they had loved each other? Did it mean why had the brutal beatings and the stony defiance borne such bitter fruits as the slaughter of a father by a secretly beloved son? He did not know. But he did care.

And the word continued to echo from the lifeless lips of his dead father, a terrible incantation, "Whywhywhywhywhywhy*why*?"

He shuddered, his blood once again like ice in his veins, as he fought down the memories, battered them into submission, and rode on, his lips a tight line, a muscle in his jaw jumping.

Later, when he rode in among the scattered agency buildings, he headed directly for the one where he had spoken to Garth and Briggs. He changed direction when he spotted Isabel Bonner just coming out of the back door of the mission building to stand vigorously pounding a dust mop against the porch railing. He rode up to the porch and touched the brim of his hat to her. "How do, Isabel?"

"Good morning." She continued to pound the mop against the railing, raising tiny clouds of dust.

"You sound about as chilly as today's air, which has a definite nip in it. Have I done something to offend you?"

"You're a man," Isabel answered cryptically.

"That's plain enough to see. That's as plain as the nose on my face." Or as plain as the ramrod I got swinging between my legs, he thought. "But has that turned into some kind of crime?"

Isabel huffed in apparent exasperation and turned a withering glance on him, the dust mop drooping in her hands. "You're all alike, every last one of you, where women are concerned. You ride roughshod over any woman you meet and then expect her to give you a cheerful smile and a humble curtsy when next you walk into a room where she happens to be. You men, none of you, have any respect for a woman's tender feelings. You are all"—she seemed to be struggling to find a word—"*merciless!*"

Cimarron sat his saddle and stared at the empty spot on the porch where Isabel had just been standing. Then, shrugging, he dismounted, wrapped his reins around a trellis, from which hung the dead remains of last summer's wisteria, and followed her into the mission.

He found her weeping in the kitchen just inside the back door. He went to her and took her in his arms. "What's got you so upset?"

"Nothing," she said, almost choking on the word.

"You want to tell me what that nothing is? Maybe I can help straighten it out." He drew her closer to him.

She pushed him away from her. "You saw how he was at the dance yesterday. How he practically ignored me. How he went panting after that Baldwin woman!"

So that's it, Cimarron thought. "You have your eyes on Hunter, do you?"

"No! I mean—well, yes, I did. But not now, not anymore. Not after the awful way he treated me. For him, I don't even exist! I might as well be living on the moon."

"This old world'd be a sorrier place were you to take up an abode on the moon, Isabel. I can testify to that."

She looked up at him through her slowing tears.

"I'm telling you the truth, Isabel."

She burst into a fresh torrent of tears.

Again Cimarron took her in his arms and held her gently, stroking her hair with one hand. "You go ahead and cry out all your hurting. It'll do you good."

"But it won't make Clyde Hunter take notice of me!" she wailed.

"There are a whole bunch of other men in the world, honey, me among them," he reminded her, hoping.

"I'm so weary of listening to other people's troubles," Isabel confided. "We missionaries are expected to be so full of patience and kindness and so many other virtues. We're supposed to keep a stiff upper lip and our chins up all the time. But nobody ever seems to realize that we are sometimes in dire need of comforting ourselves. That we suffer pain just like everyone else! That we long for someone to show us a little tender mercy sometimes!"

"You spoke about needing some comforting. I'd like to try to comfort you, if you'll let me." Cimarron drew her closer to him, keenly conscious of the heat of her very desirable body and of his rampant erection.

"Why not?" Isabel murmured, her words almost lost as she pressed her cheek against Cimarron's chest. "Why shouldn't I take what I'm entitled to? Don't I deserve some creature comforts the same as everyone else? Some fleshly delights?"

"You bet your bottom dollar, you do!" Cimarron exclaimed quickly and maneuvered his pelvis so that his shaft was pressing hard against Isabel's thigh. "You're about the most deserving lady in the fleshly delights department that I've ever laid eyes on."

"But it would be wrong."

He quickly shook his head in firm denial of her statement. "It'll be right, you'll see."

Isabel tentatively moved closer to him. "I've been living a chaste life for so long that I feel like a field in a drought. I don't ask much of life, and I do try to give to other people more than I get. Perhaps it would be committing only a small sin."

"Small or big, it'll be worth it for you to let go and kick over the traces, honey, if only just this once."

"Is that a guarantee?" Isabel asked him in a suddenly teasing tone.

"I'd say it was, only I don't want you to think me prideful." He kissed her and then, when he raised his head, he brushed a tear from her cheek. "Where can we go?"

By way of answer she took his hand and led him out of the kitchen, up the stairs to the second floor, and into a sparely furnished bedroom. And then she did an abrupt about-face and started out of the bedroom. But Cimarron caught her by the arm and, before she could free herself from him, he kissed her again, and this time his tongue forced its way into her mouth. A moment later she began to moan, and a moment after that she was sucking lustily on his tongue and he was leading her, their lips still locked together, toward the bed. When he reached it, their lips parted and he eased her down upon it. His right hand burrowed under her skirt, and his fingers caressed her calf, her thigh, and finally her hot mound.

He lay down beside her and, after fumbling about for a while, managed to get his hand beneath her undergarments and the middle finger of that hand well into her. He was not surprised to find her responding eagerly to him. He smiled to himself, thinking that missionary women were a whole lot like pent up dams bursting when the right—or even the wrong—man managed to get them in bed on their backs.

His thoughts were interrupted as Isabel pulled away from him and his finger slid out of her squirming body. She was up off the bed, and then so was he, ready to grab her if she again got cold feet and started to flee. Such a move proved to be unnecessary because she was tearing off her clothes and flinging them in every direction until at last she was naked, back in bed, and urging Cimarron to hurry up and undress.

He shucked his clothes as fast as he could, happy to oblige the lady watching him with fiery eyes. Then he flopped back down beside her and she grabbed him and her hands began to explore his body. A moment later, her lips joined the exploratory expedition. Shudders shook him as wave after wave of pleasure washed over him. He was about to cover her when she scrambled up onto her knees and, straddling him, touched the tip of his shaft with the tip of her fingers, causing it to throb. He reached up and took her breasts in his hands. She moaned with pleasure as he fondled them, thumbing their nipples into erect life. She lowered her body toward him, and he took her left breast in his mouth and began to suck on it, causing her to moan even louder. Then she withdrew from him and eased up along his body until the cleft between her legs was directly above his lips.

As she lowered herself upon him, his tongue shot into her and began to snake its way about in the hot darkness. She cried out as he continued his arousing ministrations, while at the same time he caressed both of her breasts. As the scent of sex rose around them, Isabel drew back until her knees were once again pressing against Cimarron's thighs. Slowly, she lowered her head. Her lips parted.

He watched as her lips closed around the head of his shaft. He continued watching as she lowered her head still further until her lips were pressed against the hairy thatch at the base of his shaft. And then, as her head began to rise and quickly descend in a swift rhythm, she made soft mewling sounds, and Cimarron, his head thrown back and his eyes closed, felt himself ascending ecstatic heights until at last he erupted and he cried out, his toes curling, as Isabel's tongue continued to lave the long quivering length of him.

She straightened and looked down at him, a faint smile on her face as she positioned herself above his shaft and then lowered herself onto it, and it gradually disappeared within her.

Cimarron had no time to relax after his orgasm because Isabel was writhing on him, twisting her pelvis in every possible direction, as she grunted, "Uh, uh, *uh!*"

She cried out, a piercing sound, as she achieved the first of what proved to be a pair of orgasms, and she cried out even louder as Cimarron also climaxed when she did for the second time.

Only gradually did her movements begin to slow down, and it was several minutes before she rose and he slipped out of her. Then, lying down beside him, her fingers caressing his chest, his navel, his now semistiff shaft, she sighed and said, "It was all you guaranteed me it would be—and more."

"Thanks in no small measure to yourself," he told her sincerely.

"But I feel terrible."

He propped his head up on one hand and looked down at her. "You mean I hurt you?"

She shook her head. "I feel as if I have betrayed Clyde."

"Are you two engaged?"

"No. But—it's just something I feel inside. I feel as if I somehow belong to him."

"That may be on account of you want so bad to belong to him."

"Yes, I suppose that's it. But there's no use my thinking that way since Clyde is obviously enamored of Miranda Baldwin."

"You're not going to let a little thing like that stop you, are you?"

"What can I do in the face of his feelings?"

"Women know more about what to do in a situation like that than any man does. But there must be something you can do if you want to get your rope on Hunter."

"I'm so ashamed of myself."

"What's wrong now?"

"Here I am with you like this, and all I can talk about is another man. It must make you feel terrible and me appear totally insensitive."

"I've not got you hobbled, honey. What you and me just did—well, it was a kind of friendly thing to do, don't you think?"

"Well, I suppose 'friendly' is one way to put it."

He playfully touched the tip of her nose. "Hunter sure doesn't know what he's missing."

"Cimarron, I'm worried about him."

"I reckon you've got one or two good reasons to feel that way about him. One of them's named Baldwin, and the other one's named booze."

"One or the other could kill Clyde."

"That's the sad truth of the matter, as I see it."

"Oh, if there was only some way that I could save him!"

"Maybe you could—"

"My word, what was that?" Isabel cried, sitting up in bed at the sound of the wordless roar that could be heard in the bedroom even though its windows were closed.

Cimarron got out of bed and went to the nearer of the two

windows, and peered through it. "It's Hunter," he told Isabel who then quickly joined him at the window.

"It looks like Hunter and Earl Briggs are bent on braining each other," he commented as he watched the two men fighting in front of the agency building.

"Stop them, Cimarron!" Isabel cried, clutching his arm.

He glanced at her, saw the pleading look in her eyes, and hurriedly began to dress. Minutes later, he was bounding down the stairs of the mission and out of the house, heading for the two battling men, who were almost invisible as a result of the clouds of dust they were raising as they viciously fought each other.

When he reached the warriors, Cimarron asked no questions. He simply waded into the middle of the battle, delivering a powerful right uppercut, that knocked Briggs unconscious. He turned and was about to do the same for Hunter, when his attention was distracted by the sudden appearance of the Indian agent, Abel Garth. Garth staggered out onto the porch of the agency building and, pointing a shaking finger at Hunter, shouted, "*Arrest that man!*"

Hunter let out an enraged roar and dodged past Cimarron, heading for Garth. But before he could even begin to mount the steps leading to his quarry, Cimarron caught up with him, seized him by the collar, spun him around, and hit him in the head with both fists. Hunter dropped as if he'd been struck on the skull with a nine-pound sledge.

"What the hell's been going on here, Garth?"

"That Indian," Garth replied, pointing to the unconscious Hunter, who lay on the ground by Cimarron's boots, "tried to murder me. He came here with a gun. He was roaring drunk as usual, and he began making wild and totally unfounded accusations against me. I would not, I am certain, be alive now were it not that my trusted associate, Mr. Briggs, came so bravely to my assistance and disarmed Hunter. Then Briggs drove that wild Indian out here into the open and was in the process of giving him the sound thrashing he so richly deserves when you arrived. I want Clyde Hunter arrested, Deputy."

"On what charge, Garth?"

"For being drunk and disorderly. For defaming my good

name with his insane accusations. Most of all, for attempting to murder me.''

"That's quite a list of charges," Cimarron commented blandly as he bent down and picked up the limp body of the still unconscious Hunter. "What kind of accuastions was the man making against you, Garth?" he asked and tossed Hunter over his shoulder.

"I would really rather not say. They don't bear repeating."

"I'll need to know them for my official report on this," Cimarron lied.

Garth, looking annoyed, said, "He accused me of profiting illegally through the granting of Fox land leases."

Cimarron nodded and, carrying Hunter, began to walk away.

"Deputy!" Garth called out to him and he halted and looked back. "If this matter is too much trouble for you to handle, I shall be happy to turn it—and Hunter—over to my Fox Lighthorsemen.''

"I'll see to it, Garth." Cimarron resumed his journey.

"There is one other thing, Deputy." When Cimarron halted a second time and looked back, Garth continued, "Hunter should also be charged as the prime suspect in the shooting of Mr. Paul Baldwin.''

Cimarron nodded noncommittally and then made his way past the still-unconscious Briggs, who lay awkwardly sprawled on the ground. When he reached the hitchrail behind the mission, he freed his black and tossed Hunter over the animal's withers. He was about to swing into the saddle when Isabel, clad only in a woolen wrapper, dashed out onto the back porch.

Clutching her wrapper tightly about her with both hands, she stared speechlessly for a moment at the unconscious Hunter and then, turning to Cimarron, asked, "What happened?''

He told her.

"Is Clyde badly hurt?"

"Not so bad he won't mend, given time." Cimarron climbed aboard the black.

"Where are you taking him?"

"Somewhere out of sight so Garth won't get exasperated and send his Lighthorsemen after him." Noting the dismayed expression on Isabel's face, he added, "Now, don't you fret, honey. I'll do my damndest—beg pardon—my best to see to it that no harm comes to Hunter."

"Oh, I'm sure you will, Cimarron, only—" Isabel's words trailed away into silence.

"Only what, honey?"

"Only I can't help wondering if your best will be good enough in the light of all that's happened."

Cimarron also wondered if his best would be good enough to protect Hunter from the combined wrath of Paul Baldwin and Abel Garth. He touched the brim of his hat to Isabel and rode away from the mission, wondering if he was taking on the task of protecting the wrong man. Maybe, he thought, I ought to be protecting men like Baldwin and Garth and Briggs from this Indian, who does seem to have a fondness for going on the warpath with the help of a little too much firewater.

Seven

Cimarron drew rein in a wooded area about a mile from the agency when Hunter groaned and raised his head. He picked Hunter up by the belt and the scruff of his neck and eased him down to the ground, where Hunter stood blinking foolishly up at him and swaying unsteadily on his feet.

"Why didn't you let me finish my fight?" he barked at Cimarron. "Why the hell did you interfere?"

"To keep you from making a wanted man out of yourself, that's why I interfered. Now, tell me something. What's this I hear about you going gunning for Garth?"

"It's true. I had a gun and I told the bastard I was going to shoot him, although I didn't intend to. I just wanted to scare him. But Briggs stopped me and took my gun."

"From where I sit it looks like a damned good thing he did disarm you. Drunk as you were you could have shot somebody by accident—maybe killed them."

"Maybe that wouldn't have been so bad."

"You do seem keen on taking chances with your life, not to mention your liberty, Hunter. First Baldwin. Now Garth."

"I didn't shoot Baldwin!"

"You expect me to believe that, do you, after what you admit you just did back at the agency?"

"I told you. I was bluffing. I thought if I merely threatened to shoot him—"

"Why exactly did you threaten to shoot him?"

"Because of that scheme of his I told you about. The way he sells Fox land leases to whites and splits the take with whoever it is in the Indian Bureau who has to approve his grants. I thought if I could put a good enough scare into him, maybe he'd hightail it out of here and we might get some-body decent in as the new agent."

"It strikes me that you'd be a whole lot better off, Hunter, were you to get some proof of your charges against Garth and then lay that proof out in a court of law. Or maybe send it to the head of the Indian Bureau. That way you'd have a chance of getting what you want without foolishly risking your own and other folks' necks in the process."

"At the moment, I have very little proof. I told you when we first met about the white rancher named Loomis who promised me he'd testify against Garth and Briggs; Loomis, as I also told you, has disappeared. However, I did run into a man yesterday who just might be willing to back me up in what I'm charging."

"Who might that be?"

"An Indian—one of the Mesquakie. I mentioned him to you the first day we met. His name is Pushetonequa. He used to be one of Garth's Lighthorsemen."

"Used to be?"

Hunter looked down at the ground. "Like me, Pushetonequa is a drunk. So Garth got rid of him. But he knows the truth about Garth's operation. He was the one who first told me about it. That was right after Garth fired him."

"This Pushetonequa, he might not be the best of witnesses. Sounds to me like he might be telling tales about Garth just to get even with the man for canning him. And those tales, well, they might or might not be true."

"He's telling the truth. Pushetonequa doesn't have any axe to grind, not where Garth's concerned. He doesn't have to try to keep up appearances. He's perfectly content to be a drunk. In fact, he's *glad* Garth fired him!"

Cimarron considered what Hunter had said for a moment and said, "Maybe I ought to have a talk with Pushetonequa. Let's you and me go see him."

"You go."

Cimarron gave Hunter a questioning glance.

"I need a drink," Hunter said, avoiding Cimarron's eyes. "There's a still not far from here. And then I should go to see my uncle. I promised to pay him a visit yesterday, but I forgot all about it."

"Why not skip the drink and come with me instead?"

"Don't you tell me how to live my life, and I won't tell you how to live yours!" Hunter snarled, his temper flaring.

"You sure can be a snotty sonofabitch, Hunter. Maybe I just ought to arrest you to keep your ass out of trouble."

"Do it, then!"

"Don't push me or I might." Cimarron silently counseled himself to simmer down. "Where can I find Pushetonequa?" he asked, and Hunter sullenly gave him the directions he had sought.

It took Cimarron the better part of two hours to locate Pushetonequa's wickiup, which was nine miles north of the agency in a box canyon. The entrance was also almost completely hidden by a tangled stand of cedars and the dense undergrowth beneath them. He had passed the entrance to the canyon several times without seeing it. It was not until he heard slurred singing in a language he did not understand that he was able, by following the sounds, to locate the entrance. Once inside the canyon, he followed it to the wickiup, which was built of bare tree limbs covered with cured hides. From inside it, the unseen singer sang on, the monotonous melody of his song interrupted from time to time by rumbling belches.

Cimarron halloed the dwelling. The song continued. He halloed it again. The song continued. Finally, he drew aside the hide that was flapping in the breeze over the wickiup's entrance and went inside. There he found an Indian he estimated to be no more than twenty years old seated cross-legged by the ashes of a long-dead fire, an uncorked jug resting between his legs.

The man's long black hair was unkempt, his clothes were little more than rags, and his eyes were glazed and barely focused. He greeted Cimarron with a wave and then paid no more attention to him as he went on alternately singing and drinking from his jug.

Cimarron introduced himself. "I'm a deputy marshal here in Indian Territory. Are you Pushetonequa?"

At the sound of the name, the Indian looked up at Cimarron and grinned. He took another long swallow from his jug and resumed his singing.

Cimarron reached out and forcibly took the jug away from him. "What's your name?"

"You just spoke it, white man. Give me—"

But Cimarron refused to surrender the jug. "Clyde Hunter told me about you. He told me you used to ride for Abel Garth the same as I ride for Judge Parker."

"And I was one hell-for-leather Lighthorseman in my time too, let me tell you," Pushetonequa said with pride. But then his face fell as he added, "When I was sober."

"Hunter also told me you claim that Garth and his right-hand man, Briggs, are running a crooked land-lease scheme here on the reservation."

"Sure, I did."

"How does Garth's scheme work?"

"Deputy, since I've got no gainful employment at the moment, I sure could use a loan. What would you say to two dollars?"

Cimarron hesitated only briefly and then paid Pushetonequa the bribe he had asked for. "How's Garth's scheme work?" he repeated.

Pushetonequa pocketed the two dollars. Smiled. Said, "Simple. A white man comes to the reservation. He looks around, sees plenty of good grazing land. Decides he'd like to settle himself down on some. So off he goes to Garth and tells him what he has in mind, and Garth tells him he's welcome—so long as he's willing to pay a nice price for the land he's been coveting. So much money up front and so much each and every month. Garth keeps most of the money, but he has to split his take with Briggs and the man in the Indian Bureau in Washington—the one who's got the power to grant the leases."

"What's his name?"

"Samuel Barstow." Pushetonequa gave Cimarron a searching stare. "Are you interested in Garth's operation as a lawman or have you a hankering to become a big-time rancher?"

"I had me a bellyful of punching cows a whole lot of years ago. Does that answer your question?" When Pushetonequa nodded, Cimarron asked, "Where and how exactly did you fit into Garth's land-lease picture?"

"That'll cost you another two dollars, that information will." Pushetonequa smirked at Cimarron, who dug down in his pocket and handed over two more dollars. "Us Light-horsemen," he said as he pocketed the money, "we were soldiers, and Garth, he was our general. He gave the orders and we obeyed them."

"That don't tell me a damn thing. What kind of orders?"

"Say some rancher ran short of funds one month and couldn't shell out to Garth like he'd agreed to. No problem, not for Garth. Garth would just send some of us boys out to pay a visit to that rancher, and by the time him and us got all through visiting it was likely we had collected the money he owed Garth. But if we hadn't for one reason or another, it was even more likely that the rancher we'd visited would find himself with a broken arm or maybe a leg. Word got around fast that Garth wasn't a man to fool with. He didn't have much trouble collecting his money. When he did—well, like I said, some of us Lighthorsemen were there to see he got what was due him."

"For a cut, no doubt."

"A man's got to live. The annuity payments us Foxes get from the government aren't all that much. And a Lighthorse-man—at least here on the reservation, he doesn't earn but fifteen dollars a month. Like I said, a man has to live."

"Clyde Hunter's hell-bent on calling a halt to Garth's game. He told me when we first met that he'd talked to you about testifying against Garth and Briggs if he files charges against them, but he said you two couldn't work out an arrangement on that score. Is that true?"

"It's true. I told Clyde I'll be more than glad to tell a judge and jury everything I know. All Clyde has to do, I told him, is come up with fifty dollars to pay me for my time and trouble, and I'll testify against Garth and Briggs any old time. But Clyde didn't have the cash at the time, and so far he's not been able to come up with it. Which gave me an idea. When I was at the agency to get my annuity payment the other day I told Garth what Clyde wanted me to do. But I told him I wouldn't do it if *he* would pay me fifty dollars."

"What did Garth say to that?"

"He just laughed at me and told me to go ahead and testify to my heart's content. He said nobody would believe drunken Indians making claims against a respectable man like him. And I guess you know that by drunken Indians, he meant Clyde and me. Now, Deputy, I've not got another damn thing

106

to tell you, so would you mind handing over that jug of mine?''

Cimarron did and watched Pushetonequa upend it on his bent arm and drink noisily from it, before he turned and left the man's wickiup.

The following morning Cimarron sat at the breakfast table with Baldwin and Miranda and ate heartily of the flapjacks he had doused with apple butter.

"Ask him, Paul," said Miranda.

Cimarron looked up at her and then across at her brother, seated on the opposite side of the table.

When Baldwin remained silent, Cimarron spoke. "Ask me what?''

Baldwin leaned back in his chair. "Cimarron, Miranda wanted me to ask you why you have not seen fit to take Clyde Hunter into custody.''

Cimarron shoved a forkful of flapjacks into his mouth, chewed, swallowed, took a drink of coffee from his cup, and only then answered, "On account of I'm not so sure he's guilty of shooting you, Baldwin. And on account of there's a whole lot going on around here that I want to get to the bottom of before I go off half-cocked and do something dumb like arresting the wrong man in this case.''

"Surely you don't mean that you think Clyde Hunter is innocent of the charge of shooting my brother?" Miranda exclaimed incredulously.

Cimarron ignored her. "Baldwin, how come you didn't see fit to tell me that you were paying bribes to Abel Garth?''

"I don't know what you're talking about!''

Cimarron sighed. "Baldwin, I do wish you wouldn't dance me around the barn on this matter. I know you paid Garth a fee to get your land lease. I also know you pay him a monthly fee to keep on using your grazing land. What I don't know is why you didn't tell me so when we first talked over the matter of what's been happening around here lately.''

Cimarron was keenly aware of the way Miranda was studiously avoiding looking in her brother's direction. He waited.

Baldwin scratched his head nervously. He stroked his chin and looked everywhere but at Cimarron. Finally, "I didn't think it was important—or germane to the matter of the shooting.''

"It might be," Cimarron commented laconically.

"In what way?" Baldwin inquired, frowning now.

"Don't know. Maybe it doesn't have any bearing on the matter. The point I'm trying to make is you've been a lot less than aboveboard with me, Baldwin, and I got to tell you that makes me wonder what else might be going on around here that folks might be hiding from me."

"We weren't hiding anything!" Miranda protested. "It was a simple business arrangement between my brother and Mr. Garth and, as such, we felt it was none of your concern."

"I must say," Baldwin declared, "I fail to see what Abel Garth's dishonest little scheme to make a few dollars has to do with the fact that someone tried to kill me."

Cimarron emptied his coffee cup. "First off, Baldwin, let me ask you something. What makes you so sure somebody wanted to kill you?"

"He was shot—wounded!" Miranda cried in evident exasperation.

"Maybe whoever it was shot him meant to wound, not kill, him," Cimarron pointed out to her. "And, as to why I might be making a connection between the bribes you've been paying to Garth and the fact that somebody shot you— well, consider this angle, Baldwin. If you failed to make your payments, Garth would have tried some tough tactics to get you to come up with the money you owe him."

"Why, that's an absolutely preposterous idea!" Baldwin spluttered.

"I had me a talk yesterday with an Indian by the name of Pushetonequa," Cimarron continued. "He used to be a Lighthorseman. He told me Garth was in the habit of sending some of his Lighthorsemen out to rough up white ranchers who reneged on the debts they owed him."

"The man's a liar!" Baldwin practically shouted. "He—"

Before he could finish what he had been about to say, there was a loud knock on the back door, and Miranda rose in response to it. She opened the door to admit one of Baldwin's hired hands who pulled off his hat and announced, "Abel Garth's dead, Mr. Baldwin!"

Cimarron stared at the man as Baldwin repeated, "Dead?"

"Me and two of the other boys was driving stock past the agency just after first light this morning, Mr. Baldwin. Well, sir, there was a commotion of some kind up there, and I rode over to see what it was all about. It turned out, according to Mr. Briggs, that Clyde Hunter had come to the agency real early in the morning and started a fight with Mr. Garth same as he did the day before when Mr. Briggs disarmed him. Well, he'd gotten himself another gun, and this time he shot and killed Mr. Garth and—" The man blushed and glanced at Miranda.

"And?" prompted Baldwin impatiently.

"I don't like saying in mixed company what else Mr. Briggs saw Hunter do to Mr. Garth, Mr. Baldwin."

"Tell us what happened," Miranda directed her brother's employee, who was nervously twisting his hat in his hands as he stood in the doorway.

The man looked questioningly at Baldwin and, when Baldwin nodded, he continued, "Mr. Briggs said Hunter held him at bay with a six-gun while he cut off Mr. Garth's head and his—" The man blushed an even brighter shade of crimson and glanced again at Miranda.

"He did what?" Baldwin cried.

"Hunter took Mr. Garth's head—and some of his other parts—away with him when he lit out, is what Mr. Briggs said."

"Did anybody else see Hunter do the killing and mutilating besides Briggs?" Cimarron asked.

Baldwin's hired hand shook his head. "Mr. Briggs said him and Mr. Garth were both asleep upstairs in the agency building when Hunter busted in on them. He said, Mr. Briggs did, there wasn't another soul around at the time. He said he had to stand and watch what Hunter did to Garth after Hunter had killed him, and he couldn't do a thing on account of Hunter warned him in no uncertain terms that he'd blow his head off if he made a wrong move."

"Has anybody seen Hunter since?"

"No, sir, not that I know of. But Mr. Briggs, he said he was sending for as many of the agency's Lighthorsemen as he could round up on short notice, and he was going to set them to tracking Hunter down. Maybe they've found him by now for all I know."

"Thank you for bringing us the news," Baldwin told his employee. When the man had gone, both he and his sister stared in silence at Cimarron.

It was Miranda who finally broke the strained silence by saying, "Well, it seems that the matter of Clyde Hunter is now out of your hands, Cimarron. And I for one am glad it is. Now, it seems, we can expect some action when Mr. Briggs's Lighthorse police set out after Hunter instead of the shilly-shallying about we've had from you so far."

Cimarron rose and started for the door. On his way to it, he took his hat down from a wall peg and clapped it on his head. At the door, he halted. Addressing Miranda, he said, "You're dead wrong about the matter of Clyde Hunter being out of my hands. When an Indian kills or otherwise harms a white person here in the Territory, that crime comes under the jurisdiction of the District Court of the United States for the Western District of Arkansas, which is the one run by Judge Parker and the one I happen to work for."

Miranda and her brother exchanged glances before she asked Cimarron, "Then you intend to arrest Hunter for the murder of Abel Garth?"

"I'm going to try to get my hands on Hunter before the Lighthorsemen do," he replied.

"That is not a direct answer to my sister's question," Baldwin pointed out testily.

"I might arrest Hunter," Cimarron said, "after I've heard his version of what happened this morning up at the agency."

"You *might* arrest him!" Baldwin exclaimed. "Good Lord, Cimarron, you heard my man say that Earl Briggs was an eyewitness to the crime!"

"Yep, I heard what your hired hand had to say. Now I intend to hear what Hunter has to say about the matter." Before either Baldwin or Miranda could utter another word, Cimarron left the house and headed for the barn to get the black ready to ride.

Hunter had him a reason to do in Garth, Cimarron thought as he galloped north. Namely, to stop the man from running his corrupt land-leasing scheme. Maybe Hunter got drunk and

110

figured it was time to put an end to the dirty business once and for all, so he got him a gun and went after Garth.

But you turn the whole thing around another way, and you come up with a whole different way of figuring out what happened. Maybe Briggs decided to get Garth out of his way so he could pocket all the money coming in from the ranchers instead of splitting it with his boss. Maybe he shot Garth and claimed he saw Hunter do the deed. That way Briggs would have killed two pesky birds with one stone: his boss, who was taking the lion's share of the grazing fees, and a trouble-some Indian who was trying his damndest to blow the whistle on the operation.

Cimarron lashed the black with his reins, and the horse, its body lathered with sweat, raced on gamely. As he rode, Cimarron kept his eyes peeled, expecting trouble but hoping he wouldn't meet any in the form of Lighthorsemen out chasing Hunter. To his relief, he saw no one else on the plain during the entire time it took him to reach his destination—Mokohoko's wickiup.

When he did reach it, he quickly dismounted and called the old man's name. When Mokoholo emerged a moment later, Cimarron asked him if Hunter was inside the dwelling.

Mokohoko shook his head.

Unwilling to accept the old man's denial at face value, Cimarro entered the wickiup—and found it empty. Back outside he asked, "Where's your nephew?"

"You might as well ask me where is the wind. Now it is here, now there. One never knows where or when he will find it."

"Hunter's not been here? He told me yesterday he intended to pay you a visit."

"He was here yesterday. Today he is not here. Why do you seek him?"

Cimarron told Mokohoko about the murder of Abel Garth, concluding his account of it with, "Briggs says he saw your nephew shoot, kill, and mutilate Garth, and he's been rounding up Lighthorsemen to hunt him down. So if you know any-thing about his whereabouts, Mokohoko, I'd advise you to tell me so I can maybe keep a Lighthorse rope from going around your nephew's neck."

"You think the Lighthorse will hang Clyde?"

"Let me put it to you this way, Mokohoko. I've known of cases where somebody gets accused of a crime—a crime he didn't commit—and the real committer of that crime, he sees to it that the accused dies before he can be tried or can prove he didn't do it. Case closed and the real criminal walks around a free and easy man."

"Then you think Clyde did not kill the agent?"

"I won't go so far as to say that. He had a motive—to put Garth out of the land-leasing picture."

"Clyde has many faults, drunkenness among them," Mokohoko murmured. "But he is not capable of killing another human being—not even in self-defense. Find him, Cimarron. Save him."

Cimarron noted the tears glistening in Mokohoko's eyes. "That's what I'm trying to do. I thought he might be here. But maybe he's with that friend of his—Pushetonequa."

"No, he is not."

"How come you sound so sure he's not?"

"When Clyde came here late yesterday, I told him what I had heard, which was that Pushetonequa has disappeared. He was shocked. He asked me what had happened. All I could tell him was that the man had suddenly vanished from the face of the earth."

Like the rancher named Loomis that Hunter and Isabel told me about, Cimarron thought, and Hunter's two friends, Neapope and Poweshiek. What the hell is going on around here? How come people seem to keep falling off the edge of the earth, never to be seen again? "I'll head for the mission," he told Mokohoko. "Maybe he's holed up there with Isabel Bonner."

Cimarron went to the black and was about to swing into the saddle when Mokohoko pointed to the east and said, "Someone comes."

Cimarron stared at the two riders on the horizon who were rapidly approaching the wickiup, but he was unable to make out their features. It was not until they came much closer that he recognized Clyde Hunter and Isabel Bonner. They're riding like old Lucifer himself was on their backtrail, he thought, watching them.

Minutes later, as they both drew rein in front of the wickiup, Clyde said, "Uncle, I'm in big trouble. I—"

"I know," Mokohoko said. "Cimarron told me."

"Then you know what has happened this morning at the agency?" Isabel asked Cimarron.

He nodded. "Hunter, what's your side of the story? Did you kill Garth?"

"I did not!" Hunter promptly replied at the same time that Isabel said, "Clyde was with me at the mission during the time Mr. Briggs says Mr. Garth was murdered. So he has a valid alibi, one I will support by court testimony in his behalf should that ever become necessary."

Cimarron, noting the defiant glance Isabel gave him, wondered if she were lying. He hoped she wasn't. And if she's not, he thought, maybe Hunter's finally got his eyes open to the fact that the lady loves him. "Hunter," he said, "I think you and me had best be making tracks out of this part of the country until I can sort things out and—" He frowned.

"What is it?" Isabel asked him anxiously. "What's wrong?"

"Look yonder," he replied, pointing to the horizon.

The other three people did and then Isabel said, "I don't see anything."

"See that little puff of what looks like smoke just this side of the horizon?" Cimarron said tensely. "Well, it's not smoke. It's dust. Dust that's being raised by a bunch of riders who're all heading this way."

Hunter turned back to stare at Cimarron. "Lighthorsemen?"

"That'd be my guess." They'd be likely to come here hunting you." Thinking fast, Cimarron rejected his original plan to ride off with Hunter in tow. "You three had best get yourselves out of here before the company comes. Isabel, you go back to the mission, where you'll be safe. Take a roundabout route so nobody sees you and connects you with any of this. Hunter, you and your uncle head for Pushetonequa's place and hole up there till I can join you and we can figure out what move to make next."

Cimarron helped Mokohoko climb up behind the cantle of his nephew's saddle and then, as the two men rode west and Isabel rode south, he broke a branch from a nearby tree and dragged it along the ground to eliminate from the dust in front of the wickiup all sign of Hunter's and Isabel's horses.

Six Lighthorsemen, Cimarron thought, as the riders came closer and he was able to make out their faces. "Howdy," he said cheerfully to the men when they drew rein in front of Mokohoko's wickiup.

"Where's the old man?" asked one of the lawmen who seemed to Cimarron to be the leader of the group.

"What old man?"

"Mokohoko's his name, and this wickiup is where he lives."

"Don't know the man," Cimarron lied. "I was just riding by and stopped to see if whoever lives here'd be good enough to give me some water for my mount."

As the leader of the group continued to stare suspiciously at him, Cimarron gave the man a smile. "You boys hunting somebody, are you?"

"Since when's that any of your business?" snapped the Indian.

"Well, I reckon it's not any of my business, but I was just trying to be friendly. You see, boys, you Lighthorsemen and me, we're in the same business."

"How do you know we're Lighthorsemen?"

"Why, that's easy enough to answer. You've got the look of lawmen about you, same as me. It's a kind of mean look, I'm told by folks who say I've got it."

"That's him!" one of the other Lighthorsemen muttered.

"Your name, it's Cimarron?" inquired the group's leader.

"It is. I take it you've heard of me. Nothing bad though, I hope." He grinned.

The leader of the Lighthorsemen made a curt gesture. In response to it four revolvers and one rifle suddenly appeared in the hands of the other five Lighthorsemen, all of which were aimed directly at Cimarron, who threw up his hands, his grin collapsing.

"Hey, now, what's this all about?" he asked.

"Mr. Briggs told us about you," replied the leader of the Lighthorsemen. "He don't much like the way you coddled Clyde Hunter even though the word was out about him shooting Mr. Baldwin. If you'd run Hunter in, Mr. Garth might be alive and kicking, only he ain't because Hunter killed him early this morning. So Mr. Briggs told us before we set out after Hunter to be on the lookout for you and, if we found you, to make sure you stayed out of our way. He was afraid you might try to help that murderer get away from us."

114

The Lighthorseman gestured again, and all of his men dismounted. While four of them held their six-guns on Cimarron, the fifth pulled Cimarron's rifle from its saddle boot and ordered him to hand over his gunbelt, which he reluctantly did. Then the Lighthorsemen reached for a length of rope that hung from his saddle horn.

The leader of the Lighthorsemen swore. "What the hell are you intending, Smoky? You plan on tying him up right out here in the open so somebody can easy find and free him?"

"Inside!" ordered the man named Smoky, and Cimarron turned and entered Mokohoko's wickiup, followed by the other five Lighthorsemen.

"Sit down on that chair!" Smoky ordered.

Cimarron did as he had been ordered, and when he was seated on the chair, Smoky ordered him to put his hands behind him.

Minutes later, Cimarron's hands were tightly tied to the slats in the back of the chair, and his ankles were tied as tightly to the chair's front legs.

"That ought to hold him," commented one of the other Lighthorsemen who had not spoken before, and then all of them left the wickiup.

Cimarron, cursing under his breath as he listened to the sound of the Lighthorsemen riding away from the wickiup, strained mightily against the ropes that held him prisoner in the chair.

But they held.

Eight

Cimarron silently damned the ropes that would not give and himself for having gotten into such a situation. He flexed his fingers and tried again—and failed—to pull one of his hands through the ropes that bound him to the slatted back of the chair.

Then, no longer straining against the ropes, it occurred to him that the chair might be weaker than the ropes. His fingers closed on one of the narrow slats that formed the back of the chair. He pushed it in one direction and then pulled it in another. It bent slightly under the heavy pressure he was applying to it. He continued bending it, a little farther each time, and at last the thin wood snapped, and his hands, although still bound behind his back, were at least free of the chair.

He bent over backward, his hands groping, until his fingers managed to close on the left rear leg of the chair. Gripping it in both hands, he pulled hard on it. It took him several tries, but he finally managed to tear the leg free. When he did, the chair tilted, and he fell to the floor. Moments later, he had ripped the chair's right rear leg from the seat, and soon he had succeeded in snapping the chair seat free of its remaining two front legs.

He lay for a moment on the floor until he caught his breath amid the wooden wreckage that had recently been a chair. Then, by contorting his body, he was able to pull his bowie knife from his boot. Working it free of its sheath, he got a grip on its handle with both hands and began to apply its blade to the ropes that bound his wrists. It was a painstaking process and once, when he dropped the knife, it took him

116

considerable squirming about on the floor before he could retrieve it and begin again to try to sever his bonds. But he kept at it, and he almost let out a whoop of pure joy when the bowie's blade finally sliced through his bonds and he shook the rope free of his wrists. Then, sitting up, he proceeded to remove the rope from around his ankles. He sheathed his bowie, returned it to his boot, sprang to his feet, and hurriedly left the wickiup.

He ran to where his black was browsing at the base of a tall elm and mounted. He rode away from the wickiup at a gallop as he headed for Pushetonequa's wickiup and his planned rendezvous with Hunter and Mokohoko.

When he arrived, he found the wickiup empty and no one in the surrounding area. Where the hell are they, he asked himself, trying not to face his worst fear: that the Lighthorsemen, after leaving Mokohoko's wickiup, had come to this one in search of Hunter and—

And what?

Maybe they hanged Hunter, he thought. Or shot him to death. But would they shoot Mokohoko? he wondered. Sure, they would, he decided. They would if they had killed Hunter. They'd not want any witnesses around to tell anybody about what they'd gone and done. But maybe Briggs ordered them to bring Hunter in alive, he speculated. That hopeful thought spurred him into action.

He turned his horse and set out for the agency in the hope that he would find Hunter and his uncle there—and both of them hale and hearty. Names flitted through his mind as he cat-tracked his black with his spurs to urge the animal into an even faster gallop. *Pushetonequa. Poweshiek. Loomis. Neapope.* All of them gone, he thought. Like they fell off the edge of the earth. Another name darted through his mind: *Briggs.* And one more: *Garth.* They're like pieces in a jigsaw puzzle. Put them all together, and you get a picture.

The three Indians and the white rancher, he thought. Those four pieces of the puzzle have one thing in common. They were all a threat, in one way or another, to the land-leasing scheme Garth and Briggs were running. Now let's put Garth into the picture. Let's say Garth wipes them out somehow or other to keep them from making trouble for him. Then we slip in the last piece of the puzzle—Briggs—and what have we got? What we've got is Briggs killing Garth so Briggs then has the whole land-leasing show to run all by himself. All he has to do then is frame Hunter for the murder of Garth, and that way he gets rid of just about the only threat left to the scheme he's taken over from his former boss.

That could be the way things went, Cimarron thought as he rode on. At least it ties up all the loose ends, and it explains a lot of what's been happening around here. He frowned. Only trouble is there may be one or two other ways to explain the same things—maybe even better ways. But my way points to one thing for sure, and that's that Briggs has got to get rid of Hunter, who's like a knife at his throat.

He rode on, his teeth grinding against one another as he thought of what Briggs had done to Garth—if his theory was right—and what such a man would be capable of doing to Hunter and Mokohoko. No, he thought grimly. They've got to be at the agency. They've just got to be.

However, when he reached the agency, they weren't there either. And neither was Briggs.

Cimarron left the empty agency building and was making his way to the mission when Isabel suddenly came running from the building.

"Cimarron!" she cried, and when she reached him, she practically fell into his arms. "Where's Clyde?" she asked breathlessly.

"I don't know."

"What happened after I left Mokohoko's place?"

He told her, concluding his account of what had happened with, "Then, when I went to meet Hunter and Mokohoko at Pushetonequa's wickiup like we'd planned, neither one of them was there. I thought maybe they'd come here instead but I was just at the agency and nobody's in there, not Briggs nor anybody else."

"What do you think happened to Clyde and his uncle? I mean where else could they have gone?"

Cimarron hesitated a moment before answering, not wanting to alarm Isabel. But neither did he want to hide from her his worst suspicions, believing it was always better for a person to know the truth, no matter how bad that truth might be, so that it could then at least be squarely confronted and

118

dealt with. "I'm beginning to wonder if Hunter and Mokohoko haven't gone the way of some of the other men who've disappeared like Loomis, that rancher you and Hunter talked about to me, and some Indians I've also heard about."

Isabel gasped and clasped a hand to her chest.

"Are you all right?"

"Yes, I think so. "I just—for a moment there I felt quite faint. Cimarron, in my concern for Clyde and Mokohoko I completely forgot to tell you. It wasn't until you mentioned Mr. Loomis's disappearance that I remembered."

"Remembered what?"

"Miranda Baldwin was here waiting for me when I got back to the mission late this afternoon. She was distraught. It seems that Paul Baldwin has also disappeared."

Cimarron's eyes narrowed. "What did she have to say to you?"

"As I said, she was very upset. I gathered though that she has not seen her brother since early this morning when he left to join his men out on the range."

"I saw Baldwin this morning. He and some of his boys were driving in some stock. He told me how to find Mokohoko's wickiup. Maybe Miranda's got no good reason to be upset about her brother. It's less than a whole day he's been gone. He could have decided to spend the night out on the range with his men."

"He didn't. Miranda said his men arrived at the ranch with the stock, and when she questioned them about her brother's whereabouts, they were surprised to learn that he'd not come home. She said that they told her Mr. Baldwin had decided to take a shortcut home and, while doing so, check a spot along the way where the stock tended to stray because there was a salt lick in the area."

"Where's Miranda now?"

"She told me she was returning home, and she asked me to tell you if I saw you that she needed your help. I'm truly sorry I didn't tell you about this right away. I would have but it completely slipped my mind because I was so worried about Clyde—about Clyde and Mokohoko."

"I understand. Honey, you stay put right here. If I find Hunter and his uncle, I'll be sure to get word to you as soon as ever I can."

"Where are you going now?"

"Down south to the Baldwin ranch. I want to have a talk with Baldwin's men to see if they can shed any light on his disappearance."

As Cimarron turned and headed for his horse, Isabel called his name. "What about Mr. Briggs?" she inquired when he turned back to her.

"What about him?"

"I haven't seen him since I returned to the mission, and you just said he isn't at the agency. Cimarron, do you think he too has disappeared like the others?"

"Could be. But he's not my main concern at the moment. I'm a whole lot more interested in finding out what's happened to Hunter, Mokohoko, and Baldwin."

"Be careful, Cimarron," Isabel told him as he swung into the saddle of the black and touched the brim of his hat to her.

Cimarron was barely out of sight of the agency when a rifle shot rang out. His mount nickered and began to strain at the bit. Cimarron, unarmed and holding tightly to the reins to check the startled horse, turned the animal and rode in the opposite direction from which the shot had been fired. Whoever fired at me, he thought, ought to buy himself a pair of eyeglasses. He missed me by nigh on to a mile.

The gunman fired a second time, and again the shot went wide of its mark. If he tried missing me, Cimarron thought with grim satisfaction, he couldn't've done better. He flinched as a third shot sounded, and then he realized as he swung around in his saddle that the shot had not come from behind but from in front of him. What the hell—

A mob of mounted Indians led by the leader of the group of Lighthorsemen Cimarron had encountered earlier came riding out of the woods on both sides of the trail. They seemed to him to be an army, there were so many of them. More than a dozen, he estimated. Closer to two dozen.

"We got him dead to rights, Bigler!" crowed one of the men, addressing the leader of the group. "You sure had his moves figured out right."

"I figured he'd show up at the agency sooner or later," drawled the man named Bigler. "That's why I staked it out and why I posted Carlin up there on that hill to shoot the wild way he did—to drive this deputy right into our arms."

120

Bigler gave Cimarron a cold stare. "We went back to Mokohoko's place to round you up, only to find out you'd flown the coop. So we got ourselves some reinforcements and came looking for you."

"I thought you Lighthorsemen were looking for Hunter," Cimarron remarked, his hands in the air.

"We were. But once we'd found him and his uncle at Pushetonequa's wickiup, we got orders to get you too."

"Orders from Briggs?"

"Move him out!" Bigler ordered his Lighthorsemen, ignoring Cimarron's question.

Cimarron found himself riding between two columns of Lighthorsemen. Bigler rode at the head of the double column, and two other men brought up the rear.

"Where are you boys planning on taking me?" Cimarron asked, addressing no one in particular.

"He wants to know where we're taking him, Bigler," one of the men called out. "Shall I tell him?"

"You go and tell him," Bigler called back, "and you'll spoil the surprise."

Odd laughter then from the Lighthorsemen, mirthless and ragged.

The journey continued as evening became night and the stars and moon appeared. A chill wind rose and swept over the land. The Lighthorsemen and their prisoner rode in silence.

As they headed northwest and began to make their way among the foothills of a low mountain range, Cimarron thought once again of the men who had disappeared—Loomis and the others. Now it's my turn to disappear, he thought, wondering if there could be a connection between what was now happening to him and what had earlier happened to the other men who, he had been told, had vanished without a trace.

They continued to follow a long and tortuous trail through the foothills. Twice they were stopped by sentries posted on peaks who let them pass only when Bigler identified himself and his men.

It was close to midnight, Cimarron estimated after a glance at the polestar's position in the sky, when they topped a ridge and rode down into a small valley that was dotted with several glowing furnaces.

121

Furnaces? Cimarron, as he and his captors came closer to them, wondered what they were used for and by whom.

"Welcome to Death Valley," Bigler said to Cimarron as they rode out onto the floor of the valley.

Cimarron coughed as the wind suddenly shifted, and he inhaled throat-searing smoke that was rising from the furnaces. When Bigler called a halt, Cimarron was able to make out the forms of men moving about near the furnaces which, he could now see, were retort smelters. The men, wraithlike figures with haggard faces and emaciated bodies clothed in rags, fed wood to the furnaces, while other men, many of them trembling uncontrollably, set out rows of iron flasks on wooden tables placed near the smelters. Overseeing them were armed guards.

Bigler eyed Cimarron, who was watching the workers at the smelters. "Maybe you wonder why we call this place Death Valley, Deputy."

Cimarron said nothing.

"We call it that because men die here. Men like the ones over there working the furnaces."

Cimarron, his gaze fixed on the silent workers, became aware that most of them were not only trembling uncontrollably, but they were also slavering. Their skins, lit by the glow of the flames in the fireboxes of the smelters, were livid and oddly mottled, and their teeth were a sickly green color. The men were of all ages, but even the youngest of them seemed aged and stooped.

"What kind of an operation are you running here, Bigler?" he asked.

"We mine cinnabar," Bigler replied. "We dig it out of that big open pit over there."

Cimarron looked in the direction Bigler had pointed and saw the deep bowl-like depression that was illuminated by the light of the full moon. "We sell the quicksilver we get when the cinnabar's been smelted down and stored in those iron flasks you see over there," Bigler added. "It's a profitable business, Deputy, believe me, especially considering the fact that we've got real low overhead in the labor department."

Cimarron gave him a questioning glance.

"We don't pay those boys you see smelting the ore. Nor do we pay those who dig it out of the pit over yonder. We don't even pay the men we set to gathering wood for the smelters or the ones we've got weaving the baskets we use to carry the ore from the pit to the smelters."

"Where do you get men willing to work for nothing?"

Bigler smiled and answered, "We got our ways of recruiting laborers. We recruited you, didn't we?"

"Slave labor," Cimarron said softly, hating the sight of the twisted smile on Bigler's face.

"You got it, Deputy. Those are some of our slaves you're looking at over there. We recruit men who stray into the area and get themselves caught by the sentries that we've got posted on the range that runs all around this valley. We also put a lot of rabble-rousers and trouble-makers to work here in the valley."

Bigler's use of the words *rabble-rousers* and *trouble-makers* sparked a thought in Cimarron's mind. "You mean men like Loomis and Pushetonequa and Neapope and Poweshiek."

"Them—and men like you," Bigler added, his smile widening. "You'll be working right alongside them."

"Those men at the smelters," Cimarron said. "They look to me to be in pretty bad shape."

"Oh, they are," Bigler agreed amiably. "They're being poisoned from roasting the ore. Most of them have tried to escape or else they've given the guards headaches of one kind or another. So we tame 'em by putting them to work on smelting the cinnabar, and that tames 'em fast, I can tell you. They also die just about as fast. But that's no big problem for us. We can always recruit new men to take their places. Big strong men like you are the best. Such men usually last a good long while. Maybe you will, Deputy, before you finally drop."

Bigler gave commands to his men, and they proceeded to disperse, most of them heading for a large cabin that was situated on a stretch of level land between the smelters and the cinnabar pit, the others taking the horses to a corral that was off to one side of the cabin, and three men relieving the men who had been guarding the slave laborers at the smelters.

"Stand down," Bigler ordered Cimarron as he leaned over and ripped the black's reins from Cimarron's hand. "Find yourself a spot to bed down for the night."

"Out here in the open?" Cimarron asked, aware of the cold bite of the wind.

"We don't run a first—not even a second-class—hotel here in Death Valley," Bigler retorted.

Cimarron watched Bigler lead the black in the direction of the corral, which was crowded with horses. He looked around and finally chose a spot to the east of the smelters since the wind was blowing the poisonous fumes from the smelters in a westerly direction. And the smelters, he had noticed, gave off heat which, because of the cold night, he welcomed. As he lay down on the ground, he became aware of several other men lying huddled together in the vicinity. He considered waking them. There were questions he wanted answered. But he suppressed his impulse to awaken the men. If they were as malnourished and sick as those working the smelters, he thought, they needed their sleep more than he needed immediate answers to the questions that were plaguing him.

He lay for a long time looking up at the stars but not seeing them as he began to think about escaping from the valley. But escape, he told himself, would have to wait until he had answers.

Cimarron slept fitfully during what remained of the night. He was already awake at first light when the clanging of an iron bar against a metal triangle hanging from a post in front of the cabin shattered the early-morning stillness.

In response, men rose from the ground to shamble stoop-shouldered toward a shed north of the smelters, where an armed Indian distributed picks and shovels. Then they trudged slowly toward the huge cinnabar pit and climbed down into it, disappearing from Cimarron's sight like condemned souls wending their weary way down into hell.

"Don't they give a man breakfast here?" Cimarron asked a man shuffling past him. The man merely shook his head and moved on. Cimarron rose, joined the other slave laborers at the shed, taking a pick from the Indian and making his way to the pit.

He halted at its rim and stared down at the men who were making their way down the pit's sloping sides, some of them stumbling and rolling down to the bottom. No one stopped to help anyone else. No one paid any attention to those who fell.

The fallen picked themselves up and went silently to work with their picks and shovels.

Cimarron suddenly found himself toppling down into the pit because one of the guards ringing its perimeter had slammed a boot against his buttocks and shoved.

He collided with one of the workers in the pit when he hit bottom and knocked the man to the ground. Cimarron got to his feet and helped the man up as the guard who had kicked him shouted at him: "That'll learn you not to shilly-shally when there's a day's work to be done!"

Cimarron glared up at the guard in silence, retrieved the pick he had dropped, and began to dig into the side of the pit. He dislodged chunks of earth that were speckled with bright red crystals and occasional red or brown masses of earth. The color of the crystals reminded him of something, but of what he wasn't sure. He continued to dig as a man appeared at his side and began to shovel the cinnabar into a crudely woven basket, which when he had filled it to the rim, he carried up the slope, making his way to the smelters.

Cimarron worked on, sweat beginning to run down his face and body as the sun rose higher in the sky. And then, as he stared at the red earth he was digging into, it came to him. He had seen dust of that color on Earl Briggs's clothes and boots the first day he had gone to the agency and talked to Garth.

A coincidence? Or did Briggs have something to do with the mercury mine? Cimarron had no time to consider the question because at that moment someone whispered his name. He glanced over his shoulder and found himself staring into the haggard face of Clyde Hunter.

"Keep working," Hunter advised him, "or one of those guards up there will give you trouble. What the hell are you doing here, Cimarron?"

"The Fox Lighthorsemen caught me. They were following somebody's orders. Do you happen to know whose?"

"No." Hunter began to shovel the ore that Cimarron had torn loose from the sides of the pit with his pick into a basket. "They came to Pushetonequa's wickiup—the Lighthorse, I mean—and they disarmed me and brought my uncle and me here."

"The top man—the one named Bigler—he told me the rancher named Loomis you told me had disappeared is here

125

along with Pushetonequa and your two friends, Neapope and Poweshiek.''

"None of us will ever get out of here, Cimarron," Hunter intoned. "Not alive, we won't."

"I'm not so sure about that. I for one don't intend to die here."

"My uncle may already be dying. Mokohoko has had trouble breathing for some time now. I guess they saw that he wasn't all that fit or that strong and wouldn't be much good at digging down here. So they put him to working the day shift at the smelters. He's sick with mercury poisoning, Cimarron."

Cimarron heard the pain that lurked behind Hunter's words. "We've got to get Mokohoko out of here. You get your three friends, and I'll try to round up some more men for our side. Then the bunch of us can try taking control of this place."

Hunter, bent over his ore basket, shook his head. "They've got sentries picketed in the mountains. Any one of them would shoot you down like a dog. What's more, none of us have any weapons to defend ourselves."

"I've got a bowie knife in my boot," Cimarron said as he tore loose a section of red-speckled earth from the side of the pit. Hunter then smashed it with his shovel and loaded into his basket. "All of us have got picks or shovels."

"What good is one knife and a few picks and shovels against guns? Face it, Cimarron. We're trapped here, and there's only one way to get out of this place they call Death Valley, and that's by dying." Hunter hoisted his basket onto his left shoulder and began to climb slowly up the sloping side of the pit.

Cimarron worked on doggedly. Hours later, when the sun reached its zenith, he straightened and dropped his pick. He stretched to try to untie the knots that had formed in the muscles of his arms and shoulders.

He didn't see the stone that was flung at him by one of the armed guards up the rim of the pit, but he felt it strike the side of his head and break the skin there, releasing a thin stream of bright red blood. He swore and, with his hands fisted at his sides, he turned to stare up at the guard who had thrown the missile.

"That's what you get for loafing!" the guard yelled down

to him, and then he patted the stock of his rifle. "This *here's* what you'll get if you don't keep digging, gopher!"

As if to prove the validity of his shouted threat, the guard raised his rifle to the level of his waist and fired a shot that plowed into the side of the pit no more than a foot from where Cimarron stood.

Cimarron, almost choking on the rage that was rising within him, retrieved his pick and returned to work, trying to ignore the guard's triumphant and clearly mocking laughter that drifted down to him.

A little while later, another shot sounded. Cimarron stiffened, but the man working not far from him groaned and muttered, "Praise the Lord for small favors."

Cimarron looked up and then joined the other workers who were climbing up out of the pit to receive from an iron kettle some of the soup that one of the guards was ladling into tin bowls and passing out to the workers. When he had received his ration of soup, he made his way, searching for Mokohoko, among the smelter workers who were slumped on the ground as they ate. He found the man on the far side of the nearest smelter. Mokohoko lay prone on the ground, his eyes closed, his normally dark skin pale and badly mottled. Cimarron hunkered down beside him, touched him on the shoulder, and spoke his name.

"He's a goner, mister," volunteered a man on the far side of Mokohoko as he slurped soup from his bowl. "He's got not much more than a few days left at best. It's a sin to put an old man like that to working these god-awful smelters."

It's a crime, Cimarron thought. A crime called kidnapping. "Mokohoko," he repeated and gently squeezed the old man's shoulder.

Mokohoko stirred. His eyes fluttered open and tried to focus.

Cimarron shifted position so that his body provided shade for the old man to lie in. "It's me, Mokohoko. Cimarron."

Mokohoko managed to raise an arm. His hand came to rest on Cimarron's wrist. "I am sorry to see you here, Cimarron, because this is a place of death."

"I just had a talk with your nephew, Mokohoko. I told him I'm going to get you out of here."

Mokohoko coughed. His lips trembled and his eyes began to water. "And old man like me—forget me, Cimarron.

127

Clyde—he is young. He has his life, most of it, yet to live. Get him out of here. Help him escape. Promise me you will."

"What I'll promise you, Mokohoko, is I'll do my damndest to get the both of you out of here along with me."

The man who had commented on Mokohoko's deplorable condition earlier sighed and said, "Mister, you're having pipe dreams. Nobody gets out of here. They've got ways to make sure nobody gets out of here alive." He sighed again. "Awful ways. Believe me, I've seen some of 'em since I been here."

"Sometimes I think the Great Spirit plays tricks on both his red and white children, Cimarron," Mokohoko whispered. "Mr. Baldwin is also here. A prisoner like the rest of us."

"Baldwin's here? Where?"

"I do not know where. But Clyde told me he has been assigned to the smelters."

"Mokohoko, how come you don't have any soup?"

It was the man on the far side of Mokohoko who answered Cimarron's question. "Because he's too far gone to try to eat any, that's why."

Cimarron helped Mokohoko up into a sitting position, placing him so that his back was braced against a wheel of an ore wagon.

"No," Mokohoko protested feebly as Cimarron raised his own bowl to the aged Indian's lips. "Save your soup for yourself. You will need strength if you and Clyde are to escape from this place."

"I don't intend to argue with you, old man," Cimarron stated firmly. "Now, drink some of this soup before it spills and neither one of us gets to gain any benefit from it."

Mokohoko tried to push the bowl away but Cimarron kept him from doing so. Finally, Mokohoko took a sip from the bowl which Cimarron continued to hold to the old man's lips until it was empty.

"I thank you, Cimarron," Mokohoko murmured. "And I give you, for whatever it may be worth, an old man's blessing. It is all I have to give you."

"You hold on as best you can, Mokohoko," Cimarron said, getting to his feet. "Don't give in to the bastards that are running this hellhole. You and me, we're going to take this place over, and then we're getting out of here. "That's a promise. So promise me you'll try hard to hang on, will you?"

"I will try to." Mokohoko's eyes flickered shut.

Cimarron thrust a hand into a pocket of his jeans. He handed the money he came up with to the man sitting nearby. "Give the old man any help you can. Try to lighten his work load."

"You really intend to try busting out of here?" the man asked him as he took Cimarron's money. When Cimarron nodded, he added, "Count me in on whatever plan you come up with. My name's Charlie McLeod."

"I'll be in touch, McLeod. But if I should find out you've let the old man down, you'll have me to reckon with, and you sure as hell won't be in on any plan I come up with to get our asses out of here. You got that?"

"I got it. I heard the old man call you Cimarron. Well, sir, Cimarron, I got to say you're like a breath of fresh air blowing around these parts. Most of the men here are about broken—their spirits as well as their bodies. The fight's gone clean out of most all of them. But you're still stiff-spined and full of ginger, I'm real glad to see."

Cimarron turned away and scanned the faces of the smelter workers. Then, not finding Baldwin among them, he made his way in and out among the smelters until he finally came upon Baldwin on the far side of the work area. He went up to where Baldwin was sitting on the ground with his shoulders hunched, his face, hands, and clothes streaked with red ore. He sat down beside Baldwin and spoke his name.

Baldwin looked up at him, his eyes listless and registering no surprise. "Baldwin," Cimarron said, "I'd heard you'd disappeared, and I'm sorry to see this is where you disappeared to."

"So they got you too."

"Looks like they got both of us."

Baldwin nodded. "I guess Garth decided it was time to get rid of me."

"What do you mean?"

"First, he had me shot. Then, when I didn't run, he tried poisoning my stock. It was Garth who moved that fence in the hope that my stock and men—and me as well—might get caught in the quicksand like we all did. When even that didn't send me hightailing it back to New Orleans with my tail between my legs, he had his police pick me up and put me down here in his Death Valley.''

Cimarron wasn't sure he had heard correctly. Or, if he had indeed heard correctly, he thought, maybe Baldwin was too sick from the poisonous mercury vapors to be making any sense. Before he could raise the questions that were on his mind Baldwin gave him a sidelong glance and remarked, ''You heard me right, Cimarron. It wasn't Hunter who shot me that day. It was Earl Briggs.''

''Earl Briggs?''

Baldwin nodded. ''I saw him.''

''But you led me to believe you thought Hunter was the one who shot you.''

''I know I did. And I was wrong to do that. But I didn't want any trouble with Garth and Briggs. I believed I could find a way to deal with them before they could do me any real harm. And then you arrived on the scene, and I didn't want you stirring up trouble either, so I tried to talk you into letting sleeping dogs lie.'' Baldwin looked away for a moment before continuing, ''By the way, Briggs wasn't out to kill me. He just wanted to scare me off my land. He was acting under Garth's orders, I later learned from Garth himself.''

''Why?''

''That's easy enough to answer. I happened to stumble on this cinnabar mine quite by accident one day when I was out trailing strays on my own. I saw Garth and Briggs here. Later, I confronted Garth with what I'd seen—the Lighthorse guards, the slave laborers—all of it. He admitted what he was doing and said he was making a small fortune on the quicksilver he was selling. He got almost three dollars for each one of those iron flasks he sold, and he sold them all, he said. He warned me I'd be in trouble if I talked about the mine. Later, he obviously decided he'd better get me out of his way, so he tried to scare me into leaving the poisoned stock and so on.''

After a pause Cimarron said, ''Wait a minute. I heard you disappeared yesterday after Garth was murdered. But you just said Garth was the one who ordered you picked up and put here.''

"That's right, I did say that."

"But that makes no sense. Dead men don't give anybody orders."

Baldwin's response was drowned by the sound of shouts, which were quickly followed by several rounds fired in rapid succession from a guard's carbine.

As Cimarron and Baldwin both sprang to their feet, they spotted the cause of the disturbance, which was a scarecrow of a man, whose bony arms were flapping and whose ragged clothes were fluttering as he fled from the rim of the cinnabar pit toward the distant mountain range.

"He's making a run for it," Cimarron commented, excitement in his voice. "I hope the poor bastard makes it."

But the would-be escapee didn't make it. A round from the guard's carbine struck him, lifted him off the ground, and then threw him face down upon it.

Nine

"The wheel!" shouted the guard who had shot the prisoner who had tried to escape. He barked an order, and the two slave laborers he had designated detached themselves from the crowd and picked up the limp body of the man on the ground and carried it away. Other guards herded the other workers, Cimarron and Baldwin among them, in the direction the two men carrying the wounded man had gone.

"What the hell's going on?" Cimarron asked Baldwin as he surrendered his soup bowl to a guard who was moving among the prisoners collecting the bowls.

"I don't know for sure," Baldwin answered, "but I've heard some of the men talk about the wheel. They said—that must be it."

Cimarron gazed in the direction Baldwin was pointing and saw a wagon wheel mounted on its axle, which had been driven into the ground so that the wheel was parallel to the ground and some two feet above it. Spaced beneath a portion of the wheel's circumference, two iron stakes sprouted a good five inches out of the ground.

"What the hell kind of a contraption is that?" Cimarron asked as he halted near the wheel but Baldwin, instead of answering him, merely shook his head.

"Put him on it!" ordered the guard who had shot the would-be escapee.

Obeying the guard's order, the two men carrying the hapless prisoner forced him down on the wheel. Once his back was upon it, they proceeded to tie his hands above his head to two of the wheel's wooden spokes with lengths of ropes given them by the guard.

132

The man on the wheel struggled feebly. He cried out first for help, then for mercy. He received neither. Blood flowed freely from the bullet wound in his shoulder and soaked his torn shirt. He kicked at his captors as each of them seized one of his legs, but they managed to tie his ankles to the two stakes that were driven into the ground. When their task was completed, they stepped back and melted into the crowd of prisoners surrounding the wheel, who were being closely watched by the armed guards.

"I told you they had some pretty awful ways of discouraging men from making a run for it," McLeod, who suddenly appeared beside Cimarron, muttered.

"What are they going to do to that poor bastard, do you know?" Cimarron asked him.

"I know, I seen them do it to another fellow one time. They—"

But before McLeod could say anything more, two burly guards stepped up to the wheel, got a grip on it, and then began to turn it slowly in a counterclockwise direction.

"No!" cried the man tied to the wheel as his body began to twist to one side because his feet were tied to the stakes in the ground. "Oh, sweet Jesus, *don't!*"

He began to scream then, his piercing screams the only sound to be heard except for the faint creaking of the wheel as it continued to turn on its obviously unoiled axle.

"My God!" Baldwin muttered under his breath, his face pale. "They'll tear him apart."

"That's the general idea," responded a grim-faced McLeod.

The man on the wheel twisted his head from side to side, his body grotesquely contorted. His lips worked wordlessly and then a long drawn-out moan issued from between them. His moan became a shrill scream when the two sweating guards gave the wheel another half-turn.

Cimarron took a firm step forward and then another, his hands fisted at his side.

Baldwin seized him by the shoulder. McLeod grabbed his arm. They stopped him in his tracks.

"Don't do it!" McLeod muttered as he and Baldwin dragged Cimarron back into the crowd.

"They'll shoot you for sure if you interfere," Baldwin warned.

Cimarron knew Baldwin was right, but still he wanted to—

He stood stiffly and stared as the left thigh bone of the victim tied to the wheel tore through the man's flesh. He couldn't take his eyes from the awful sight of the blood running down the broken white bone as it jutted upward at an ugly angle from the imprisoned man's leg.

"That ought to do it!" shouted the guard as the man being tortured gave a series of shrill screams.

The two men who had been slowly turning the wheel moved away from it.

The guard who had just given the order to halt the terrible proceedings scanned the faces of the prisoners. Then, shouting above the sound of the screams of the man on the wheel, he said, "Now, should any of you jaspers take a notion to try what he just did"—he pointed to the broken body bleeding on the wheel—"that there's what you'll get when we catch you. And catch you we damn well will! Nobody's ever escaped from Death Valley. Now, back to work, all of you. *Move!*"

"Let's go," Baldwin said, but Cimarron stood his ground, his eyes fastened on the man on the wheel, who seemed to have fainted.

He didn't move a muscle as the other prisoners began to return to their labors. He strained to make out the words the prisoner who had become conscious again, was murmuring as his head lolled from side to side and he bared his teeth in a lip-twisting grimace. Cimarron took a step closer to the bound man, ignoring Baldwin and McLeod, who were both urging him to return to work.

"Help me."

The breathy and barely audible plea reached Cimarron's ears, but he could think of no way to help the man. At that moment, as the broken man's head flopped to one side, his half-closed eyes came to rest on Cimarron, who now stood alone where a moment ago there had been a crowd.

"Shoot me," the man pleaded pitifully.

Cimarron's right hand dropped to his hip—and touched the worn spot on his jeans where his holster had rested before he had been disarmed.

"Please! The pain—" A scream ripped past the victim's lips.

Cimarron could barely endure the agonized look the tormented man gave him. He could only stare at the man's thigh bone that was jutting skyward through sundered flesh—a ghastly symbol of the awful agony the man had endured—and was still enduring.

"Have mercy on me." The man's words were a desperate entreaty.

More words then, harsh and brutal words from a guard who was fast approaching the spot where Cimarron stood: *"Get back to work!"*

Cimarron glanced to his left. He saw the guard and the Remington .45 in the man's dirty hand. His eyes flicked back to meet the imploring eyes of the man stretched on the wheel, the eyes that were crazed with unendurable pain. He waited another split second until the guard was almost upon him, and then he lunged at the man, ripped the gun from his hand, turned, took swift and accurate aim, and fired.

The body of the man on the wheel lurched. An abortive cry escaped his lips. And then he went limp, his agony at last ended by the bullet Cimarron had put in his brain.

Cimarron spun around, the guard's gun still in his hand. Before he could use it the guard he had taken it from seized his wrist and twisted it. Cimarron's trigger finger convulsed and the gun roared. The shot went harmlessly into the ground just as another guard appeared. Cimarron saw that guard's rifle stock come slamming down toward him. Before he could get out of its way, he felt it strike his skull. He grunted as pain roared through his head, and darkness came rushing toward him in the pain's red wake, sending him spinning away into a world where there were no guards and no wheels on which living men could be shattered.

Horses were kicking his skull. He tried to move away from them. Couldn't. He tried to ward off their hooves. Couldn't. He wondered why his skull did not shatter and spill his brains on the ground of the sunless and cold land where he lived.

Light.

His eyelids flickered. He saw a slice of sun from where he lay on the ground. It blinded him, forcing him to close his eyes. He turned on his side, trying not to hear the pain that was screaming inside his skull. Someone—something—touched him. His eyes opened and he saw the boot butting his ribs. He groaned and tried to seize it. It withdrew. He turned his head, looked up—and knew at once that he was in hell, not in the world he had once known. He knew because leering above him was the owner of the boot that had just butted him in the ribs to bring him back to consciousness. He knew that man's name and the man's face, so he knew he had to be in hell. Because the dead man looking down so smugly at him was Abel Garth. So there's sunlight in hell, he thought with surprise, same as there is up on earth.

"I knew you for a troublemaker the first day I laid eyes on you, lawman," Garth muttered. "Even here you make trouble. It must be something bad in your blood."

"I don't know how to be docile, Garth," Cimarron rasped, his voice weak, as he marveled at his realization that two dead men—himself and Garth—could carry on a conversation here in hell.

Then, as other men came into view and Cimarron recognized Bigler and a few of the other Indian Lighthorsemen who also served as guards at the cinnabar mine, he realized that they were not dead. And if they weren't dead, well, then, he thought, maybe neither am I. He managed to sit up and look around. He saw the familiar sights of the cinnabar pit, the smelters, the slave laborers going wearily about their assigned tasks, the log house that sheltered the mine's guards. He noticed that the gun he had taken from the guard was no longer in his possession. When he looked up again at Garth he recalled the conversation he had had with Baldwin when he'd wondered how Garth could have given any orders after he'd been murdered. He remembered that Baldwin's response had been drowned out by the disturbance caused by the laborer who had chosen that moment to try to escape.

"Who was it?" he asked Garth.

"Who was what?" Garth responded. Then, as an understanding smirk spread across his face, "You must mean who was the headless dead man all dressed up in my clothes back at the agency."

Cimarron nodded, his hand gingerly exploring the spot where he had been struck with the rifle butt and finding caked blood covering it.

"A drifter," Garth replied offhandedly. "I never knew his

name. Bigler and his boys rounded him up for me. We forced him to put on some of my clothes and then Bigler shot him and used a cavalry saber to decapitate the unfortunate fellow. Bigler then used the same cavalry saber to relieve the man of his private parts, for which he obviously, being dead, had no further use.''

"You killed him just so you could blame Clyde Hunter for murdering you.''

"That is only partly true,'' Garth stated. "I wanted to frame Hunter but my main purpose, was to disappear so I could operate my cinnabar mine without the distraction of also having to operate the Sac and Fox Agency. Of course, I'm not out of that latter situation altogether. Briggs, who's taken it over, still collects fees from the white ranchers leasing Indian land, and he splits those monies with me as I did with him. But this''—Garth gave a wave of his hand that took in all of the area—"is by far the more lucrative enterprise, and I'm now free to devote my entire attention to making it more successful than ever.

"But you, Deputy, do seem bound and determined to plague me with trouble—right here like you did with your investigation on the reservation. I refer, of course, to your recent interference in our little disciplinary affair. When I arrived here a little while ago following a trip made to find new buyers for my quicksilver, I learned what you'd done.''

Cimarron, concentrating on every move he made, laboriously got to his feet and stood somewhat unsteadily, staring at Garth.

"Now, it is your turn to be disciplined, Deputy,'' Garth continued. "But at least you shall have a chance to save yourself, unlike that poor wretch who was put on the wheel.''

Cimarron waited.

"This man here—the one from whom you took the gun—wants to get even with you for embarrassing him. His name is Packler, and he was once, so he informs me, a Comanchero. During that enterprising time he managed to learn a Mexican trick or two. Tell him, Packler.''

Packler unwound the dirty white sash he wore around his waist. Then he took a knife from his belt. He held out his hand, and another guard handed him a second knife. "You know how to duel with a sash and a knife?'' he asked Cimarron.

"I know." Cimarron thought of the time he had seen two men in old Mexico fight over a girl. Each man had held one end of a sash in his left hand and a knife in his right. Then the two men went at each other, slashing and slicing each other's flesh, until one of the men gave up and let go of the sash, thereby automatically condemning himself to death at the hands of his opponent in the deadly duel.

"Then you know that this is a duel to the death," Garth declared. "A regrettable affair, but one Packler insists must take place if his honor is to be restored. But''—Garth sighed and made a theatrical gesture of despair—"I stand to lose no matter who wins this match. I shall lose either a sturdy slave laborer or a highly competent guard. But such are the ways of fortune."

"Take it!" Packler muttered, and held out one of the pair of knives to Cimarron. When Cimarron had taken it from him, Packler flicked the white sash, and Cimarron caught the free end of it in his left hand.

Packler's arm drew back so that the sash stretched tautly between the two men. Then he lunged at Cimarron, his blade flashing in the bright light of the sun.

Cimarron twisted his body so that the thrust went wide of him; then he parried Packler's second attempt to stab him by bringing his own knife down in a sharp arc. Packler made no sound as his shirt sleeve and then the flesh of his right forearm were slashed by Cimarron's knife.

Both men then began to circle one another, their knives poised, the sash stretched between them. Cimarron danced out of the way of Packler's sudden lunge, and again he ripped the flesh of Packler's right forearm. This time Packler let out an involuntary yelp, and then he clamped his mouth shut, his face coloring either from rage or embarrassment or both. Warily, the two men faced each other, prancing at times like boxers, standing stolidly in place at other times, the knives in their hands gleaming, Cimarron's blade bright with Packler's blood.

Packler was breathing heavily, his lips drawn back over his yellowed teeth, as his eyes darted from Cimarron's knife to his face and then back to his knife again. Cimarron was ready for him when Packler suddenly rushed him. He adroitly stepped to one side while maintaining a firm grip on the sash. But Packler, not to be denied blood this time, determinedly swiveled in the direction Cimarron had moved and deftly swung his blade, the tip of which punctured Cimarron's left bicep.

The intense pain that erupted where Packler's knife had penetrated his flesh flared its hot message to Cimarron's brain, but he ignored it, swiftly retaliating with an upward thrust of his knife while simultaneously jerking on the sash to draw his opponent toward him and his blade. Packler managed to sidestep, and Cimarron's knife cut only air. Before he could try again, Packler put out one booted foot and tripped him. Cimarron went down hard, but he did not release his hold on the white sash, which was now flecked with blood. As Packler raised his knife to deliver another blow, Cimarron jerked hard on the sash, and Packler fell on top of him.

Cimarron pushed Packler aside, scrambled to his knees, and was about to plunge his blade into Packler's chest, when the man managed to wrap the sash once around Cimarron's knife hand. Momentarily prevented from attacking his assailant, Cimarron fought to free his hand of the sash. As he did so, Packler leaped to his feet, and his knife sped down toward Cimarron's body. To defend himself, Cimarron bent down low and, his shoulder hunched, used it to deflect the descending blow. As his shoulder struck the underside of Packler's wrist, Packler screamed a string of obscenities and, his balance lost, fell again to the ground.

Cimarron sprang to his feet. His hand and knife came free of the sash. "You couldn't stick a trussed-up pig with that Arkansas toothpick of yours, Packler," he taunted his opponent, knowing that a mad man was a reckless man, and that a reckless man took chances and often made dangerous mistakes. Packler, still on the ground, slashed at Cimarron's legs but succeeded only in cutting a piece of leather from the heel of his right boot. He tried a second time to trip Cimarron, but Cimarron was too fast for him. Then, as Cimarron hauled Packler to his feet by means of the bloody sash, Packler made a feeble effort to cut him again but failed. Cimarron's blade swooped up and entered the flesh of Packler's left shoulder. Packler screamed and frantically struck out, desperately and obviously aiming this time for Cimarron's eyes. Cimarron's head swiveled out of the way of the man's flashing blade, but not before it had ripped open the lobe of his left ear.

Packler tried again for Cimarron's eyes, and Cimarron, enraged at the man's attempts to blind him so that he could kill him more easily, moved in on Packler. His knife sank into Packler's chest, glanced off a rib, and then withdrew. It immediately went back in, even deeper this time, as the men stood toe to toe, the sash now hanging limply between their two tense bodies.

Packler sighed. He made a half-turn as if he were about to abandon the battle and desert the battlefield. He shivered as if in a cold wind. He coughed, and a small geyser of blood spurted from between his lips. His knees buckled, and he began to sag. He went down, still coughing, blood still pouring from between his lips.

Cimarron let go of his end of the sash. He hardly noticed it when one of the guards took the knife away from him. He watched Packler in a stony silence, and when the man's blood no longer flowed, he knew that Packler's heart had stopped.

"Well done!" exclaimed a jubilant Garth. "You fought the good fight, Cimarron, and you won!" Garth's tone and expression turned suddenly somber. "And you shall reap a fitting reward. *Bigler!*"

As Bigler scurried up to Garth in response to the man's sharp summons, Garth pointed to Cimarron and said, "Put him to work at the smelters."

"The smelters, Mr. Garth?" echoed Bigler. "I reckon you know what you're doing, but I feel I ought to point out to you that he won't last nearly as long working the smelters as he would down in the cinnabar pit."

"You don't understand, do you, Bigler?" Garth asked, sadly shaking his head in the face of what he apparently considered to be Bigler's obtuseness. "You saw him kill your colleague just now. Consider what might happen to you—or me—if he should get his hands on another weapon. As long as he's alive, he's a threat to all of us, Bigler."

"I see your point, Mr. Garth. Maybe I ought to just shoot him now and have done with it. I always say the only good deputy, is a dead deputy."

"No, Bigler, don't shoot him. I don't want him to be a total loss. Besides, I want to repay him for the trouble he was on the verge of causing me. Work him hard, Bigler, for as long as he lasts!"

"Yes, sir, Mr. Garth, I'll do that." Turning toward Cimarron, Bigler gestured peremptorily with the gun in his hand. "March, mister!"

Cimarron marched to the smelters, where he spent the rest of the day shoveling cinnabar ore mixed with lime into the firebox of his assigned smelter, and periodically feeding its fire with cordwood he took from a nearby stack. He was given no chance to tend to the wounds in his left bicep and left earlobe. Blood mingled with sweat streamed down his neck and arm as he worked steadily in silence under the hot sun. His mind soon became numb as he continued performing his repetitive tasks until he was aware of nothing but the occasional cackling cough of one of the nearby workers, the crackling of the flames in the smelters' fireboxes, the debilitating heat thrown off by those fires, and the stench of the fumes from the cinnabar ore, which seared his throat and nose and made his eyes water badly.

That night, after wolfing down a bowl of thin gruel and devouring a hard piece of bread from which he first had to pick out the weevils infesting it, Cimarron stretched out on the ground and closed his eyes. But sleep would not come despite his exhaustion. Pain throbbed in his wounded ear and arm, which were crusted over with dried blood. Anger drummed in his mind as he vowed vengeance against Garth and every man who did Garth's bidding.

"Cimarron? You awake?"

"I am." Cimarron turned his head and stared at Baldwin, who was kneeling on the ground beside him.

"I'm glad you weren't killed in that fight today."

"So am I." Cimarron clasped his hands behind his head and stared up at the stars, which were hard to see because of the bright red glow of the flames in the smelters' fireboxes.

"You made me ashamed of myself, Cimarron. You made all of us ashamed of ourselves."

"I don't follow you, Baldwin. What are you getting at?"

"The way you fought that guard. The way you wouldn't be stopped from doing the only thing you could to end the suffering of that poor sonofabitch they put on the wheel. And you did it knowing they'd make it hot for you for trying to help him. What I'm getting at is you made the rest of us—Hunter, and his friends, Loomis, Pushetonequa, Neapope, and Poweshiek—and me—seem like a pack of cowards."

"Wait a minute, Baldwin. You're making a mistake. You can't go through life measuring yourself against other men you meet. You do and you lose two ways. If you come out looking better in your own eyes than the man you measured yourself against, you get to feeling smug and self-satisfied on account of you think you're better than him. So you lose because you ease up on trying to make yourself any better than you already are. Or if you fall short when stacked up against some other man, then you figure you're worthless, and like as not you'll decide there's no use trying to be as good as that other fellow because maybe you won't be able to bring it off. So you lose on that score too 'cause you give up trying to better yourself. No two men are cut from the same cloth, Baldwin. My killing that guard don't make me any kind of hero. And it don't make you or anybody else a smaller man than me because it was me and not you who killed the sonofabitch."

"What I came here to tell you is we're all with you if you still want to try to take control of this place."

"All of you are?"

"Hunter and his friends, yes. Not Mokohoko though. He's too sick. But even he says he'll do whatever he can to help us. What do you say, Cimarron? Shall we try it? Will you be our leader?"

Cimarron stared at Baldwin for a long moment. And then, solemnly, "There's bound to be bloodshed. On both sides. Are you boys prepared to bleed? Maybe die?"

Baldwin hesitated before answering. "I don't want to die—"

"Nobody does, I reckon."

"—but I don't want to live like this either. And even if I don't fight I'll still die if I stay here. All of us will. We'll be worked to death. So even though I don't have the courage that you have, Cimarron—"

"There you go again, Baldwin, taking your own measure by sizing up another man. No man really knows how much, if any, courage he's got till he's tested. And think on this. You came to me. I didn't try to force you into anything."

"Then you'll do it—you'll lead us?"

"Go round up the rest of the men you mentioned and bring them here. We'll have us a war council."

Baldwin started to say something but instead he reached and mutely squeezed Cimarron's shoulder. Then he was gone, a shadow moving swiftly among other shadows.

Cimarron hadn't long to wait. They came to him one by one, stealthily, silently. The first to arrive was Neapope. He had barely given Cimarron his name when he was joined by another Indian, whom Neapope identified as his friend, Poweshiek. Both men were dark-skinned, black-eyed, and black-haired. Both had the high cheekbones and narrow foreheads typical of the Foxes. To Cimarron, they looked like brothers, so similar in facial characteristics, height, and body build were they. But Neapope's nose was straight, whereas Poweshiek's was hooked.

Cimarron made a mental note of that difference to help him keep tell the two men apart. "How come you're here?" he asked them.

It was Neapope who answered him in a voice that, though even, could not entirely hide the man's anger. "Garth knew that we backed Clyde up in what he was trying to do so he sent his Lighthorsemen to pick us up."

"We'd told Clyde we'd testify against Garth if he ever came to trial," Poweshiek added. "Both of us had seen him and Briggs make the rounds of the white ranchers, and we saw money change hands."

"I'm no lawyer," Cimarron mused, "but what you saw, it wouldn't hold a helluva lot of water in court."

Neapope said, "We spoke to the ranchers afterward."

"To three of them," Poweshiek said.

"All three told us they were paying Garth to stay on the land they'd leased from him," Neapope declared. "And all three also said they'd paid to get their leases from Garth in the first place."

"So now both you boys are ready to break out of this hellhole?"

As Poweshiek and Neapope both answered in the affirmative, they were joined by a third man.

"Howdy, Pushetonequa," Cimarron greeted the newcomer.

"Hunter just told me you were here. He said he's rounding up some boys to light a fire under Garth and his guards."

"That's right," Cimarron said. "I take it you wound up here on account of how you were trying to work both sides of the fence, Pushetonequa. I mean you went to Garth to get him to pay you to keep quiet about this setup—you told me so yourself—when Hunter couldn't come up with the fifty dollars you wanted him to pay you to testify against Garth."

"You got it right, Cimarron. I should not have tried to blackmail Garth. But I did it, and that's why he saw to it that I was put out of his way. I hope you and Hunter aren't planning on holding my mistake against me."

"I reckon a man's entitled to a mistake or two," Cimarron remarked mildly. "I know I've made some in my time and paid dear for a few of them." Cimarron fell silent as another figure materialized out of the darkness.

"I'm Ned Loomis," announced the man who had just arrived. "Hunter told me you boys were planning on turning the tables on Garth and his police."

Before anyone could say anything, another white man appeared; Cimarron recognized McLeod, the man he had met earlier.

"I heard Baldwin and Hunter talking to Loomis," McLeod volunteered. "I want to join the party if you fellows'll let me."

"You're welcome, McLeod," Cimarron said. "The more the merrier."

"There's not likely to be anything merry about what we're planning," said Clyde Hunter as he, with Baldwin beside him, joined the group.

"On the contrary," said Baldwin, "things are more likely to wind up on the grim side."

"That's a fact," Cimarron agreed. "And each one of you fellows ought to know that. There's no use in any of us trying to fool either ourselves or each other about what we're facing. The guards have guns. We've got nothing but our fists,

144

our guts, a few picks and shovels, and a bowie knife I've got stashed in my boot. The odds are against us right from the outset.''

"The odds are against us if we do not try to save ourselves,'' Poweshiek pointed out. "Two men have died since I have been a prisoner here.''

There were murmurs of assent among the others.

"Well, then, let's us get right down to it,'' Cimarron suggested. "Any of you fellows got any ideas about how we ought to go about taking over this place?''

Cimarron's question set off a discussion that lasted for the better part of an hour. Numerous proposals were put forward and either accepted or rejected by a consensus of the group after the pros and cons of each had been judiciously weighed and debated.

"Then this is what we've got,'' Cimarron stated when they all had finally agreed on the outlines of their escape attempt. "We'll make our move at first light, which is only hours from now, when the guard changes—when the day men take over for the night men. It ought to be a good time because both sets of guards'll be sleepy, both those coming off duty and those just about to go on duty.

"Poweshiek, your job is to be with Mokohoko. The minute we make our move you whisk him the hell out of here.'' When Powshiek nodded, Cimarron continued, "Neapope, you and Pushetonequa tip over the smelter that's nearest the cinnabar pit just before we make our move. That'll catch the guards' attention for sure, and while they're wondering what the hell happened to upset the smelter, Loomis and McLeod will jump one of the guards and disarm him.''

"Maybe Loomis and me, we should each jump a guard,'' McLeod mused. "That way, if we don't get ourselves killed, we'll wind up with two guns.''

"One guard,'' Cimarron insisted. "With two of you against one of them, you'll have a better chance of getting that one gun than if you try to bite off more than you can chew. Agreed, McLeod?''

McLeod nodded his assent.

"Hunter, Baldwin, and me,'' Cimarron went on, "we'll go for the cabin where Garth and the rest of his Lighthorsemen'll hopefully still be sleeping. I'll give a whistle and then all of you—*go!*''

"I wish you'd whistle now—right this very minute," Hunter muttered. "I'm feeling so fidgety I don't think I can wait till first light."

Cimarron said nothing, but he shared Hunter's feeling. It was a feeling he had experienced before when he had been a soldier in the Civil War and he had had to wait for the night to die and the day to be born before going back into battle against the enemy. It was a feeling that ate at a man, one that was almost as deadly in its own way as the armed men to be faced the following day.

"Look at the wait this way," Neapope suggested. "Let it be a time for all of us to think of the blood we will spill in the morning. A time to think of how sweet revenge will be to each of us who has suffered at the hands of Garth and his men."

Cimarron saw a faint smile, more of a grimace, appear on Loomis's face as he settled in with the others to wait for first light.

And wait they all did. Through what remained of the night, some of the men talked in low tones about anything but the impending battle, but most of them sat in silence, each alone with his own thoughts.

All of them glanced continually toward the east. They turned as one toward Cimarron when the first gray streaks of light began to brighten the eastern horizon.

Cimarron neither moved nor spoke until several more minutes had passed and the first of the guards began to emerge from the cabin to begin the new day's shift. Then, led by Cimarron, they all rose and made their way to their prearranged positions. Poweshiek strode purposefully toward the spot where Hunter had earlier told the group Mokohoko had bedded down for the night. Neapope and Pushetonequa went to the smelter that stood closest to the cinnabar pit as McLeod, with Loomis at his side, made his way toward one of the day guards who stood yawning and stretching not far from the cabin.

"You boys ready?" Cimarron asked. When Baldwin and Hunter both nodded, he said, "Let's go, then."

The three men started for the cabin, wending their way

among the laborers, who were being prodded awake by guards' rifle butts and boots.

Cimarron, as he walked, glanced over his shoulder and was pleased to see that Neapope and Pushetonequa had reached the smelter. Looking to the left, he saw Poweshiek helping Mokohoko to his feet while whispering in the old man's ear. Cimarron glanced to his right and saw that McLeod and Loomis had positioned themselves on either side of the still-yawning guard they had chosen as their target.

Cimarron walked a few more steps and, putting two fingers between his teeth, he gave a shrill whistle and began to run, Hunter and Baldwin right beside him.

"What the hell—" he heard either a guard or a prisoner shout as he ran. He saw Neapope and Pushetonequa use pieces of cordwood to tilt and then overturn the smelter, sending a shower of sparks and clouds of smoke up into the air. He saw Poweshiek and Mokohoko hurrying away from the cinnabar pit toward the mountain range in the distance. He heard the excited shouts of the guards and saw the figure of a Lighthorseman, who was wearing only long johns, appear in the open doorway of the cabin. Without breaking stride, he pulled his bowie knife from his boot and hurled it at the Indian, who stood blinking dazedly in the cabin's doorway. He ran on, his expression grim, as the Lighthorseman, clutching the hilt of the bowie in both hands, went down.

At the sound of shots, Cimarron looked over his shoulder and saw Loomis reel away from the guard he had been struggling with, blood from a shoulder wound soaking through his shirt. As the guard turned and prepared to fire again, McLeod kicked the guard in the shin, and seized the man's gunhand in one hand and the cylinder of the gun in the other to keep it from firing. Cimarron almost cheered as McLeod wrested the gun from the guard and used it to hold the man at bay.

Cimarron, Hunter, and Baldwin were approaching the cabin when an Indian suddenly appeared in the doorway. Seeing the three men sprinting toward him, the Indian pushed the body of the dead Lighthorseman away from the door and slammed it shut. The sound of a bolt being shot on the inside of the door was followed by yelling from within the cabin which, in turn, was followed by the appearance of gun barrels in the loopholes of the cabin's front wall.

One of the first shots fired from inside the cabin hit Baldwin in the left calf. He staggered and went down. Cimarron, carried forward by his own momentum, threw himself down behind the body of the Indian he had killed. He ripped his bowie knife from the dead Indian's body, booted it, and then crawled along the ground toward Baldwin. Before he could reach Baldwin, Hunter had the man up on his feet and was half-carrying and half-dragging him behind the thick trunk of an old maple tree.

Ten

Pinned down, dammit, Cimarron thought as he lay prone behind the makeshift breastwork formed by the corpse of the Indian he had knifed to death. Got to get my ass out of here. He surveyed the scene before him and considered his options. A moment later, he got to his feet and made a run for it, ducking each time he passed a loophole to avoid being shot by the men whose guns were poking through them. He reached an elm next to the one Hunter and Baldwin had taken refuge behind.

"You okay Baldwin?" he asked, noting the tourniquet made from a bandanna that was now tied around Baldwin's leg just above the knee.

"The bleeding's just about stopped," Baldwin replied, "thanks to Hunter here."

"The bullet—is it in you?"

"No. It went right through."

"Hunter, loosen up that tourniquet every once in a while so some blood can get through to Baldwin's lower leg."

Hunter nodded. "It looks like we're finished, Cimarron. They've got enough firepower inside that cabin to blow us all right through hell's front door."

"It's not over yet," Cimarron commented. "Look."

Hunter and Baldwin looked in the direction he had pointed as the men inside the cabin ceased firing.

"Picks and shovels," Hunter muttered. "Those laborers won't win with what they've got. Besides, they're all too weak to keep fighting much longer."

Cimarron, his eyes on the melee taking place between the laborers and their guards around the smelters and in the cinnabar pit, said, "I'm going to get me a share of that action."

"I'm coming with you," Hunter announced as he got to his feet.

Cimarron hesitated, but then Baldwin waved him and Hunter away, saying, "I'll be fine here. I'd join you fellows but I'd only slow you down if I did. Good luck to you."

"Let's go!" Cimarron said, and with Hunter right beside him, he went racing toward the battle taking place between the laborers and the guards.

Seconds later, Hunter and Cimarron were in the thick of it. Cimarron gave and took a number of blows. He wondered for a moment why the guards had stopped firing, and then he realized that they had all been disarmed. When he spotted a gun lying on the ground just beyond the field of battle he made a dive for it. When his fingers closed on its butt, he rolled over on the ground and yelled, "Hoist 'em and stand hitched!"

The guard he was aiming at threw his hands into the air and stood immobile. Just as Cimarron was about to get to his feet, one of the laborers struck a guard on his left with a haymaker. The guard staggered backward, fell over Cimarron, and knocked the gun from his hand.

Cimarron lunged for the gun, but he was too late. The guard he had just had under the gun retrieved the weapon Cimarron had just dropped and, snickering, aimed it at him.

Cimarron, staring over the man's shoulder, yelled, "Get him."

The guard with the gun spun around to see who Cimarron had addressed. By the time he saw that no one was there and realized he had been tricked, Cimarron was upon him. He dropped like a stone as he spun around and the bowie Cimarron had slid from his boot burrowed in his gut. He doubled over, dropped the gun, and grunted as blood began to bubble from between his thick lips. He clutched his gut with both hands, swayed slightly, and, as his knees gave out on him, slumped to the ground, where he stared dully up at Cimarron's face and then down at the bloody knife in Cimarron's hand.

Cimarron bent down, thrust his knife back into his boot, picked up the dropped gun, turned . . .

And couldn't believe his eyes.

Heavily armed men were riding down out of the mountains and heading directly for the battling guards and laborers. As the riders neared their destination, they began firing, and their volley of shots sent both laborers and guards scurrying. But then the man riding at the head of the advancing horde shouted an order, and the guards rallied, ended their flight, and turned back to resume their battle with the laborers.

Cimarron recognized the leader of the rapidly approaching riders: Earl Briggs. Loomis took aim and fired at Briggs, missed, and turned to run as his fire was returned tenfold. Poweshiek and Mokohoko ran as fast as they could to get out of the way of the riders and Cimmaron swore as he saw one of them fire and hit Poweshiek. The Indian raised his arms in mute protest before he fell face down in the dirt.

Cimarron thrust his gun into his waistband and began to run toward Mokohoko when one of the riders swung his rifle, striking the old man on the side of the head, sending him sprawling. Gunfire erupted all around Cimarron and he ran in a ragged course to avoid a confrontation with any of the armed guards who were now forcing the laborers down into the cinnabar pit. He dashed in among the smelters, dodging from one to the next, and then left them behind as he headed for the horse corral. Behind him now were the shouting Lighthorsemen who had been barricaded in the cabin. Off to his left rode Briggs with some men, who, Cimarron suspected, were sentries posted in the mountain range that surrounded the valley to keep the slave laborers from escaping.

When he reached the corral, he climbed between its poles, shouldering horses out of his way as he made his way to his black. He vaulted into the saddle and spurred the horse up to the corral gate, which he leaned down and opened before riding out of the corral.

When he reached Mokohoko, who was still lying on the ground, he slid out of the saddle, scooped up the unconscious old man, and draped his limp body over his horse's withers. He was headed for the mountains when someone behind him shouted, "Stop him! He's getting away!"

A shot whined harmlessly past him. He glanced over his shoulder and saw that the battle, for all intents and purposes, had just about ended with the laborers being rounded up by the guards. He saw no sign of Baldwin or Hunter. Poweshiek still lay on the ground where he had fallen. Loomis, McLeod, and Neapope were among those being herded into the cinnabar pit by the guards as Briggs, still astride his horse, supervised the operation.

Cimarron wondered, as he galloped away, how many sentries were still on duty in the mountains. Briggs must have been on his way to see Garth, he thought. No doubt he heard or maybe even saw the commotion at the cinnabar pit, so he went and rounded up some sentries and decided to sit in on the game. Damn the man, he thought. We could have won had he not showed up when he did with his reinforcements.

He rode on through the foothills and toward the summit of the mountain. Got to watch for sentries, he reminded himself. Who the hell knows if there are any more of them up here. He slowed the black slightly as he entered a grove of scrub oak because the low-hanging branches were like whips striking his head and shoulders.

Suddenly, he halted. He listened for a moment, then turned his horse and began to ride at a right angle to the course he had been following. He had just caught sight of a mounted man who was heading toward him. He did not know if the man was friend or foe, but he could not take the chance that he might turn out to be a sentry. He took cover beneath an outcropping of shale and clapped a hand over Mokohoko's mouth as the old man regained consciousness and began to groan.

"Quiet!" he ordered as a plainly bewildered Mokohoko stared up at him. "No noise," he admonished and then took his hand away from Mokohoko's mouth.

"How came I here, Cimarron?"

After he had answered the question, Cimarron said, "There was a fellow prowling around here a little while ago. He might be one of Garth's sentries. Once I'm sure he's gone we'll light a shuck."

"It is an odd thing to say, but I am glad you were a prisoner too. If you were not, I would still be a prisoner, no doubt. Where are you taking me?"

"I hadn't given much thought to that question, to be truthful about it. You can't go back to your wickiup. Garth might send somebody there after you. Tell you what. I'll take you

152

to the mission. Isabel Bonner'll be glad to look after you till things settle down.''

"What are you going to do?"

"I'm going back and try to finish what I started at the cinnabar pit.''

"Alone?''

"I don't know of anyone I could get to ride with me so, yep, I guess I'll be going back alone.''

"Many of the Mesquakie would ride with you, Cimarron. Young men. Brave men. Let us hurry to the mission. We can send the children to tell some of the Mesquakie to come to your aid.''

"That's the best news I've heard in a long time, Mokohoko. To tell you the truth, I wasn't exactly relishing taking on Garth, Briggs, and all the rest of those boys back there on my own—though I hoped I'd be able to come up with some way to outwit them. In fact, I—''

The throaty chuckle that suddenly sounded behind Cimarron caused him to stiffen, and he noticed that Mokohoko was staring in alarm at someone behind him.

"You fellows ought to have kept your voices down,'' said a male voice from behind Cimarron. "I thought I heard somebody groan when I was riding by here awhile ago. So I came back to scout. And what did I find? Two of Mr. Garth's slave laborers on the loose, that's what.'' The man chuckled again. "Did y'all know that Mr. Garth pays us sentries two-fifty apiece for each escapee we round up and hand back to him? So you two are worth five dollars to me.''

"Let the old man go,'' Cimarron said without turning around as his right hand eased toward the gun he had earlier thrust into his waistband. "You do and I'll give you five bucks for him. That money plus the two-fifty you'll get from Garth for me'll put you way ahead of the game.''

With no hesitation, the sentry said, "Make it ten and you've got yourself a deal, mister.''

"Ten it is, then,'' Cimarron agreed as his hand continued to ease toward the gun in his waistband.

"Lets see your money, mister,'' barked the sentry.

But what the man saw instead was a burst of flame from the gun in Cimarron's hand.

The sentry was thrown backward by the impact of the two

bullets entering his chest. His gun flew from his hand, and his hat fell off. As the dying man went down, Cimarron eased the hammer of his gun back into place and returned it to his waistband.

He helped Mokohoko to his feet, and then, after mounting his black, helped the old man climb up behind the cantle of his saddle. The pair rode away then, leaving the dead sentry behind them as they headed for the mission and Isabel Bonner.

At the mission later that day, Cimarron was helping Mokohoko up the steps of the building when the door flew open and Isabel Bonner burst through it.

"Cimarron, what's wrong?" she cried. "What's happened to Mokohoko? Where have you been?"

Before he could reply, Miranda Baldwin came through the door and cried, "Cimarron, you're hurt."

He was about to deny it until he saw her point to the spot on his head where the stone thrown by one of the pit guards had struck him. "I'm fine," he assured her.

Without warning, Mokohoko sagged and started to fall. Cimarron picked the old man up in both arms and carried him inside the mission. "Where can I put him down?" he asked Isabel who, with Miranda, had followed him inside.

"The guest room upstairs," Isabel said.

Cimarron followed her up the stairs to the second floor, both of them trailed by Miranda. In the guest room, he gently placed Mokohoko on the bed.

"The poor old man looks terrible," Isabel whispered.

"But he'll recover," Cimarron assured her. "Men who've been mercury-poisoned, they start getting better as soon as they stop inhaling the fumes from the ore smelters. Once he's had a few days' rest and some good food, he'll be all right."

"I have some soup that I made the other day," Isabel said. "I'll warm some up for him."

That night, after Mokohoko had been fed and was resting comfortably, Cimarron sat in the parlor with Isabel and Miranda, who were both bombarding him with questions. "Hold it," he said and proceeded to outline all that had happened to him since he had last left the mission.

"How badly is Paul wounded?" Miranda asked anxiously when he had concluded his account.

"Not too bad," he answered. "But a visit to a good doctor wouldn't do him any harm at this point." He turned to Isabel. "Mokohoko told me he knows some Foxes who'll lend me a hand when I try to take control of that mine Garth's running. I'm going upstairs now and ask him for those names. I'll be right back, ladies."

When Cimarron returned to the parlor, Miranda said, "You'll need all the help you can get, judging by what you've just told us about that terrible place, Cimarron. I am therefore going to return to the ranch and get our men to back you up. I know they'll be glad to do it. They are all devoted to Paul, and I'm sure they'll want to do whatever they can to help you rescue him."

"I'm obliged to you, Miranda. The more guns I can go after Garth and his gang with, the better the odds are that I can do what I want to."

"You mean kill those men?" Isabel asked, her voice little more than a whisper.

"Nope. That's not what I meant. There'll be killing, sure. But there's no way that can be avoided. But what I want to do is arrest Garth and Briggs and those guards of theirs. I want to see to it that they stand trial, every man jack of them, for kidnapping, unlawful imprisonment, and for acting as accessories in at least one case of assault and battery that I know about."

"You're referring to that poor man you told us about," Isabel observed. "The one they tortured so horribly."

When Cimarron nodded, Miranda got to her feet.

"I'll go and tell the men what has happened to Paul," she volunteered. "Shall I have them meet you here, Cimarron?"

"This is as good a place to meet as any, I reckon. Tell those who are willing to risk their necks with me to be here by midnight." When Miranda had hurried out of the room, Cimarron turned to Isabel. "How come she was here when I arrived?"

"She's been frantic with worry about her brother. She didn't know where else to turn. Actually, she came here after you left in the hope that she would find you here. When I told her you had left here intending to visit her, she became even more frantic. She thought—we both did—that you might, if

155

you could, return to the mission. So she decided to wait here in the hope of seeing you again."

"I got the names of some Foxes from Mokohoko who he said will be willing to side with me. Could you send some of your students to round up these boys and tell them to meet me here by midnight if they're game and tell them too why I need their help?"

"Yes, of course I can. School is still in session. If you'll excuse me, Cimarron."

He rose as Isabel did and he was standing by the window looking out when she returned several minutes later. "I've dispatched several very reliable young boys who come to school on horseback to alert the Foxes," she said.

"I'm obliged to you, Isabel." As she sat down with a soft sigh, he turned from the window. "That sigh—you're fretting about Hunter, are you?"

To Cimarron's surprise, Isabel shook her head.

"Oh, don't get me wrong, Cimarron. It's not that I'm indifferent to what has happened to Clyde. It's just that— well, I think I've behaved rather foolishly where he and I were concerned."

"I don't follow you."

"I told you that when Miranda came here she was frantic with worry about what might have happened to her brother. She desperately needed someone to talk to, someone who could sympathize with her plight. I was that someone, as it turned out. As we talked—actually, she did almost all of the talking—I learned from her that her brother does not exactly like Indians, including halfbloods. To my surprise, I learned from Miranda that she has been seeing Clyde Hunter secretly for some months—until her brother was shot and she began to suspect that Clyde might have done the shooting. She even admitted to me that she had fallen in love with Clyde during the time she was seeing him."

"Hey, wait a minute! You lost me at the last turn. Miranda Baldwin in love with Clyde Hunter? I don't believe it."

"It's true whether or not you believe it."

"But every time she talked to me about him she sounded like she wanted him dead because she believed he had tried to kill her brother. It was Miranda who came to Fort Smith to get a deputy to come here to investigate the shooting!"

"When you were upstairs with Mokohoko just now, she explained to me that she had tried to deny her feelings for Clyde because she suspected him of having tried to kill her brother. She felt obligated to file a complaint against Clyde in Fort Smith. Cimarron, you can't imagine how relieved she was to learn from you that it was Briggs and not Clyde who had shot Mr. Baldwin.

"And there is another reason why Miranda had to hide her feelings for Clyde even before the shooting. Why she had to scorn him during the handkerchief game we all played at the Meeting Hall, for example."

"I think I can guess what that other reason is. It goes by the name of Paul Baldwin."

"Yes, that's correct. Mr. Baldwin, according to Miranda, does not think well of Indians. And Clyde had still another strike against him where Mr. Baldwin was concerned—his drinking. Miranda told me she thinks Clyde drinks in part because of her. Because she would not—could not—publicly acknowledge her love for him."

Isabel continued, "Well, as I listened to Miranda describe her feelings for Clyde, I realized what love really is. It isn't what I felt for him. What I felt for him, I came to understand as I listened to Miranda, was pity. I felt sorry for Clyde and tried to help him, and in the process I began to imagine myself in love with him."

"Pity's fine in its place," Cimarron ventured, "but it comes in a poor second to love as a thing to bind a man and a woman together."

"You're right, of course, Cimarron. I understand that now." Isabel looked down at the floor.

"You're blushing," Cimarron observed.

"I was thinking about Barney Mitchell."

"Who might he be?"

"He's one of the Baldwin ranch hands. He comes to Sunday service here at the mission and even to Evensong on Wednesdays when his duties permit. He—we—Mr. Mitchell and I have walked out together now and then."

Cimarron grinned as Isabel's blush deepened. "I take it it's not pity you feel for this Barney Mitchell?"

"Oh, no, not at all!" Isabel responded quickly and then,

apparently disconcerted at the sight of Cimarron's grin, she looked away.

"I'd like to meet up with this Barney Mitchell some time."

"You would? Why?"

"I'd just like to have a chance to shake the man's hand and tell him what a lucky buckaroo I happen to think he is to have the power to bring a blush to the cheeks of a pretty woman such as yourself, honey."

Isabel managed a shy smile. And then, "Are you hungry, Cimarron? Yesterday was my baking day. There are apple turnovers and all sorts of other pastries, not to mention fresh bread, in the larder. And there's still some soup left. I could boil some potatoes, mash some turnips— the mission's garden provided a bountiful harvest this year and our root cellar and pantry shelves are filled with vegetables, both fresh and canned."

"I am hungry," Cimarron admitted, "so I can promise you that anything you see fit to set before me, I'll polish off in a hurry."

"Come along into the kitchen then," Isabel said and Cimarron followed her out of the parlor.

Eleven Indians armed with guns arrived at the mission a few minutes after eleven o'clock that night. Cimarron stood on the porch with Isabel at his side to greet them.

One stepped forward and said, "I am Appanoose, war chief of the Fox clan. Me and my warriors come here because Mokohoko called us. You are the man called Cimarron who sent Mokohoko's message to us?"

"I am and I'm glad to make your acquaintance, Appanoose," Cimarron shook hands with the broad-faced and fiery-eyed war chief of the Fox clan, whose face was daubed with bright red paint.

"The others who wear red paint like me," explained Appanoose, "are also members of the Fox clan. The men whose faces are painted green—they are of the Bear clan."

"Which one is their chief?" Cimarron asked.

"They have no chief," Appanoose answered. "Not here. Not tonight."

"Why's that?"

"Chief of Bear clan must be always a peaceful man. This night we make war, so he does not come here."

"You're surely right about that," Cimarron remarked grimly. "It's war we'll be making tonight, and if my ears don't deceive me there are more soldiers on their way to join us."

As five riders—four men and Miranda Baldwin—rode up to the mission and drew rein, Appanoose turned to Cimarron and said, "White woman thinks she is a soldier?"

"Nope. That's Miranda Baldwin. Her brother, Paul Baldwin's a slave laborer at Garth's cinnabar mine. Those fellows with her are Baldwin ranch hands. She brought them here to help us in the night's work we've got ahead of us."

Miranda dismounted and hurried up to Cimarron. "The men—they're anxious to help try to free Paul and the others at the mine. I'll introduce you to them." She turned back to the men she had brought with her. "This is the deputy marshal I told you boys about—Cimarron." Then she pointed each man out to Cimarron as she named them: "Bud Avnet, Curly, Denver, and Barney Mitchell."

Cimarron's gaze lingered on the man named Mitchell, who was sandy-haired, blue-eyed, and seemed dazed as he stared longingly at Isabel Bonner. "Glad to meet you boys," Cimarron said. "These fellows here who are all painted for war," he continued, indicating Appanoose and his men, "they're Foxes. Some of them are members of the Bear clan—they're the ones with the green paint on their faces— and some of them belong to the Fox clan—they're the ones with red paint on their faces."

"But all of us are Red Earth People," Appanoose declared proudly.

"Now that we all know each other," Cimarron continued, "I reckon it's time I told you all exactly what we're going up against tonight." He then proceeded to describe the mining operation, carefully explaining where everything in the area was located—the cabin that housed the guards, the cinnabar pit itself, the smelters. "What we'd best do is strike before daybreak. They've got fewer guards on at night than they have during the day when everybody's up and about. But they've got a night shift that works the smelters so the place won't be completely shut down. The main thing we've got to watch out for is the sentries they've got posted in the range that rings the valley. I don't know how many there are at any given time or where exactly any of them are located. But we've got to get safely past them before we can raid the valley. If we do have the bad luck to run into any of the sentries, I don't want any shooting. It might alert the guards down in the valley to the fact that trouble's on its way to plague them. You boys got that?"

There were murmurs of assent and nods from the assembled men.

"Cimarron."

Cimarron turned to face Appanoose, who had just spoken his name, and asked, "What's on your mind?"

"Let the Foxes have Garth and Briggs. Let us repay them for what they have done to us."

"They both deserve to die!" shouted one of the green-painted members of the Bear clan, brandishing the gun he was carrying.

"They steal our land and the wealth that lies under it—the cinnabar," cried a member of the Fox clan. "That cinnabar belongs to us!"

"No!" roared Appanoose. Then, addressing the man who had just spoken, he continued, "You forget that the Great Spirit told the Red Earth People a long time ago that we may plow only the top six inches of the earth, which is all of it that belongs to us. The rest must not be touched."

"About Garth and Briggs, Appanoose," Cimarron said. "I'd like to oblige you and hand them over to you, but the fact is I've got first claim on them. Both of them, once I get my paws on them, are going to stand trial on a whole bunch of charges when I get them back to Fort Smith. And that brings up another matter. I don't want you boys killing for the simple sake of killing. What I want is prisoners, not dead bodies."

There was some grumbling among both the Indians and the Baldwin ranch hands, but Cimarron, refusing to back down, reiterated his points and finally received assurances from both Appanoose and Barney Mitchell that there would be no killing—except in self-defense.

"I guess we've covered about all the ground we need to," Cimarron commented then. "So let's ride."

"Take care—"

"I'll be sure to do that, honey," Cimarron told Isabel.

"—of yourself, Barney," she concluded. Then, noticing the crestfallen expression on Cimarron's face, she added, "And you be careful too, Cimarron."

Miranda followed Cimarron as he went to his horse. "I shall pray for you, Cimarron. For you and Paul."

"I reckon you'll also be saying a prayer or two for Clyde Hunter, judging by what Isabel told me tonight about you and him."

"Isabel told you about—"

"Now there's no need for you to look so flustered, Miranda. Your secret's safe with me." He patted her cheek, swung into the saddle, and rode away from the mission with the eleven Indians and four Baldwin ranch hands following close behind him.

When the foothills of the range that surrounded Death Valley came into sight, Cimarron held up a hand and called a halt. Turning his horse, he spoke to Appanoose, who had been riding directly behind him. "I told you about the sentries Garth's got posted up in those mountains. I don't relish one bit the idea of running into any of them. What I'd like you to do is send two of your men on ahead to scout the area. Should they come upon any sentries they can try putting them out of comission before they can cause us any woe. Only they've got to remember to do it real quiet so there's no shooting that might alert our enemy to the fact that we're on his trail. Tell them to double back and rejoin us once they've scouted down the other side of those mountains."

Appanoose spoke briefly to two of his men, and when he had finished, they put heels to their horses, rode away, and soon disappeared among the foothills.

Cimarron set out after them, the remaining men riding behind him. They moved into the foothills and began to climb toward the peaks looming above them. When they finally reached the summit, they started down the other side. Cimarron was the first to spot the man whose arms were wrapped around a tree trunk and whose back was pressed up against it. He stiffened in the saddle, but then when the man neither moved nor made a sound, he relaxed. As he and the others rode on, he noticed that the man's mouth was stuffed with moss, which served as an effective gag.

"Is he a sentry?"

"He's one of them," Cimarron answered in response to Appanoose's query.

"You are sure?"

Cimarron nodded and pointed to the bound man's boots, which were caked with red cinnabar ore.

Later, when they were halfway down the mountain, they were rejoined by the two scouts Appanoose had dispatched at Cimarron's direction.

"We saw only a single sentry," declared one of the scouts.

"And I thank you for taking care of him," Cimarron said. He dismounted and signaled to the men with him that they were to do the same. He led them to a rocky ledge that jutted out from the side of the mountain and overlooked Death Valley below.

"That's it," he told the men, pointing at the cinnabar pit and then at the smelters that glowed like giant fireflies in the night. "That cabin down there, it's where the guards hole up along with Garth and Briggs—if those two are still down there."

"Bleeding Jesus Christ!" muttered Barney Mitchell as one of the slave laborers below them tossed wood into a smelter and stoked its fire, causing flames to flare up and brighten the dark night. "Will you take a look at that!"

Cimarron stared at the tall wooden stakes he had not been able to see before the fire in the smelter illuminated them. On each was impaled a decapitated head.

"Who the hell were those poor bastards?" the man named Curly asked in a breathless whisper.

"I recognize the one on the end," Cimarron answered. "His name was Poweshiek. He was shot and killed when we were trying to take control down there. My guess is that Garth or Briggs—somebody in charge—ordered the heads of the laborers who got killed in the fight stuck up there on those stakes to remind the living not to make another try to clear out of the valley.

"Now I've got a few suggestions to make about how we ought to try taking control down there," Cimarron continued. "I'd like to see if they meet with your approval. What I've got in mind is this: instead of just a frontal attack, I think we ought to come in from the front and from both flanks. I'd like to see a man on each flank who don't make their move till the rest of us attack from the front. Then each flank man can go around behind that cabin down there in case anybody tries climbing out the back windows.

"There's only the usual three guards on night duty down there. Those of us who ride in from the front can take them out first thing. Then—except for the two men back behind the cabin—we've all got to concentrate on the ones left inside the cabin who'll try to stay put in there as long as they can. But we'll flush them out."

"How?" Barney Mitchell asked.

Cimarron told him and his answer brought a grin to the faces of the men surrounding him. "You boys ready?" When everyone was once again mounted, Cimarron gave the signal to move out, and as he did, one of the Indians rode to the left, and the ranch hand named Denver rode to the right. Cimarron and the remaining men continued in a straight line down the mountainside.

Half an hour later, Cimarron and his men had formed a long line that ran parallel to the mining camp. He held them in position as he watched the activity in the camp, and then, when the backs of all three night guards were turned to him, he signaled to his men, and all of them rode forward at a fast gallop with some of them, Barney Mitchell included, yelling at the top of their voices.

Cimarron bent down over his black's neck as the three guards, obviously startled, spun around and went for their guns. The black's mane flew in his face, but Cimarron managed to guide the animal toward a guard who was standing several yards away from his companions. The smelter workers stood stiffly and stared in apparent disbelief at the approaching raiders.

Several shots rang out, all of them fired from the guards' guns, but none hitting any of their targets. The guards began to fall back, two of them taking shelter behind the nearest smelter.

Cimarron rode between a small group of smelter workers and the guard he had chosen as his quarry. He waved the workers away, and, as if suddenly energized by his gesture, they turned and fled the scene. He pulled one booted foot from his stirrup, thrust it straight out, and rode on. The heel of his boot smashed into the face of the guard who was turning toward him, his gun clutched tightly in both hands.

The guard let out an anguished scream as blood poured from his broken nose and ripped lips. He staggered backward and went down, his hands clawing at his ruined face. Cimarron drew rein, slid out of the saddle, and scooped up the guard's gun. He thrust it into his waistband, climbed back into the saddle and rode on.

"Rope them!" he shouted to the men who had been riding with him when he saw that they had taken the other two guards prisoner. "Take their guns and hog-tie both of them."

Cimarron dismounted when he reached the woods, and leaving his black ground-hitched, he crouched down behind the trunk of an elm. He scanned the area around the cabin and eventually made out the figures of a Fox flattened against the left sidewall of the cabin and the ranch hand named Denver sheltering behind a growth of chokecherry brambles on the right side of the cabin. Ignoring the shouts of the laborers who were now milling about in obvious confusion, Cimarron rose and ran to the tall pile of cordwood that was stacked beside one of the smelters. He took two lengths of wood from the pile and thrust both of them into the firebox until they were both ablaze. He was about to return to the woods when he caught a glimpse of Hunter in the distance. He yelled the man's name and ran toward him.

"Cimarron!" Hunter cried when he saw who it was who had called his name. "What—"

"Take the gun I've got in my waistband," Cimarron ordered, interrupting Hunter. "But don't shoot anybody unless you have to to save your own ass. Where's Baldwin?"

"Over there with those men he told me work for him."

"His hired hands and those Foxes and me, we're here to finally put an end to Garth's cinnabar mining. You can do me a favor, Hunter."

"Name it."

"Get the workers out of harm's way. I don't want any of them hurt. Round them up and herd them over there on the far side of the horse corral."

"Where are you going?"

Cimarron didn't hear Hunter's question because he was already sprinting back to the woods. He made his way through

164

them until he was beyond the rear wall of the cabin. Then he turned right and ran up to the men he spotted kneeling in the underbrush behind the cabin.

"You made it," crowed Denver as Cimarron handed him one of the two firebrands he was carrying and gave the other one to the Indian next to Denver.

"Let's go," Cimarron said and began to angle toward the rear wall of the cabin, keeping away from the windows. When all three men reached the cabin, Cimarron silently gestured, and Denver and the Indian took up positions next to the two windows set into the rear wall. Cimarron, using the butt of his gun, smashed the window nearest him, and the Indian hurled his firebrand into the cabin. Cimarron darted across to where Denver crouched beside the second window. He swiftly smashed that window and watched Denver toss his torch inside the cabin.

"That ought to burn those boys out of their burrow," an enthusiastic Denver cried as flames began to leap up beyond the cabin's windows.

"You two stay here," Cimarron directed Denver and his Indian companion. "Make sure nobody gets out this way. If they try it, use your guns to drive them back. I'm going out front to get ready for them when it gets too hot inside and they're forced to make a run for it."

Cimarron bounded around the side of the cabin and took up a position behind the trunk of a maple tree. He scanned the area and found it deserted. It's as if, he thought, as he stared up at the decapitated heads topping the stakes, the living have left this place to the dead.

Suddenly, the door of the cabin burst open and guards, all of them only partially clothed, came streaming out. They scattered, firing blindly as they went. Behind them, a red glow emanated from the interior of the cabin.

Cimarron studied their faces, searching for Garth and Briggs. Disappointment welled up in him when he saw no sign of either man. But, only a moment later, two more men burst from the cabin to follow in the wake of the others.

Cimarron exulted as he recognized Garth in the lead with Briggs right behind him. They sent their Lighthorsemen out to clear a path for them, he thought. He stepped out from behind the maple, yelled, "Round them all up, boys!" and raced after Garth and Briggs, his gun in his hand.

"Garth!" he yelled. "Briggs! Stop or I'll stop you both dead in your tracks!"

Neither man obeyed his order. Instead, both turned and fired at him. Then, as Briggs suddenly swerved to the right, Cimarron halted, took careful aim, and fired at the man.

Briggs went down with Cimarron's bullet in his left leg.

"Hunter!" Cimarron yelled. When Hunter appeared in the distance, he pointed to Briggs and ran awkwardly on as Hunter made his way to Briggs and stood over the downed man with the gun Cimarron had given him earlier.

Garth suddenly disappeared around the side of a smelter. He took up a position there and fired again at Cimarron. Dodging the bullet, Cimarron swerved to the left, intending to circle the smelter and come in on Garth from the other side. But Garth foiled his plan by suddenly appearing on the left side of the smelter and firing at him again. This time he hit his mark and Cimarron, struck in his left thigh, lost his balance. His hands flew out before him to cushion his fall. But, instead of hitting the ground, he crashed into the smelter, causing it to tilt precariously. As he bounced off it and fell to the ground, the smelter toppled over, spilling sparks and burning brands from its metal belly.

Garth screamed. He screamed again.

Cimarron sat up and saw the fiery apparition that was Garth go running away toward the woods, flames streaming out behind him from his clothes and hair—a result of him having been in the direct path of the falling smelter. He watched Garth stop, spin around, flail at the flames that were rapidly consuming his hair, then run a few more steps before dropping down to his knees. Cimarron grimaced as Garth turned toward him, for he saw the smoking flesh of the man's face, saw Garth's mouth open in an anguished cry, saw the flesh of his face begin to char. A moment later, Garth, a living torch, fell face down on the ground, where he lay writhing for less than a minute before becoming still as the flickering flames continued to consume him.

"You hurt bad?"

Cimarron looked up at Paul Baldwin, who had suddenly materialized beside him.

"Took a round in my leg. Which reminds me. How's your leg holding up?"

Baldwin patted the makeshift bandage that covered the wound in his leg. "Hunter makes a good nurse. He's a man of many talents."

Barney Mitchell came running up to them then to announce, "Cimarron, we've got the guards rounded up, every last one of them."

"Anybody hurt?"

"Appanoose got nicked in the shoulder, but he'll be okay."

Cimarron looked up at the grisly display of staked heads.

Baldwin, noticing what he was looking at, said, "Garth ordered that done."

"He couldn't even let the dead rest in peace," Cimarron commented bitterly as he got to his feet.

"You think they were all dead when they were decapitated?" Baldwin asked him.

"You mean—"

"Poweshiek wasn't," Baldwin stated somberly, "although most of them were. Garth gave the order to decapitate them. Briggs was the one who did the deed."

"It's time we got out of here," Cimarron remarked, shaking his head in disbelief at what he had just heard. "But first I've got to find the Lighthorseman who relieved me of my Winchester and Colt when him and his boys had me outnumbered at Mokohoko's wickiup. Then, once we're on our way, we'll pick up that sentry the Fox scouts have hog-tied up in the mountains. Mitchell, make sure none of those guards gets away from us. Mount them on horses from the corral. Do the same for the prisoners. We're getting out of this hellhole right now."

Back at the mission late the same morning, Cimarron was given an enthusiastic reception by both Isabel and Miranda. The Indians and Baldwin's ranch hands stood guard over the prisoners they had taken, and Miranda busied herself caring for the men who had been held captive at the cinnabar mine. Isabel cleansed and then bandaged the flesh wound in Cimarron's thigh.

His bandage secured, Cimarron went up to Baldwin, Hunter,

167

and Miranda, who were engaged in a low-toned discussion. They all fell into a strained silence as he joined them.

"I don't mean to butt in on your private business," he told them, preparing to leave.

"Don't go, Cimarron," Miranda pleaded. "Maybe you can talk some sense into my stubborn brother's head."

"What kind of sense did you have it in mind for me to talk into him?"

"I told him I was going to marry Clyde Hunter no matter what he said, and all he could say was no. Please Cimarron, try to make him understand that I am not a bigot as he so obviously is."

Before Cimarron could say anything, Baldwin said, "Miranda, if you'd be still for more than thirty seconds at a time, I'd be happy to explain my position to you."

"You hate Indians," Miranda accused.

"It's true that I never had much liking for them before," Baldwin admitted. "But now—well, I told you Clyde saved my life during the first battle back at the mining camp and how he cared for me afterward. And I saw the way Appanoose and his Foxes fought like the very brave men they all are to save not just the Indians Garth had imprisoned but the white men like myself as well.

"By the way, Miranda, I should tell you that I have apologized to Clyde for not telling the truth right from the start about the fact that it was actually Briggs who shot me. I shouldn't have put Clyde at risk of being arrested for a crime he didn't commit.

"When I said no before," Baldwin continued, still addressing Miranda, "I intended to go on to explain that I don't want you to marry Clyde—" Baldwin scowled at his sister as she opened her mouth to protest. Then, when she remained silent, he continued, "I was going to ask you to wait awhile before marrying Clyde. Until he and I can set up a partnership to run the ranch together. *Then* you can marry him with my blessing."

"Partnership," Miranda repeated, beginning to smile.

"And another thing, Miranda. I know you've been upset about the way I ran father's real estate business in New Orleans," Baldwin added in a soft voice. "I intend to pay off the men I cheated from the future profits—my share of them—that result from the operation of the ranch. It will take some time, but I'll do it."

"Oh, Paul!" Miranda cried happily and threw her arms around his neck. "That's wonderful. You are!"

Cimarron, as brother and sister hugged one another, shook hands with Hunter and wished him luck. Then, "Baldwin, I'll be needing that black you've been letting me use to get me back to Fort Smith. I'll pay you a good price for him."

"Nonsense, Cimarron. Take him. He's yours."

"That's real nice of you, Baldwin. I thank you."

"Let's go back to the ranch and have a drink to celebrate," Baldwin suggested.

Hunter shook his head.

"Why, Clyde, what's wrong?" Miranda asked him. "Nothing's wrong," he replied. "In fact, everything's as right as it could possibly be. Including me not wanting a drink. I neither want nor need one—now that I've got you." He put his arm around Miranda's waist and drew her close to him.

"I hope they give you an honest agent to replace Garth," Cimarron said. "One who won't try getting rich by leasing Indian land the way he did. Which reminds me—I intend to see to it that Samuel Barstow, who was in cahoots with Garth, gets booted out of the Indian Bureau. By the way, Hunter, now that you're well rid of Garth, what are you planning on doing about the other white ranchers who are holding leases issued by Garth?"

"Baldwin and I are going to set up a Landholder's Association here on the reservation and see to it that every non-Indian rancher makes a substantial contribution to both the Sac and Fox tribal treasuries for the privilege of working reservation land."

"We felt that would be the best way to handle the ranchers already here and any our association might let come in later on," Baldwin explained. "We'll lease only a relatively small portion of Indian land and see to it that the Indians benefit from that leasing, not some crooked federal employee like Garth was."

"Glad to hear you two have got things all smoothed out between you." Cimarron shook hands with Baldwin, and then turned to Miranda.

She threw her arms around his neck and kissed him on the

cheek. Then he turned and made his way back into the mission in search of Isabel. He found her in the kitchen in the arms of Barney Mitchell, who was kissing her ardently. Cimarron cleared his throat, and when Isabel and Mitchell drew apart, he said, "I'm sorry to interrupt what you two were about, but I wanted to bid you both good-bye."

"If you're ever out this way again, Cimarron—" Isabel began as he shook hands with Barney Mitchell.

"I'll be sure to look you both up," he told them as she planted a kiss on his cheek.

Outside again, he took charge of his prisoners and said good-bye to Baldwin's ranch hands and to Appanoose and his Foxes.

"You look like one of us," Appanoose said to him as he swung into the saddle of the black.

"I don't follow you, Appanoose."

The Indian pointed to Cimarron's boots, his clothes, and finally his face. "You have red cinnabar ore all over you. It makes you look as if you were formed from the red earth by the Great Spirit as our ancestors were. You look like one of the Red Earth People."

"Which, as far as I'm concerned, is a pretty proud thing to look like." He gave Appanoose and his Foxes a wave before riding out behind Briggs and his other prisoners as he began his long journey back to Fort Smith.

SPECIAL PREVIEW

Here is the first chapter
from

**CIMARRON
AND THE MANHUNTERS**

twenty-first in the action-packed
CIMARRON series from Signet

One

Cimarron rode up to the small frame house on the eastern side of the Katy railroad's tracks and drew rein. He hallooed the house, and a man came out of it to stand staring suspiciously at him. Cimarron dug into a pocket of his jeans and came up with a nickel star, which he displayed. "Name's Cimarron," he told the man. "Asked around in town and folks said you could be found out here. I've come about Bob Tucker."

"How much'll you pay me?"

"Ten dollars."

"There's a *fifty*-dollar bounty on Bob Tucker's head, so how come you're offering me a measly ten dollars?"

"On account of that's what it's worth to the law—to me—to find out where Bob Tucker's at. The fifty-dollar bounty, that's to be paid to the man who can bring Tucker in. I don't reckon you're the man to do it, but maybe I can if I don't happen to get my head blowed off by a backshooter like Tucker."

"I don't rightly know if I should tell you what I know for just ten dollars," the man whined, shifting his weight from one foot to the other and his chaw from one cheek to the other.

"Mister, when I stopped at the sheriff's office back in McAlester I was told about you and that you were itching to sell some information on the whereabouts of Bob Tucker and—"

"Only to a federal starpacker though," the man interrupted. "They're the only kind with any money to spend these days it seems. That sheriff in McAlester wouldn't—claimed he couldn't—pay me a dime for what I know."

"Here I am," Cimarron concluded, ignoring what the man had just said. "Now, I don't like wild goose chases one little bit. When I find out I'm on one, well, what I generally tend to do is grab the goose I've been chasing and wring its neck. Do you follow me, mister?"

The man nodded. He swallowed. His right hand rose, and his fingers encircled his scrawny neck. "The Faber farm," he croaked.

"That's where I'll find Tucker?"

"He's been working there ever since last month when he drifted through these parts. I recognized him right off when I was out to Faber's one day to buy some turnips. I have a pretty good memory for the faces I see printed on dodgers. Once I see such a face, I don't as a rule forget it. It's Tucker for sure." The man held up a hand to Cimarron, who pulled a gold eagle from his pocket and handed it to him. "Where's the Faber farm?" he asked and, when he had been given directions to it, he turned his black and rode away while the man stood busily biting the gold coin to make sure it wasn't counterfeit.

Later, as Cimarron crested a hill and drew rein, he sat his saddle and stared down at the fields below him where withering corn shocks and orchards, now stripped of both fruit and leaves, stood under the thin November sun. He surveyed the area, noting the men who were cutting timber some distance away and the two-story house and outbuildings beyond the orchards. His gaze returned to the men who were piling the cut wood in the bed of a spring wagon. They were too far away for him to make out their faces, so he couldn't be sure if Bob Tucker was among them.

Cimarron put heels to his horse and started down the hill toward the farmhouse. When he reached it, he hallooed it and gave the grizzled man who emerged from it a cheerful "Good day."

"What can I do for you, stranger?" the man asked.

"Are you Mr. Faber who owns this farm?"

"I am. How come you know my name?"

"I asked around in town about where I might find me some

work," Cimarron lied. "Somebody mentioned you and your place so here I am, Mr. Faber, ready and willing to work at anything you want done."

"Folks in town talk without knowing what they're talking about more than half the time," Faber grumbled. "I'm in no need of any hands. Got a bunch of them. Besides, winter's a-coming on, and those hands I've got, half of 'em I'll be letting go before the first snow flies."

Cimarron let the disappointment he was feeling show on his face. He wondered if he had failed in his mission before he had barely begun it. If he couldn't hire on here at the Faber farm, he knew, he had no other way of getting close to Bob Tucker. And if he couldn't get close to Tucker, there was no way in the world he could hope to get evidence to prove that Tucker had murdered Lucy Brandt as he was suspected of having done. And without such evidence, Tucker would probably never be convicted of the crime.

"You say you want work," Faber mused, stroking his bearded chin.

"I'll do whatever needs doing," Cimarron volunteered quickly. "Haul manure, slop hogs—"

"You need work, I take it?"

"And the money it'll put in my empty pockets, yep, I surely do."

"Some of the boys I've hired are about as useless as tits on a boar hog," Faber grunted. "So I'll tell you what I'll do. I'll hire you at half the going rate since I'm doing you a favor taking you on at all this late in the season. Fifty cents a day. Is that agreeable to you?"

"It sure is, Mr. Faber," Cimarron declared enthusiastically, thinking: you old skinflint.

"Then ride on out there to where those boys are working and give them a hand."

Cimarron turned his black and went galloping away toward the cluster of woodcutters in the distance. When he reached them, he dismounted and asked who was in charge of the crew.

"Me," said a burly man. "What business have you here, mister?"

"I was just hired by Mr. Faber to lend you boys a hand."

"Then you'd best get cracking," advised the man in charge as he handed Cimarron an axe. "Start splitting wood."

Cimarron took the axe and made his way to where the man he recognized from having seen his pictures on dodgers was using a bucking saw to cut up felled trees. "Howdy," he said to Bob Tucker as he placed a piece of wood on a chopping block and split it in two with his axe. "My name's—" He hesitated, thinking that an owlhoot like Tucker just might be familiar with his name. "It's Smith. Ed Smith."

"Mine's Tom Fenway," Tucker answered without looking at Cimarron, who had to suppress a smile as he thought that Tucker was every bit as good a liar as he was.

"Glad to know you, Tom."

No response from Tucker.

Cimarron worked on in silence for awhile. When sweat began to stream down his face, he wiped it away and commented, "This kind of work's sure to bust a man's back before long. I sure'd rather be back dealing three-card monte on some fancy Mississippi sternwheeler." The provocative comment elicited an appraising glance but no comment from Tucker.

Later, the woodcutters made their nooning on food that had been brought from the farmhouse on a flatbed wagon. Cimarron, when he had filled his plate with boiled beans, sourdough biscuits, and a hearty portion of a thick beef-and-rice stew, made his way to where Tucker was seated alone beneath a blackjack oak. "Mind if I join, you, Tom?" he asked, using the assumed name Tucker had given him earlier.

"Suit yourself."

Cimarron sat down next to Tucker. "Grub's real good. Is it always or is this meal an accident?"

"It's passable most days. I've had better—and worse."

"You a logger by trade, Tom?"

"At the moment I am, yes."

Cimarron sopped up some of the stew's broth with a biscuit, which he devoured. He sighed mournfully. "Where'd you work before here, Tom?"

"You sure do ask a man a whole lot of personal questions."

"No offense meant. Didn't mean to pry into your personal business. Meant to find a way to make the time pass easy between us."

Tucker remained silent for a moment, then, apparently mollified, "I've seen better days as, I take it, you have from what you said before about being a riverboat gambler."

"I played my last ace on those old riverboats some time

back," Cimarron commented with a wistful note in his voice. "There were some who said I cheated, and try as I might I couldn't clean the mud some men kept flinging at me off my reputation."

"You didn't cheat?"

Cimarron gave Tucker a sly grin. "Well, maybe I did use a card pricker from time to time." He shrugged. "So maybe those old boys were right in running me off the river. But I took it all in stride. What the hell else could I do? I mean if a man gets his ass skinned all he can do is sit on the blister, right?"

Tucker smiled, put down his empty plate, and pulled the makings from his shirt pocket. He offered them to Cimarron.

"I don't smoke. That's one vice I never took to. Just about the only one, I reckon."

"Let's go, boys!" yelled the man in charge of the woodcutters.

The afternoon passed slowly for Cimarron as he continued chopping wood, which another man piled in the bed of the spring wagon.

"What's Faber fixing to do with all this wood he's put us to chopping?" Cimarron asked. "He's got himself enough to keep the fires of Hell stoked for a good long time by the looks of it."

"He sells it," a man working beside Cimarron answered. "Hear he gets a good price for it too. A lot of the land around here's not timbered, and so folks are sorely in need of fuel come winter. Faber supplies it to them."

"Faber, he must be a mighty rich man to have him as fine a spread as this one," Cimarron commented idly.

"I reckon he does all right," the man who had spoken earlier speculated.

"I never had much of a way with money," Cimarron remarked as he continued chopping wood. "It came and it went, and it never stayed around long enough for me to really make its acquaintance. I don't understand for the life of me how men like Faber do it—get rich, I mean."

"By taking advantage of other folks," Tucker interjected while furiously working the bucking saw he had in his hand. "By buying cheap and selling dear," he growled. "It's not fair, if you ask me, for some men to have so much and others so little."

Which leads, Cimarron thought, to a man turning into a

rider of the long trails like you, Tucker. But he said nothing more.

After supper that night Cimarron lay on his bunk and watched Tucker shave in front of a cracked mirror nailed to a wooden roof support. Tucker wiped the lather from his face, took off his shirt, washed his face and upper torso, and put his shirt back on.

"What for are you duding up, Tom?" called out one of the men in the bunkhouse as he winked at the others.

When Tucker made no reply, one of the other men said, "You're wasting your time, Tom, if you think a homely *hombre* like yourself can hope to turn the heads of the whores in McAlester."

Still Tucker said nothing, and after a few more taunts from the men in the bunkhouse, he headed for the door.

Cimarron got up from his bunk, grabbed his hat, and followed Tucker outside. He noted that Tucker was not carrying a gun. "Where are you headed, if you don't mind my asking?"

"Those bastards!" Tucker muttered without answering, "I may not be Beau Brummel, but I wish to hell they'd keep their mouths shut about the way I look."

"Don't let their joshing get to you," Cimarron advised. "It's not always what a man looks like that lets him ram his stopper into one jug after another. It's more a matter of can he sweet-talk a woman and get her as hot as a hen trying to lay a goose egg."

"You're right on that score," Tucker declared enthusiastically. "And this old stopper of mine's plugged more jugs than those old boys in there have probably ever even seen!"

"I guess you wouldn't be wanting any company tonight, would you?"

Tucker clapped Cimarron on the shoulder. "You're welcome to ride into town with me if you want to."

"On account of I'm about as horny as a six-pointed buck I do believe I'll join you," Cimarron said. "I washed up before supper, so let's go."

As the two men made their way toward the barn, Cimarron asked, "Where exactly are we going?"

"South McAlester," Tucker answered as they entered the barn and proceeded to get their horses ready to ride.

"You're heading for that part of town folks call Chippy Hill, is that it?"

"That's it," Tucker said, and climbed into his saddle. "With a little bit of luck and an expenditure of a few dollars, both of us are likely to have something a lot sweeter than a sweaty old horse between our legs before the night's over."

"Want another one, gents?" asked the bar dog in the illegal saloon that was discreetly situated behind a tin shop in the heart of South McAlester.

"Fill 'em up," Tucker directed, and the bar dog promptly filled both glasses.

"To success," Tucker said, raising his glass to Cimarron's.

"To success."

"Their glasses touched, and then both men drank. Before they could put their glasses back down on the bar, two women sauntered through the batwings and into the saloon, where they paused only briefly before exchanging knowing glances and then headed directly toward Cimarron and Tucker.

"Evening, ladies," Cimarron greeted the two women as they arrived at the bar. "Won't you join us?"

"And have something to drink?" Tucker added. "Me and my friend here we sure could use the sight of some feminine pulchritude such as you both have to offer."

Cimarron and Tucker made room for the two women and summoned the bar dog. When two beers and a bowl of raw oysters had been placed in front of the women, Cimarron handed the bar dog a dollar.

"I'm Ella," announced the blonde woman with a saucy toss of her sausage curls, "and this here's my friend, Ida."

The auburn-haired and chestnut-eyed Ida giggled and took a dainty sip from her glass. She patted her full lips with the back of her hand and said, "Ella and me have rooms in the hotel right next door."

"Are you fellows looking for a little fun?" inquired Ella with a coy lifting of her plucked eyebrows.

"You just bet we are," Cimarron replied, "and you two look like you're both chock full of fun."

"What kind of fun did you have in mind?" simpered Ida.

"A quickie or an all-nighter?" Ella asked bluntly.

Cimarron glanced at Tucker, who said, "I've got me some serious drinking to do, so I'll put my money on a quickie."

"What about you, mister?" Ella asked, batting her eyelashes at Cimarron.

"I reckon I'll have the same as my friend here. How much?"

"Two dollars—each," Ida said.

"Two dollars!" Tucker exploded. "Why, a man can buy the selfsame thing in almost any parlor house here on Chippy Hill for anywhere from four bits to a dollar."

"You're welcome to go to one of those houses, I'm sure," said Ida, quickly downing her beer, "and see if we care. Come along, Ella."

"We're independents," Ella explained as Ida grabbed her arm and tried to pull her away from the bar. "We have to charge a higher price than most of the other whores in the houses around here. We have our hotel rooms to pay for and—"

Cimarron chucked her under the chin, silencing her. "Why, sure you do, honey. I understand. Let's you and me go to your place."

"What about me?" wailed Ida as Cimarron began to guide Ella toward the batwings.

"Come on," Tucker said, and grumbling all the way about Ida's price, he followed Cimarron and Ella out of the saloon with Ida walking haughtily beside him.

They made their way into the lobby of the hotel next door and up the stairs, where the women led Cimarron and Tucker down a dreary hall. They stopped at the end of it, and Ella announced, "This here's my room," and Ida said, "Mine's the one right next door."

Ella unlocked her room and, taking Cimarron's arm, she led him into her room and closed the door behind her. She held out her hand to him. He came up with two dollars, which she tucked between her breasts.

"I don't get undressed for quickies," she informed him. "Neither do you," she added, and flopped down on her back on the bed.

"That wasn't what I had in mind."

Ella propped herself up on her elbows and stared at Cimarron. "What wasn't what you had in mind?"

He told her what he had in mind.

"Why not?" was her professional response. She got up from the bed and approached him. "Why don't you have a seat— take a load off your legs?"

He sat down in the only chair in the room, and Ella dropped to her knees before him. She unbuttoned his fly, thrust a hand into his jeans, and came up with his already stiff shaft, which she proceeded to stroke, eliciting a contented sigh from Cimarron. She lowered her head, the tip of her tongue protruding from her mouth.

Cimarron, his hands resting on the arms of the chair, watched her tongue snake out to touch his swollen flesh. He spread his legs wide as Ella's tongue teased and tickled him. He was about to order her to get on with it before he exploded, but then she opened her mouth wide, lowered her head, and engulfed him. He laid his head against the back of the chair, closed his eyes, and listened to the wet gurgling sounds Ella was making. As her hot tongue skillfully laved him, he tightened his grip on the arms of the chair.

Then he opened his eyes, raised his head, and looked down at her. Her cheeks were drawn in and her lips were tightly pursed around him as her head bobbed up and down in a wildly arousing rhythm. He felt himself growing hotter, felt his face flushing, felt the tingling in his groin as Ella continued using her lips and tongue on him. A kind of giddiness almost overcame him as he felt the sudden surging within him. He moaned. He thrust upward, causing Ella to gag. But she quickly recovered and began to fondle his testicles as her lips continued to grip him.

He couldn't help it; he cried out as he erupted. At first, as he began to flood Ella's mouth, he stiffened, but then, with each successive upward thrust and hot spurt, he began to relax until finally, completely spent and totally satisfied, he lay limply back in the chair and stered up at the ceiling without really seeing it.

Ella released him and sat back on her heels. She swallowed, licked her lips, and said, "I thought I was going to choke to death when you rammed it down my throat."

"I got carried away, honey. Didn't mean to cause you any trouble."

Ella smiled. She reached out and playfully pinched Cimarron's still-erect shaft. "I bet this thing has caused more than one girl more trouble than she could handle. Am I right?"

"I always try to look on the bright side of things," he responded with a grin. "I've been told by more than one woman that that thing of mine gave them nothing but pure pleasure."

"I can believe it," Ella said and got up.

Cimarron stuffed his softening flesh back into his jeans, buttoned up, and got to his feet. Ella threw her arms around him, her hands running up and down his back, caressing his hips, groping between his legs. He stood there, enjoying her attentions, as she continued her stroking and provocative petting of his body.

Then, stepping back, she said, "Well, it's time I was getting back to work."

Once outside the room, Cimarron knocked on the door of Ida's room. When he got no response, he called out, "Tom, you in there?"

Still no response.

He made his way down the hall with Ella, and together they returned to the saloon, where they found Ida and Tucker drinking at the bar.

"I feel like I could lick my weight in ants," Tucker glumly declared as he and Ida were joined by Cimarron and Ella. "Now the only thing left to do to round off the night is to get drunk," he announced and emptied his glass.

"What'll you have, another beer?" Cimarron asked Ella.

"Thanks but no thanks," she answered, shaking her head, her eyes on two dandified men who had just come into the saloon. "Ida," she muttered, prodding her friend in the ribs with her elbow and pointing at the two men.

Ida turned, saw the two newcomers, and stared toward them with a whispered, "Let's go, Ella. There stands four dollars on the hoof."

Tucker didn't turn around as the two women left. "She was as loose as a stretched sheep bladder," he complained. "I kept sliding right out of her."

"Women," Cimarron muttered. "You can't do with them and you can't do without them." He ordered a drink. "They're more trouble than they're worth, take it from me."

Tucker ignored him.

"I could tell you some hair-raising stories," he whispered conspiratorially. "Some of them not so pretty. I swear off the weaker sex from time to time. They're nothing but trouble, every last one of them. A man does well to steer clear of them if he knows what's good for him."

"I've had my share of troubles with women," Tucker mused and ordered another drink as he watched Ella and Ida leave the saloon with their two new customers.

Cimarron waited for him to go on, hoping Tucker would say something about Lucy Brandt, the woman he was suspected of having murdered, but Tucker slipped into a morose silence.

Two hours and an uncounted number of drinks later, Cimarron's head was still clear because he had secretly spilled most of his drinks into the spittoon that sat on the sawdust-covered floor by his boots. He desperately searched his mind for some scheme that would cause Tucker to incriminate himself. Finally, he hit on one that he thought had a chance of working. After feigning drunkenness for some time, he suddenly began to sob. He lowered his head until it was resting on his crossed forearms which he had placed on the bar.

"Whatsh the matter?" Tucker asked him a slurred voice.

"Leave me be." Cimarron shook off the heavy hand Tucker had dropped on his shoulder. "There's no comforting a man like me who's spilled the blood of a woman, never mind that she was a conniving no-good bitch who'd had the claws of more men in her flanks than Hannibal ever had in his army.

"She said she was carrying my kid. She said I had to do right by her and marry her. Well, hell, I told her there was no way I would ever do a damn fool thing like that. She said she'd tell everybody in town what I did to her, get her pa to shoot me." He sobbed again.

"You killed her?"

"Shot her, sure. You don't know what it's like to have killed a woman, my friend. It's not the same as killing a man. It's—"

"I know."

Cimarron shifted position slightly and beckoned to the bar dog, hoping Tucker had not seen him do so. "How many women have you killed?" he asked Tucker, raising his head and throwing one comradely arm around Tucker's shoulder.

"Just one. Her name was Lucy Brandt." Tucker hiccupped. "What you've got to do is you've got to put it clean out of your mind. That's what I did."

"How'd you kill this Lucy Brandt?" Cimarron asked, aware of the gaping and open-mouthed bar dog, who was standing stock-still as he listened to the conversation taking place between Cimarron and Tucker. He motioned to the man to be silent.

"Drowned her," Tucker answered. "She was a tease, Lucy Brandt was. All talk and no delivery of the goods. I tried to make it look like she committed suicide, but the law's on my tail anyway."

Cimarron turned to the bar dog. "You heard what he said?"

"I heard him say he drowned to death a woman named Lucy Brandt." The bar dog's face was white.

Cimarron pulled his badge from his pocket and showed it to Tucker, causing the man to take several staggering steps away from him and the bar dog to blink several times in rapid succession. "I'm a deputy marshal," he told the bar dog. "This man here is named Bob Tucker, and he's wanted, like he said, for the murder of Lucy Brandt. I needed evidence against him that would stand up in court and I got it—his confession, which you heard. What's your name?"

"Edward Peters. Why?"

"There'll be a deputy who'll come to collect you. You'll be needed as a prosecution witness against Tucker at his trial since you heard his confession the same as me."

"You—" Tucker gripped the edge of the bar to keep from falling as he swayed drunkenly in front of Cimarron. "You won't take me!"

Cimarron calmly watched Tucker weave his unsteady way toward the batwings. He watched him fall to the floor before he reached them. He went to Tucker and helped him to his feet. "Let's go, Tucker. You and me are heading for Fort Smith."

But Tucker never heard him, Cimarron realized, because the man had passed out. Cimarron tossed Tucker's limp body over his shoulder and started for the batwings.

"Wait a minute, Deputy," the bar dog called out. "You and your friend haven't settled your bar bill."

Cimarron turned around. "How much is owing you?"

"Six bits."

Cimarron thrust a hand into his pocket—and swore when he realized that all his money was gone. Ella, he thought. When she was feeling me all over just before we left her room—she wasn't just being affectionate like I thought. She was stealing my poke!

He went back to the bar, retrieved a five-dollar bill he kept hidden in his left boot, and handed it to the bar dog. When he received his change, he left the bar. Outside, he looked up at the hotel's second floor. I can't leave Tucker unattended, he thought, which means I don't get to go after my stolen money. So Ella wins the game and gets to keep what she stole. Well, at least I've got Tucker, which was what I set out to do, and he's worth two dollars to me when I turn him in. He draped Tucker over the man's saddle. Then, leading Tucker's horse, he headed out of town.

As they neared the Katy depot, Tucker groaned. Cimarron looked back over his shoulder and then drew rein. "Get into that saddle of yours," he ordered Tucker, his words almost

182

drowned out by the shriek of a Katy train that was just starting to pull out.

Tucker got aboard his horse and gave Cimarron a glare before they rode out.

The two men rode without speaking as the train on their left began to gather speed, its wheels screeching and its whistle screaming. The lamp on the locomotive sent a bright beam of light into the darkness beyond the depot, but it came nowhere near Cimarron and his prisoner.

Tucker began to wave his arms and point at his horse, but the noise of the train prevented Cimarron from hearing what he was saying.

Cimarron rode up beside him and finally understood that Tucker was trying to tell him that his cinch had worked loose. Cimarron indicated with a nod of his head and a blunt gesture that Tucker could dismount and tighten it. He sat his saddle as Tucker dismounted and bent down to peer under his horse's barrel. Then, in one swift move, he ducked under his horse, came up on the other side of the animal, and went running toward the train.

"Tucker, stop!" Cimarron roared, doubting that he could be heard above the roar and iron rattle of the train.

Tucker continued running rapidly in the direction of the train, which was showering the area with cinders from its smoke stack. Cimarron heeled his black and rounded Tucker's mount as he set out after his fleeing prisoner. When Tucker increased his speed, Cimarron fired a high and wide warning shot that didn't stop Tucker, who kept running, his arms stretched out in front of him.

The train climbed a low grade and simultaneously began to round a bend as Cimarron, still galloping in pursuit of Tucker, fired another warning shot at the man. But this time Cimarron knew his shot struck Tucker because the man suddenly veered sharply to one side in a desperate attempt to leap aboard the train's caboose. Tucker stumbled, then he ran on for a few more steps. His outstretched hands clawed at the air before he let out a loud wail and went down. He rose to his knees and reached out as if to embrace the caboose that was rapidly vanishing around the bend. He fell again, and this time he did not rise.

Cimarron reached Tucker a moment later, dismounted and hunkered down beside him. He placed two fingers against Tucker's neck, and when he felt no pulse, he swore.

He stood up, thinking that the night had been a bad one. And not just for Tucker. For him as well. Ella had stolen his money. And now he had unintentionally shot and killed his prisoner, which meant two unpleasant things: One, he would have to pay, as was required by law, for the man's burial; and two, he would not get to collect the two dollars due him for bringing Tucker to the jail in Fort Smith. Two dollars wasn't all that much, he thought, but it sure was better than nothing.

As Cimarron was passing through Poteau in Choctaw Nation the next day, he was wondering how he was going to explain to Marshal Upham, once he reached Fort Smith, that he was in desperate need of a cash advance against future earnings. Upham, he was certain, would rant and rave and accuse him of being impecunious just as he had done on several other similar occasions. The last thing I need, he thought, is a holier-than-thou lecture on how to manage my money from the righteous likes of Marshal Daniel P. Upham. But somehow or other, I've got to wheedle some cash money out of the marshal, else I'll be going hungry and trail-dirty since I can't buy me so much as a corn muffin or a barber shop bath. That undertaker in McAlester relieved me of my last cent and still insisted he was losing money on Tucker's burial.

Cimarron's train of thought was derailed as he heard the shouting and saw the two men going at it knuckle and skull in the dust they were raising in the middle of the street just ahead. He was about to ride by them when a way of solving his financial problem suddenly occurred to him.

He drew rein and stared thoughtfully at the two men, who were busily battering one another to the delight of the growing crowd that surrounded them. One of the pair had a bloody nose. The other had a split lower lip. Both had numerous facial bruises and bloody knuckles. Cimarron got out of the saddle and wrapped his reins around a nearby hitchrail. He rooted about in his pockets until he came up with a piece of paper and the stub of a pencil. Wetting the pencil's lead point, he asked the man standing next to him for his name.

"What do you want my name for?"

"You're a witness," Cimarron replied, "and I'm a deputy marshal."

"That still don't tell me what for you want my name."

"You saw that fellow"—Cimarron pointed at one of the fighting men—"try to kill that other fellow and the other fellow try to

184

do the selfsame thing to the first fellow, which is, in my book, the crime of attempted murder. You'll have to come to Fort Smith with me and give your eyewitness testimony when those two jaspers go on trial."

"They're not trying to kill each other," the man protested. "They're just fighting nice and natural."

"That's not the way I see it, and I've got the eyes of an eagle when it comes to uncovering crimes. Now—your name."

The man began to back away from Cimarron.

"Stand hitched," Cimarron ordered him. "If you don't give me your name, I'll have to arrest you for obstructing justice, and you'll wind up in jail right alongside those two would-be murderers there."

Reluctantly, the man gave his name, and Cimarron wrote it down. He moved on to another man and repeated the process. By the time he was finished he had the names of nineteen witnesses to what he declared were the crimes of attempted murder.

At fifty cents a head, he calculated, that means I can collect nine dollars and fifty cents for these witnesses plus six cents a mile one way between here and Fort Smith, which'll bring me another four dollars or thereabouts. Though it sure won't make me rich, that money'll keep me from being the pauper I am now.

He drew his gun and yelled, "Hold it, gents!"

He had to yell his order a second time before the two bare-knuckled warriors paid him any attention. "You two are under arrest," he told both badly battered men, "and you're coming with me. You—what's your name?"

The man Cimarron had questioned answered, "Dawes. But what—"

"What's your name?" Cimarron asked the other man.

"Randall. Who the hell are you?"

"I'm a deputy marshal here in Indian Territory. Randall, you and Dawes are both under arrest for attempting to murder each other. I'm taking both of you to Fort Smith to stand trial on that charge along with these nineteen witnesses to your crimes that I've just rounded up."

Cimarron knocked on the door of Marshal Upham's office, and when the marshal's gruff voice yelled, "Come in," he shepherded Dawes and Randall into the office.

"Well, now, what have we here?" Upham inquired as he sat back in his chair.

"Collared these two jaspers over in Poteau in Choctaw Nation, Marshal," Cimarron answered. "You can put them down on Judge Parker's docket as attempted murderers."

"Who did they try to kill?"

"Each other, that's who. I saw what happened, and I'll testify at their trial if you need me to, but you most likely won't be needing me seeing as how I've brought to town nineteen witnesses to the crimes." Cimarron pulled his list of witnesses' names from his pocket and tossed it on the desk. "I brought them all with me so they could participate in the trial of these two would-be killers."

"Marshal," Dawes ventured with a wary glance in Cimarron's direction, "there's not a word of truth to what this deputy said."

"We weren't trying to kill each other, Marshal," Randall stated meekly. "We were just having a bit of a disagreement."

"Which we were in the act of settling when this deputy appeared on the scene and arrested us," Dawes declared indignantly.

Upham gave Cimarron a baleful glance.

But before he could say anything, Cimarron said, "Marshal, I'll just take the nine-fifty that's due me for bringing in these nineteen witnesses I told you about and the six cents a mile between here and Poteau that's also due me."

"Hold on one minute," Upham said. Turning to Dawes and Randall, he asked, "What weapons were you boys using on one another?"

"None, Marshal," Dawes replied.

"Only our fists, Marshal," Randall amended.

"Fists can be deadly weapons," Cimarron quickly pointed out. "Now, about the fees that are due me, Marshal—"

Upham held up a hand for silence. Then, summoning his clerk from an adjoining office, he handed the man the list of names that Cimarron had tossed on the desk. "Check the hotels and the saloons," he instructed the clerk. "Bring in as many of these nineteen men as you can find. I want to hear their side of this story. And make it snappy. I want you back here inside of twenty minutes."

"Marshal," Cimarron began when the clerk had departed, "I'm insulted."

"Are you now? Why, pray tell?"

"I am on account of you don't seem to be putting any credence into what I just told you about these two criminals standing before you. Why, one or both of them might be dead right this very minute if I didn't—at great risk to my own safety and well-being, I'll have you know—stop them from killing each other."

Upham merely *harrumphed*.

"Why don't you just pay me what's due me, Marshal, and I'll be moseying along?"

No response from Upham.

Cimarron was still trying to persuade Upham to pay him what he was owed when the clerk returned with three men and announced that they were the only witnesses he could locate in the short time the marshal had alotted him.

Upham proceeded to question them.

"Randall and Dawes here," drawled one of the three men, "they fight at the drop of a hat, so it ain't nothing to take so serious."

"Whenever these two meet up with each other," volunteered a second man, "they take to fightin' even before the howdies is over."

"They wouldn't try to kill each other," offered the third man, " 'cuz if'n they did they wouldn't have any chance to fight each other anymore, not with one of them dead."

Dawes grinned.

Randall guffawed.

Upham glared at Cimarron.

Cimarron tried and failed to think of anything to say.

"You gentlemen are free to go," Upham told Dawes, Randall, and the three witnesses.

Cimarron started to follow them out the door.

"You, Deputy, are *not* free to go!" Upham bellowed. "Come back here!

"That was the most obviously trumped-up case I've seen since I've been in this office, and believe me, I've seen a few such cases before," Upham thundered when Cimarron was again standing in front of his desk. "I don't know what made you think you could get away with it. And all for a matter of a few dollars in mileage and witness fees."

Cimarron suddenly exploded. "So you don't know why I did it, don't you? Well, I'll tell you why I did it!"

"Aha! Then you admit you trumped up this case."

"You're damn right I admit it. And why did I do it? For money, that's why."

"The root of all evil."

"If money's the root of all evil as some folks claim, then I must be close to becoming a saint since I always seem to have so little of it."

"Cimarron, I am ashamed of you and what you just did. Not only did you disrupt the lives of twenty-one people, albeit temporarily, but you also risked damage to the reputation of this office and Judge Parker's court. You—"

"I don't want to hear any pious preacher talk from you, Marshal," Cimarron warned, anger rioting through him now. "Not when I haven't got so much as two cents to rub against one another. Not when I'm in need of a meal I can't pay for. Not when my saddle needs repair, and I can't pay to have it fixed. Not when you pay your deputies next to nothing, and they have to stoop to stunts like this just to get their hands on enough cash to keep body and soul together."

"I know the fees we pay you deputies are low, Cimarron," Upham said sternly. "But that is no reason to risk dishonoring the judicial process and your own integrity as an officer of this court."

Cimarron leaned over the desk. "Marshal, I've been shot at—and hit—a whole lot of times in the performance of my duty out there west of Hell's fringe in what polite people call Indian Territory. I've had horses shot out from under me. I've been tormented and tortured in more ways than I care to count by villains and miscreants I was after. Sometimes I think I must be crazy to keep at it day in and day out. And now when I hear you lecturing me about how to behave—and all because I need to earn a decent wage—well, no more, Marshal. This right here and now is it. I'm through. Finished. You can hire yourself somebody else to take my place. Somebody dim-witted and foolhardy enough to want to die out there in the Territory for no good reason that anybody anywhere can think of."

Cimarron pulled his badge from his pocket and threw it on the desk. Then he turned on his heel and started for the door.

"Wait a minute, Cimarron! Let's be reasonable men about this. Let's talk it over. I'm sure we can work something out."

But Marshal Upham's words didn't stop Cimarron from storming out of the office. Once outside, he halted on the courthouse steps. What do I do now? he asked himself.

He could think of no answer to his question.

About the Author

LEO P. KELLEY was born and raised in Pennsylvania's Wyoming Valley and spent a good part of his boyhood exploring the surrounding mountains, hunting and fishing. He served in the Army Security Agency as a cryptographer, and then went "on the road," working as a dishwasher, laborer, etc. He later joined the Merchant Marine and sailed on tankers calling at Texan, South American, and Italian ports. In New York City he attended the New School for Social Research, receiving a BA in Literature. He worked in advertising, promotion, and marketing before leaving the business world to write full time.

Mr. Kelley has published a dozen novels and has several others now in the works. He has also published many short stories in leading magazines.

⊘ SIGNET BOOKS

HOLD ONTO YOUR SADDLE!

(0451)

- ☐ SKINNER, by F.M. Parker. (138139—$2.75)
- ☐ THE GREAT GUNFIGHTERS OF THE WEST, by C. Breihan. (111206—$2.25)
- ☐ LUKE SUTTON: OUTRIDER, by Leo P. Kelley. (134869—$2.50)
- ☐ THE ARROGANT GUNS, by Lewis B. Patten. (138643—$2.75)
- ☐ GUNS AT GRAY BUTTE, by Lewis B. Patten. (135741—$2.50)
- ☐ RIDE A TALL HORSE, by Lewis B. Patten. (098161—$1.95)
- ☐ TRAIL SMOKE, by Ernest Haycox. (112822—$1.95)
- ☐ CORUNDA'S GUNS, by Ray Hogan. (133382—$2.50)
- ☐ APACHE MOUNTAIN JUSTICE, by Ray Hogan. (137760—$2.75)
- ☐ THE DOOMSDAY CANYON, by Ray Hogan. (139216—$2.75)

Prices slightly higher in Canada

Buy them at your local

bookstore or use coupon

on next page for ordering.

THE OLD WILD WEST

(0451)

☐ **THE LAST CHANCE** by Frank O'Rourke (115643—$1.95)

☐ **SEGUNDO** by Frank O'Rourke (117816—$2.25)

☐ **VIOLENCE AT SUNDOWN** by Frank O'Rourke (111346—$1.95)

☐ **COLD RIVER** by William Judson (137183—$2.75)

☐ **TOWN TAMER** by Frank Gruber (110838—$1.95)

☐ **SIGNET DOUBLE WESTERN: BLOOD JUSTICE & THE VALIANT BUGLES** by Gordon D. Shirreffs (133390—$3.50)

☐ **SIGNET DOUBLE WESTERN: BITTER SAGE & THE BUSHWACKERS** by Frank Gruber (129202—$3.50)

☐ **SIGNET DOUBLE WESTERN: QUANTRELL'S RAIDERS & TOWN TAMER** by Frank Gruber (127773—$3.50)

☐ **SIGNET DOUBLE WESTERN: COMANCHE' & RIDE THE WILD TRAIL** by Cliff Farrell (115651—$2.50)

☐ **SIGNET DOUBLE WESTERN: CROSS FIRE & THE RENEGADE** by Cliff Farrell (123891—$2.95)

☐ **SIGNET DOUBLE WESTERN: TROUBLE IN TOMBSTONE & BRAND OF A MAN** by Tom Hopkins and Thomas Thompson (116003—$2.50)

Prices slightly higher in Canada

Buy them at your local bookstore or use this convenient coupon for ordering.

NEW AMERICAN LIBRARY,
P.O. Box 999, Bergenfield, New Jersey 07621

Please send me the books I have checked above. I am enclosing $_____ (please add $1.00 to this order to cover postage and handling). Send check or money order—no cash or C.O.D.'s. Prices and numbers are subject to change without notice.

Name_____

Address_____

City_____State_____Zip Code_____

Allow 4-6 weeks for delivery.
This offer is subject to withdrawal without notice.

C0-DKL-339

Friend Me!

6 get-togethers
to build Faith & Friendship

Group
Loveland, Colorado

Group resources actually work!

This Group resource incorporates our R.E.A.L. approach to ministry. It reinforces a growing friendship with Jesus, encourages long-term learning, and results in life transformation, because it's

Relational
Learner-to-learner interaction enhances learning and builds Christian friendships.

Experiential
What learners experience through discussion and action sticks with them up to 9 times longer than what they simply hear or read.

Applicable
The aim of Christian education is to equip learners to be both hearers and doers of God's Word.

Learner-based
Learners understand and retain more when the learning process takes into consideration how they learn best.

Friend Me!
6 Get-togethers to Build Faith and Friendship
Copyright © 2012 Group Publishing, Inc.

All rights reserved. No part of this book may be reproduced in any manner whatsoever without prior written permission from the publisher, except where noted in the text and in the case of brief quotations embodied in critical articles and reviews. For information, go to group.com/customer-support.

Visit our websites: **group.com** and **group.com/women**

This resource is brought to you by the wildly creative women's ministry team at Group. Choose Group resources for your women's ministry, and experience the difference!

Unless otherwise indicated, all Scripture quotations are taken from the *Holy Bible,* New Living Translation, copyright © 1996, 2004. Used by permission of Tyndale House Publishers, Inc., Carol Stream, Illinois 60188. All rights reserved.

ISBN 978-0-7644-7821-5
10 9 8 7 6 5 4 3 2 1   21 20 19 18 17 16 15 14 13 12

Printed in the United States of America.

Contents

Welcome to Friend Me!

Are you ready to move from being acquaintances who wave or nod as you pass in the halls or on the street? Ready to move into true friendship with other women and, in the process, move deeper into your relationship with Jesus? If so, *Friend Me!* is just for you!

Each week, women will gather for a session that includes food (how can you have a group of women without food included?), Bible, discussion, and prayer. Anyone can be the leader. (We call her the hostess, since that's way more fun and friendly!) Just be sure the hostess reads the session ahead of time and gathers the supplies for that session. Each woman in your group will need her own copy of *Friend Me!*

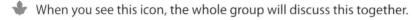 When you see this icon, the whole group will discuss this together.

 This icon means women will partner or get in smaller groups to share.

Tell Me More!

Friend Me! is a flexible six-week series for small groups that compares our friendships with others to our friendship with Jesus. The purpose is to meet new friends in a fun, friendly, nonthreatening way and discover and grow a friendship with Jesus. These get-togethers work for groups of women who are just getting acquainted, for long-time friends, for special-interest groups (such as your scrapbooking group or your prayer team), coworkers, Bible study groups, new attendee groups, and any existing group. You can meet weekly, biweekly, or once a month. You could even supplement your existing weekly small group by experiencing a once-a-month get-together using this book.

How Deep?

Yes, *Friend Me!* is great for women who are already Christians. You'll be challenged to go deeper in your faith! But it's also a good starting point for women who haven't yet accepted Christ, for those who have expressed curiosity in spirituality, and for those who have put faith on the sideline. The sessions are created to allow conversations at various levels of faith so that anyone can participate and learn.

Where Should I Use This?

Friend Me! can be used for home Bible study groups, during the Sunday school hour, or for much larger Bible study groups that meet in your church.

In more intimate settings, one person can facilitate the get-together. In a larger setting, the hostess can facilitate from the front of the room, with the discussions taking place in smaller groups. Limit each small group to no more than eight people. A group of six to eight guarantees a positive experience and maximum participation by everyone. If you have fewer than six, that's OK too. The experiences will work with smaller groups just as well.

If I'm the Hostess…What Do I Do?

You can have one hostess designated for the entire book, or you may choose to take turns being the hostess. Or you might share the role, having one person prepare the snack while another prepares the experiences. The hostess of the week will need to review the Hostess Prep box at the beginning of each session, as well as the additional tips in the back of each session.

Share the Joy (and the cooking!)
If you're meeting in homes, consider rotating from home to home, and have each home hostess prepare the meal or snack for that week.

Each session has an easy snack recommended for your group. But if you'd like to get a little more involved or make it a meal, there are additional suggestions for more elaborate foods that still fit the theme.

More Hostess Tips…

Be yourself. The best leaders are the ones who are comfortable with themselves and willing to be real, vulnerable, and authentic. You're the best you for the job! Then remember that it's not about you. It's about letting God work *through* you. God has put you with specific people in this specific time and place to represent Christ to them.

Be warm and hospitable. If you don't feel comfortable reaching out to others and initiating conversations, join a group but don't lead one.

Be open. Be willing to honestly share your own life stories.

Be willing to share the load. Find a co-leader—a friend who can partner with you.

Now, it's time to *Friend Me!* ———————————

Friend *Me!* ♥ 6 Get-togethers to Build Faith and Friendship

Week One

Getting Our Priorities Straight

Discover how to make friendship with Jesus and others a priority.

Key Verse: Luke 10:38-42

Hostess Prep

For the opening activity in "Getting to Know God," you'll need an open space for mingling. You may need to move tables and chairs to create an environment for lots of interaction.

The bolded sections of text in each session are for you to read aloud. Feel free to change the wording to make yourself more comfortable, if you need to. Or just use ours; that's what it's there for. Invite people to get their food before they sit down.

You'll need:

☐ trail mix

☐ beverages

☐ one 168-inch piece of string or rope

☐ pad of small (1½") self-stick notes

See "Helpful Hints for the Hostess" on pages 16 & 17 for additional tips and other food ideas!

Getting to Know You ✍ ───────────────
(about 15 minutes)

While everyone is arriving, this is a good time to get to know each other and enjoy the snacks while chatting.

For the next six weeks, we'll be learning how we can deepen our relationships. We'll have a lot of fun together and become good friends as we do. But there's a higher purpose here, as well—everything we do will help us explore the idea that the process of becoming friends with each other is very similar to the process of becoming friends with God. Keep that idea tucked in the back of your mind.

> Pass your books around the room, and have each person write her name, phone number, and e-mail address on the "Getting Connected" space (p. 15). You can do this either at the beginning or end of your time together.

If your group has more than six people, get into smaller groups of four. Take turns telling your first name and a true story that goes along with your name. For example, maybe you're named after a family member, or perhaps no one knows your real first name and you go by a nickname.

If you got into groups, come back together after 5 minutes and have volunteers share their stories with the larger group.

Sharing stories is a great way to get to know other people. Eating is another great thing to do together with new friends. That's why each week our food will tie into the topic we're discussing.

🍃 **What are some ways today's snack relates to friendship?**

🍃 **What are some ways the people in your circles of friends add variety?**

Getting to Know God

(about 20 minutes)

Find a partner you don't know very well. Say hello, and introduce yourself. Then determine who's wearing the most blue. That woman will share a story about a childhood friend. After a minute, switch roles.

After you've both shared, find a new partner and introduce yourselves. Figure out who's wearing the most white. This time, take a minute each to tell a story about a friend from junior high or high school.

Find a new partner, and determine who's wearing the most brown. Beginning with that person, share stories about your current best friends.

After you've both shared about your current best friend, team up with another pair to form groups of four. Take 10 minutes to discuss the following questions with your foursome. If you'd like, make notes in the space provided.

Q: What were the most interesting things you discovered during our mingling activity?

Q: Think about the stories you just told, as well as what you've just experienced while getting to know others. What normally draws you into becoming friends with someone else?

Q: How are the things that draw us to our friends like the things that draw us to explore a relationship with God? Explain.

Return to your full group after 10 minutes of discussion. Take turns sharing highlights and insights from your discussion time.

Let's look at a story that illustrates friendship. It's about two women who entertain a friend who also happens to be a very important and influential person.

Read Luke 10:38-42 aloud.

"As Jesus and the disciples continued on their way to Jerusalem, they came to a certain village where a woman named Martha welcomed him into her home. Her sister, Mary, sat at the Lord's feet, listening to what he taught. But Martha was distracted by the big dinner she was preparing. She came to Jesus and said, 'Lord, doesn't it seem unfair to you that my sister just sits here while I do all the work? Tell her to come and help me.'

"But the Lord said to her, 'My dear Martha, you are worried and upset over all these details! There is only one thing worth being concerned about. Mary has discovered it, and it will not be taken away from her.'"—Luke 10:38-42

As a large group, share your thoughts about these questions:

🍂 **As you think about each of these three friends, what do you think their words and actions say about their relationships with each other?**

🍂 **What does Jesus mean when he says "There is only one thing worth being concerned about"?**

🍂 **What words would you use to describe your relationship with your best friend? with Jesus?**

Your hostess has a 168-inch piece of string or rope. Two people in your group need to hold the ends, pulling it taut if possible.

This length of string represents one week's worth of time. There are 168 hours in a week, and each inch represents an hour in your week.

One person in your group should wrap a small sticky note around the string.

This sticky note is about an inch and a half wide. Think of it as the time you'll spend together each week as you deepen your friendships with one another and God.

Have everyone stand up and spread out along the length of string.

Think about how many hours a week you actually spend developing relationships. After you've thought of an answer, pinch the length of the string that would represent the number of hours in a week you do this.

Take a minute to talk with the people standing on both sides of you about why you spend that much or that little time developing the relationships in your life. Then discuss these questions with that small group:

Q: What do you think the goal of friendship is?

Q: How do we reach that goal?

Take a seat while your hostess puts the string away.

Getting Real 🕊 ————————
(about 15 minutes)

Each week, we'll practice making our friendships with God *and* each other a priority. Let's talk about some simple ways we'll begin doing that.

First of all, it's important for us to remember to be considerate of one another. We're in this together! It matters how we treat one another. It also matters that we spend time together. It'll be tough for us to become friends with each other if we only meet or talk once a week.

If you haven't already taken turns filling out each other's "Getting Connected" page (p. 15), do so now before moving on.

We've already taken one step by putting all our information on each other's "Getting Connected" page. Now let's make sure we use that information to connect with each other during the week.

We're each going to take a small step forward in turning what we've learned today into reality. Look at the list of options below, and select the one you'd like to take on this week—or come up with one of your own!

When you've decided on a Getting Real action, share your choice with a partner, and write what you plan to do in the space provided. Make plans to connect with your partner (by phone, e-mail, text, or in person) sometime in the next week to check in and encourage each other.

- ❧ I'll spend a few minutes getting to know a neighbor—even if it's just talking over the fence.

- ❧ I'll meet up with a new or a longtime friend for coffee or a meal and enjoy catching up.

- ❧ I'll send a friendly e-mail to each of my new friends in this group.

- ❧ I'll read 1 John 4:7-19 and spend time talking to God about what it says.

- ❧ I'll ask for wisdom as I pursue this treasure of friendship with him and with the people I'm getting to know.

Because friendship with Jesus and others is a priority, I'm going to:

_____

_____

_____

_____

_____

_____

_____

_____

_____

_____

_____

_____

_____

_____

_____

_____

_____

_____

_____

Closing

Close your time together by taking the opportunity to affirm others by praying aloud for each woman in the group.

Stand in a circle for this open-eye prayer. Each person will pray a short prayer of thanks for the person on her right. For example you might pray, "Lord, thank you for Jennie's bright smile. God, please encourage her this week."

When each person has prayed (and been prayed for), feel free to hang out, chat, eat more, and enjoy being together before it's time to head home.

Getting Connected

Name: Contact Information:

_____   _____

_____   _____

_____   _____

_____   _____

_____   _____

_____   _____

_____   _____

_____   _____

_____   _____

_____   _____

_____   _____

_____   _____

_____   _____

_____   _____

_____   _____

_____   _____

_____   _____

_____   _____

Week One

Helpful Hints for the Hostess

Especially for the first gathering, set the mood and create a relaxed atmosphere by playing appropriate background music. Consider playing some light jazz, acoustic folk, light classical, or upbeat pop music.

Make sure each woman feels welcome and at home. If you're busy getting last-minute details organized or have a large group, find a warm, friendly person to be the greeter. Remember, friend-making is a priority for this study! As each new person arrives, introduce her to those who are already there.

For extra impact: Give each woman a 7-inch piece of string as a reminder of the challenge to make friendships a priority each day of the week. The piece of string can also be used as the bookmark for this book.

Recipe Options

The point of the food choice for this gathering is that women will find a variety of ingredients in their snack or meal. Each ingredient offers something unique to the taste. In the same way, each person brings something unique to a group of friends.

Easiest Option:

- trail mix
- beverages

Purchase several varieties of store-bought trail mix, snack mix, or granola (allow ½ cup to 1 cup per person). Pour the trail mix into large serving bowls, put large spoons or scoops in the bowls, and place the bowls on a serving table with beverages. Put disposable cups and napkins nearby.

Easy+ Option:

* ice-cream sundae bar
* beverages

Purchase several varieties of ice cream, as well as toppings, fruit, candies, nuts, and whipped cream. Set everything out on a table with bowls, spoons, ice-cream scoops, and napkins. Have everyone create her own ice-cream sundae.

Getting together in the morning? You can easily adapt this to a yogurt and fruit bar. Provide yogurt and a variety of fruit and granola toppings.

Make It a Meal:

* salad bar
* beverages

Set up a salad bar with a variety of ingredients, dressings, and toppings. If you have a large group, set up the salad bar on a long table so that people can form two lines. They'll serve themselves more quickly and have more time to chat and get to know each other.

Friend *Me!* ♥ 6 Get-togethers to Build Faith and Friendship

Week Two

Getting the Right Impression
Discover how to go beyond first impressions with Jesus and others.

Key Verse: John 15:15

Hostess Prep

Read this entire session ahead of time so you know what your responsibilities are. Gather the supplies, and get ready to have a great time with others!

When we did this, we found that women were much more comfortable doing the first activity in the "Getting to Know God" section in pairs rather than in small groups. We're often much more comfortable discussing and trying things with one other person than with a larger group.

You'll need:
- [ ] surprise snack (see options on page 27)
- [ ] beverages
- [ ] pens or pencils
- [ ] name tags

See the hostess helps on page 26 for additional tips!

Getting to Know You 🕊 —————————
(about 15 minutes)

To begin your time together today, you'll enjoy a time of eating a special surprise snack. Then find a partner and discuss these questions:

Q: What were you expecting when you saw the snack?

Q: How are these expectations similar to expectations we have when we first meet someone?

After about 5 minutes of discussion, gather as a large group.

Today we're going to explore what it means to build friendships that go beyond first impressions, and we'll discuss things that can prevent us from really getting to know people and God. First let's check in on the Getting Real challenges from last week.

Share with the entire group how you followed through with your commitment and what happened as a result.

After a time of large-group discussion, gather in smaller groups of three to five, and discuss the following questions. Feel free to jot down your thoughts as you're talking.

Q: When have you been surprised by making a friend who didn't look like someone you'd typically be friends with?

Q: What's challenging for you about going beyond your first impression of someone?

Getting to Know God ✒ ──────────

(about 20 minutes)

Stay with your small group, and continue your discussion with these questions:

Q: What do you do to try to make a good first impression?

Q: How have those things worked or not worked for you in getting to know people?

Here's a simple tool that anyone can use when you meet someone for the first time.

1. **Introduce yourself by name.**

2. **Ask where the person is from.**

3. **Ask the person to tell you about his or her family.**

4. **Ask about the person's hobbies.**

5. **Ask about the person's work or school.**

Find a partner. If possible, try to find someone you don't know that well. Pretend you're meeting for the first time. Use this tool to guide your conversation and get to know each other. And see if you can tie in some of the techniques you shared with your small group that you use to make good first impressions.

After this conversation, rejoin with the entire group, and the hostess will guide you in discussing these questions:

🍂 **What did you discover during this experience? Explain.**

🍂 **How is this like or unlike getting acquainted with Jesus?**

One thing that's important in getting to know people well is to ask a lot of questions. That keeps us from making assumptions that may not be true. Let's give this idea a try!

Find a new partner, and choose one of these topics: vacation, kids, or food. The woman whose birthday is the closest to today will go first by asking the other partner questions about that topic. For each response you hear, think of another question that will help you dig deeper into why your partner answered the way she did. Try to have a 2-minute conversation where the first partner does nothing but ask questions and actively listen. That means no comments—just more questions and more listening!

After 2 minutes, switch roles and choose a new topic, repeating the activity. Afterward, stay with your partner and discuss:

Q: What was challenging for you in this exercise?

Q: What's one thing you learned that surprised you?

Q: When have you been surprised by someone once you dug deeper into a friendship?

Stay with your partner. The hostess will provide you with name tags.

Let's go even deeper now by taking a look at some of our own personal hopes, fears, and longings about friendship. Think about the things that *really* define you—the things that make up who you truly are. Think about what Jesus would say makes you who you are. Write those words all over your name tag.

HELLO
my name is
Sister God's Child Joyful
Beautiful Loved Happy
Excited Friend

After you've written words on your name tag, discuss these questions with your partner:

Q: How can you show the "real you" to people when you meet them?

Q: What might happen if you did this?

After partners have a chance to discuss, rejoin the large group.

Let's look at what Jesus says about friendship.

Read John 15:15 aloud.

> "I no longer call you slaves, because a master doesn't confide in his slaves. Now you are my friends, since I have told you everything the Father told me."—John 15:15

❧ **What emotions or thoughts does this verse stir in you? Explain.**

❧ **What are some first impressions you've had about God as your friend? How does what you've experienced today and what this verse says impact those impressions?**

Getting Real 🌀

(about 15 minutes)

We've already taken one step by letting go of some of our misconceptions about each other and about God. Now we're going to look at how we can take what we've learned and act on it this week. Look at the options below, and select the one you'd like to take on this week—or come up with one of your own!

When you've decided on a Getting Real action, share your choice with a partner, and write what you plan to do in the space provided. Make plans right now to connect with your partner sometime in the next week to check in and encourage each other.

+ I'll show genuine interest in someone by spending more time listening than talking.

+ I'll ask a friend for honest feedback about how I come across when meeting people, and I'll thank that person for the insights.

+ I'll spend at least 10 minutes writing a prayer that expresses why and how I hope to get more deeply acquainted with Jesus.

+ I'll go beyond my first impressions of God by reading 1 Corinthians 13:4-7, replacing the word "love" with "God" each time it occurs.

Because friendship with Jesus and others is a priority, I'm going to:

_____

_____

_____

_____

_____

_____

_____

_____

_____

_____

_____

Closing

Find an object in the room that can represent an obstacle you currently face in building relationships with others or with Jesus. For example, a book might represent a problem of focusing on what the "cover" looks like instead of finding out what's inside. Be creative as you look around the room or in your purse or at what you're wearing. Choose something that you can hold in your hands that will represent that obstacle.

As you hold the item in your hands, pray silently, asking God to remove this obstacle from your heart.

Once everyone has finished praying silently, close with this prayer:

God, thank you for making each of us unique and valuable. Help us put aside misconceptions of others and build intimate, lasting friendships. Show us how to get rid of any first impressions of Jesus that are preventing us from experiencing the best of all friendships. Help us get to know who Jesus really is. Amen.

Week Two

⌒ Helpful Hints for the Hostess ⌒

The discussion about being surprised by friends will work equally well for the Gelatin Drinks and Meatloaf Cake, but you could also take it a little bit further. These snacks must be actually touched in order for the surprise to be revealed, so you could ask questions about "digging into" a new friendship, such as, "When have you been surprised when you 'dug in' and got to know someone?"

If you choose the Gelatin Drinks option, don't start the discussion until everyone has discovered that the gelatin is not, in fact, liquid. (They may discover this by stirring with the straw or moving the glass, for example). Then get out the actual beverages, cups, and spoons.

When we used the five-step tool for getting to know each other, pairs wouldn't stop talking! Women who didn't know each other before the activity went beyond the conversation steps, and those who already knew each other connected in new ways. This exercise proves the power of basic and simple experiences!

For extra impact: For the prayer activity, offer inexpensive items such as candles, small rocks, or pencils. Have people take home their prayer objects to remind them of their commitments to put aside first impressions and to genuinely get acquainted with others and with Jesus.

⌒ Recipe Options ⌒

Today's discussion focuses on our first impressions and our misconceptions about God. In each of the food options, there's something people won't expect, based on the food's appearance. Today's food will help everyone talk about how our first impressions are not always accurate.

Easiest Option:
- Cornflakes
- colored milk

Purchase milk in paper cartons (not clear plastic containers). Pour the milk into a large pitcher, and tint it green or blue with liquid food coloring. Pour the milk back into the milk carton so people won't see that it's tinted until they pour it onto their cereal. Surprise!

Easy+ Option:
- gelatin "drinks"
- beverages

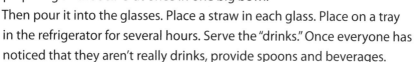

Prepare gelatin drinks using the following:
1 small package of red Jell-O for every 2 people
clear plastic glasses
straws

Prepare the Jell-O according to the package directions. Make the preparations go faster by preparing all the Jell-O at once in one big bowl.
Then pour it into the glasses. Place a straw in each glass. Place on a tray in the refrigerator for several hours. Serve the "drinks." Once everyone has noticed that they aren't really drinks, provide spoons and beverages.

Make It a Meal:
- meatloaf cake
- beverages

Prepare the meatloaf using your favorite recipe. Shape the meat into a circle or a rectangle—basically in a shape that you'd make a cake.

While the meatloaf is cooking, prepare mashed potatoes using a recipe you like.

When the meatloaf is done cooking, remove it from the oven and let it cool a bit. Press the cooked meatloaf with a wide spatula, and tilt the pan slightly over a bowl to drain off the grease. Carefully remove the meatloaf from the pan, and place it on a serving platter.

Put about a cup or so of fluffy mashed potatoes on top, and gently spread the potatoes to the edges. Spread the mashed potatoes on the top and sides of the meatloaf as you would frost a cake.

Place the remaining mashed potatoes into a pastry bag fitted with a large star or shell tip (you may need to add a bit more milk so the potatoes will pipe well). You can also use a reclosable freezer bag with a coupler and a tip. Make a shell border or small stars around the top and bottom edge of the mashed potato cake. Garnish with cherry tomatoes and green onion "leaves," if desired.

An easier option would be to purchase already-made meatloaf and mashed potatoes from the grocery store or from a restaurant such as Boston Market. Continue with the decorating instructions.

Don't let anyone in on the secret until the "cake" is cut! Serve it as if you were serving dessert. Then...once everyone has had a fun surprise, you might want to bring out rolls and a salad to make the meal complete.

Week Three

Getting Ready to Listen

Learn to listen to Jesus and others.

Key Verse: Psalm 116:1-2

Hostess Prep

Before your gathering, write several "talk starters" on slips of paper. (See the list on page 36 for ideas, or come up with your own.) Put the slips in a container.

You'll need:

- ☐ popcorn or crunchy granola bars
- ☐ beverages
- ☐ slips of paper and container
- ☐ pen

See the hostess helps on pages 38 & 39 for additional tips and other food ideas!

Getting to Know You 🌀

(about 15 minutes)

Eat the snack your hostess provides as you chat with other women. Then "officially" begin your gathering with these questions:

🌿 **What could the food we're eating today symbolize about friendship?**

🌿 **What are some real-life barriers you face when it comes to being a good listener?**

Today we're going to tackle the topic of listening. Just like crunchy foods can make it hard to hear, sometimes it's hard to listen well to our friends and to God.

First let's check in on the Getting Real challenges from last week.

Share with the entire group how you followed through with your commitment and what happened as a result.

Getting to Know God 🌀

(about 25 minutes)

Find a partner, and have the person wearing the most red have a seat and close her eyes. Stand behind your partner and imagine an arc over her head; it's equidistant between your partner's ears, starting at the nose and ending at the nape of the neck. Snap your fingers several times in various places along that arc. After each snap, the seated partner should point to where the snap came from. After a minute, tell your partner how she did, and then trade roles. When you've both had a turn, discuss the following questions together.

Q: What made listening difficult in this activity, and what did you do to overcome those challenges?

Q: What insights did you gain from this experience that you can apply to listening to others in your daily life?

Q: How can you apply these insights to listening to God?

Let's explore this concept of listening a bit more. Your hostess has prepared slips of paper with "talk starter" topics. The partner wearing the most blue should take one of these slips of paper and talk about that subject for 3 minutes. The other partner should listen. After 3 minutes, the listening partner should draw a new talk starter, and she will then talk for 3 minutes while the other partner listens.

After this experience, discuss these questions together with your partner:

Q: What did you learn about being a good listener?

Q: What do you appreciate about being listened to?

The hostess will gather everyone together. Read James 1:19 aloud as a group.

> "Understand this, my dear brothers and sisters: You must all be quick to listen, slow to speak, and slow to get angry."—James 1:19

🍂 **Tell why listening is easy or difficult for you.**

🍂 **How is listening to a friend like the way God listens to us?**

🌿 **What do you think about the idea of being silent during prayer to listen to God?**

Becoming close to Jesus is very much like becoming close to a friend. Listening is a big part of growing deeper friendships. We can be certain that Jesus wants to talk to us every day.

Read Psalm 116:1-2 aloud.

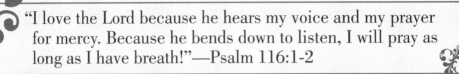

"I love the Lord because he hears my voice and my prayer for mercy. Because he bends down to listen, I will pray as long as I have breath!"—Psalm 116:1-2

This psalm writer said he'd pray as long as he had breath. Prayer is kind of like breathing. Let's spend a few minutes exploring that. We're going to have 2 minutes of silence. During that time, close your eyes and really focus on your breathing. Take big, deep breaths, and slowly exhale them. Think about how the air is coming into and going out of your lungs.

After 2 minutes, form groups of three or four and discuss the following questions:

Q: What went through your mind as you focused on your breathing?

Q: How is prayer like or unlike breathing?

Q: How could thinking of prayer like breathing change the way you pray?

If you only breathed out, you'd die. When you breathe, you need to inhale and exhale. The same is true with prayer: you need to exhale by talking to God and inhale by listening to him.

Getting Real 🍂 ───────────────

(about 10 minutes)

We've already taken one step by starting to listen better to each other and to God. Now we're going to look at how we can take what we've learned and act on it this week. Look at the options below, and select the one you'd like to take on this week—or come up with one of your own!

When you've decided on a Getting Real action, share your choice with a partner, and write what you plan to do in the space provided. Make plans right now to connect with your partner sometime in the next week to check in and encourage each other.

- ✦ I'll invite a friend to share a snack and simply listen to this friend's joys and concerns.

- ✦ I'll think of someone who needs to hear kind words from me. I'll ask God to give me just the right thing to say, and then I'll encourage that person.

- ✦ I'll take a walk with a friend and bring up the idea of listening to God. I'll talk with my friend about what God might want us to know about our friendship with him.

- ✦ For one hour this week I'll turn off the TV, radio, cell phone, music— anything that makes a sound. I'll relax in silence and listen for God.

Because friendship with Jesus and others is a priority, I'm going to:

_____

_____

_____

_____

_____

_____

_____

_____

_____

_____

_____

Closing

Find a comfortable position for prayer.

We've talked about the give and take of prayer today, and we've also talked about prayer in the context of breathing. So as we pray now, let's use our breath to help us learn to talk and to listen in our conversations with God.

Breathe out slowly, and talk silently to God as you're breathing out.

Exhale.

Now breathe in slowly, and pause when your lungs are full. Listen to God as you inhale.

Inhale deeply.

Now keep breathing in and out, praying and listening as you do.

Take 3 minutes for this breathing prayer. Then the hostess will close the prayer by thanking God that we can talk and listen to him any time we want.

Suggested Talk Starters

What always makes me laugh is...

I'm passionate about...

Someday I'd like to...

A cool vacation would be…

My favorite thing to do with friends is...

The best weekends always include...

A news story that interested me recently was...

Week Three

Helpful Hints for the Hostess

When we did this session, we had a few very quiet people in our group, and this was the day they really started to open up and share their thoughts and feelings with the others in the group. Could it be that being listened to helped them feel cared for and comfortable with others?

Some people in our group found the prayer activity deeply meaningful. Others struggled to talk and listen with each breath. Offer the option of simply sitting quietly, praying, and listening to God during these 3 minutes. This practice of praying with breath builds awareness of God's voice and presence.

For extra impact: Give everyone a small plastic bag of carrot sticks as a reminder to tune out the noise and listen to God and others this week.

Recipe Options

Since this session is all about listening, all of the food is noisy and crunchy. It'll help the group talk about things that distract them from listening.

Easiest Option:
- popcorn or crunchy granola bars
- beverages

Purchase bags of already popped flavored popcorn or a variety of crunchy granola bars.

Easy+ Option:

* tortilla chips and salsa
* beverages

Make your own salsa, or serve a variety of flavors from jars.

Make It a Meal:

* Fritos chips
* chili
* grated cheese and sour cream (optional)
* carrot and celery sticks
* beverages

Make your favorite chili recipe before everyone arrives, and keep it warm.

Have each woman put a handful of Fritos in her bowl and top with chili. Garnish with grated cheese and sour cream if you like. Serve with carrot and celery sticks to add even more crunch to your gathering.

An easier option would be to purchase canned chili for the Fritos "pie."

Week Four

Getting Right With God and Others

Experience forgiveness through Jesus and others.

Key Verse: Colossians 3:13

Hostess Prep

You'll need to set up five stations around your meeting area. Specific directions are on pages 48-50. Set up the stations so they're sufficiently far apart from one another. Expect some clumping as people gather at each station, and provide plenty of room so that women can move around freely.

Place the pillar candle and matches somewhere in the room where you'll be able to reach them easily. If possible, use low room lighting at the very end of this session to get the full effect of the candles.

You'll need:

☐ biscotti and hot chocolate

☐ pens or pencils

☐ supplies for stations (see pages 48 & 49)

☐ one pillar candle and matches

☐ one small tea light or votive candle for each woman

See the hostess helps on pages 48-51 for additional tips and other food ideas!

Note: Be sure to read Week 5 soon so you can be ready!

Getting to Know You (about 15 minutes)

Enjoy a snack provided by your hostess. As you eat, catch up with the other women in your group. Then the hostess will begin your session by having everyone discuss these questions:

🍂 **What could the food we're eating today show us about friendship?**

🍂 **How has a friendship changed you?**

Forgiveness has the power to soften and change us, just like our food has been softened and changed. Today we're going to talk about forgiveness. We'll discuss what it means to be forgiven and to forgive others, and we'll explore how Jesus' forgiveness changes us.

First let's check in on the Getting Real challenges.

Share with the entire group how you followed through with your commitment and what happened as a result.

Getting to Know God (about 25 minutes)

We've all experienced offering and receiving forgiveness. Let's get in groups of three to four and discuss those experiences.

In your small groups, discuss the following:

Q: Share about a time that forgiveness changed you.

Q: What discoveries can we make about forgiveness based on these stories?

Q: Think of someone who was hard for you to forgive. Why was that person hard to forgive? (Remember to avoid revealing names.)

Read Colossians 3:13 aloud in your small group.

> "Make allowance for each other's faults, and forgive anyone who offends you. Remember, the Lord forgave you, so you must forgive others."
> —Colossians 3:13

Q: Why is forgiving others important to our friendship with Jesus?

Q: What can help you forgive, even when it's hard?

Forgiveness is not saying that something someone's done to hurt us is OK. It's letting go of our right to revenge and freeing that person from retaliation or punishment.

Our sin is not OK, but Jesus has provided a way to free us from the punishment our sin deserves. We'll understand Jesus' forgiveness even better by transporting ourselves to the foot of the cross and experiencing the passion of Jesus.

There are five stations around the room to help you reconnect with Jesus' sacrifice and grace. You're free to experience as many or as few of these five stations as you like, in any order. You'll find all the instructions you need on pages 44 and 45.

Prayer Stations

You may do these in any order you like. Take as long as you want at each station. It's okay if you don't finish them all.

When your hostess turns off or dims the lights in the room, consider the room a sanctuary. This is a quiet time for personal reflection and intimate time with God. Take your book with you, and use the next few pages as a journal, writing your thoughts, feelings, and prayers about the experience. There are instructions at each station to help you.

It's OK if you finish before others or if you spend most of your time at one station. Your hostess will let you know when there are 5 minutes left.

Station 1 - The Painful Thorns
Before his death, Jesus received a crown of thorns.

Hold one of the items from the table, and run your thumb over its point. As you feel the sharpness, thank Jesus for enduring the pain on the cross and for taking on the thorns in your life. Pray that God will take away the pain that you suffer from not forgiving others. Write any thoughts about your experience here.

Station 2 - The Spike of Sin
The Roman soldiers hammered spikes into Jesus' hands and feet.

Strike nails with a hammer, and ask for forgiveness for a specific sin in your life. Write any thoughts about your experience here.

Station 3 - **The Bitter Vinegar**
While hanging on the cross, Jesus was offered a taste of vinegar for his thirst.

Dip a cotton swab in the vinegar, and reflect on bitter times in your life. Pray that God will help you to forgive, give you a soft and sweet heart toward others, and remove your bitterness. Write any thoughts about your experience here.

Station 4 - **Distracting Dice**
The soldiers gambled for Jesus' robe, throwing dice for his clothing, ignoring the Son of God who hung nearby.

Roll a single die. Look at the number that comes up, and name that many of the distractions that keep you from experiencing Jesus' forgiveness. Pray that God will help you focus on Jesus instead. Write any thoughts about your experience here.

Station 5 - **Remember Me**
One of the thieves hanging beside Jesus begged him to "Remember me" in heaven. The red ink symbolizes Jesus' blood, shed for you.

Write your name with the red marker under the words "Remember me," and thank Jesus for forgiving you and loving you eternally. Write any thoughts about your experience here.

Getting Real
(about 10 minutes)

We've already taken one step by experiencing what Jesus did to offer us forgiveness. Now we're going to look at how we can take what we've learned and act on it this week. Look at the options below, and select the one you'd like to take on this week—or come up with one of your own!

When you've decided on a Getting Real action, share your choice with a partner, and write what you plan to do in the space provided. Make plans right now to connect with your partner sometime in the next week to check in and encourage each other.

- ✦ I'll enjoy a meal with a friend and talk about Jesus' gift of forgiveness in our lives.

- ✦ I'll think of someone I need to forgive. Then I'll pray and forgive with God's help.

- ✦ I'll memorize Ephesians 4:32 by repeating it as a prayer, replacing the words *each other* and *one another* with the name of a person I need to forgive.

- ✦ I'll place a candle where I'll see it throughout the week. Every time I see the candle, I'll confess a specific sin and give thanks for Jesus' forgiveness and love.

Because friendship with Jesus and others is a priority, I'm going to:

_____

_____

_____

_____

_____

_____

_____

_____

_____

_____

_____

_____

Closing

Your hostess will gather everyone together for a closing time as a large group. At this time, get a small candle from your hostess.

Luke 23:46: "Then Jesus shouted, 'Father, I entrust my spirit into your hands!' And with those words he breathed his last." Jesus, the Son of God, died for our sins. But that wasn't the end of the story! Three days later, Jesus rose from the dead. He came back to life—so we can have life with him forever.

Your hostess will light the pillar candle with the lighter or match.

In John 8:12, Jesus says, "I am the light of the world. If you follow me, you won't have to walk in darkness, because you will have the light that leads to life."

Invite everyone to stand, as followers of Jesus.

In Matthew 5:14-16, Jesus says, "You are the light of the world—like a city on a hilltop that cannot be hidden. No one lights a lamp and then puts it under a basket. Instead, a lamp is placed on a stand, where it gives light to everyone in the house. In the same way, let your good deeds shine out for all to see, so that everyone will praise your heavenly Father."

Light your own candle from the pillar candle as a sign of the life and light you have in Jesus.

Place your candle near the pillar candle as a commitment to forgive others and share Jesus' forgiveness. Then step back or sit down and reflect or pray quietly.

Spend the next 1 or 2 minutes watching as all the candles are lit. After everyone has finished lighting the candles, take 1 or 2 minutes for quiet reflection.

Your hostess will close with a prayer:
Jesus, thank you for bringing light into our darkness so that we might experience your transforming forgiveness and love. Help us forgive others and spread your light into the world. Amen.

Week Four

◠Helpful Hints for the Hostess ◠

Follow the instructions below to set up the five prayer stations. Adjust the supplies and amounts for your group. For each station, provide the listed items, and make a simple station sign by writing the name of the station on a sheet of paper. Use a dark marker so it's easy to read.

Yes, this get-together requires more supplies and preparation than some of the others. But don't miss out on this powerful experience. Combine all your resources, enlist helpers, and start early! The result will be more than worth your efforts.

The stations work equally well with any number of participants— even four or five people. So don't worry about how large or small your group is; regardless of number, everyone will have a personal and meaningful time.

For extra impact: Have women take home the small candles, which symbolize Jesus' forgiveness and love.

❊ Station 1 - **The Painful Thorns**

* 2 or 3 objects with sharp points, such as a needle, pin, thistle, or thorn (you might bring in a rose that still has its thorns)

Setup: Lay the objects on a table or even on the floor so women can pick them up and hold them. Place "The Painful Thorns" station sign on the table or tape it on the wall.

❊ Station 2 - **The Spike of Sin**

* 1 or 2 pieces of scrap wood thick enough that nails won't go all the way through them (two 2x4s put together, scraps from a lumber store, or firewood from the grocery story would work)

* nails that are large enough for women to handle easily—but not so long that they'll go all the way through the wood

* 3 or 4 hammers

* floor mat, a thick blanket, or carpet (if your floor isn't carpeted)

Setup: It's best if the floor is carpeted so no damage is done to other flooring. If the floor is not carpeted, lay a thick blanket, mat, or carpet under the wood to protect the floor and reduce the bounce when women strike the nails.

Place the nails and hammers so women can easily access them. If you want to go all out, position the pieces of wood in the shape of a cross. Use nails, rope, or duct tape to secure the pieces in place. Tape the station sign to a wall or other surface, or attach it to a piece of cardboard and prop it up at the station.

— ✳ Station 3 - **The Bitter Vinegar**

- ❧ tablecloth or towel
- ❧ bowls
- ❧ bottle of cider vinegar
- ❧ cotton-tipped swabs (1 per person)
- ❧ wastebasket

Setup: Spread a tablecloth or towel over the table or area (to protect from spills). Place the bowls at either end of the table. Pour cider vinegar in the bowls. Put the cotton swabs into another bowl. Place the wastebasket beside the table so woman can discard their cotton swabs after they use them. Tape the station sign to a wall, or place it on the table.

— ✳ Station 4 - **Distracting Dice**

- ❧ 4 or 5 dice

Setup: Set the dice on the floor or on a table. Tape the station sign to a wall or other surface, or place it on the table.

— ✳ Station 5 - **Remember Me**

- ❧ large sheet of newsprint (or use the white side of wrapping paper if newsprint isn't available)
- ❧ 4 to 6 red markers
- ❧ black marker

Setup: Using the black marker, write "REMEMBER ME" in large letters in the center top of the newsprint. Place this on a table or tape it to a wall. (Be sure that your surface—either the wall or table—is protected so that if markers bleed through they won't damage the surface.) Set the red markers on the floor or table beside the newsprint. Tape the station sign to a wall or other surface, or place it on the table.

❋ Closing

We recommend you use a pillar candle for the closing activity simply for the sturdiness. Other candles may tip over easily. Be sure lit candles are not left unattended.

Recipe Options

Today women will talk about how forgiveness softens us. All of today's food options feature food that is softened before it's eaten.

Easiest Option:
* biscotti
* hot chocolate or coffee

Purchase biscotti. Serve with hot chocolate or coffee to dip the biscotti in.

Easy+ Option:
* baked brie
* fancy crackers
* sliced apples or pears (optional)

Make baked brie using the following:
1-pound round of brie
$1/3$ cup brown sugar
2 tablespoons butter
$1/2$ cup chopped pecans

Preheat the oven to 325° F. Melt the butter, and sauté the pecans in the butter until toasted. Put the brie on a baking sheet. Sprinkle the brown sugar on the brie. Then pour the butter and pecans over the top. Bake for 15 minutes until the brie is melted and the sugar begins to caramelize.

Serve with the fancy crackers, sliced apples, and sliced pears.

Make It a Meal:

* French onion soup
* toasted French bread
* Swiss cheese slices
* cookies (optional)

Prepare your favorite recipe for French onion soup, or purchase this soup from a deli. (You can even use canned if you like.) Leave the soup in the cooking pot.

Slice a loaf of French bread and toast in a 325-degree oven until well toasted on both sides.

Heat the oven to 425° F. Fill oven-proof bowls with the soup; then top with a slice of toasted bread and a slice of Swiss cheese. Put the soup bowls in the oven, and bake until the cheese is melted and bubbly. Be sure to use care—the bowls will be very hot.

You can serve this with a green salad if you like. Then end today's meal with your favorite cookies.

Week Five

Getting to Have Fun

Build companionship by enjoying time with Jesus and others.

Key Verse: Ecclesiastes 4:9

❧ Hostess Prep ❧

Read the Hostess Helps at the end of this session right away!

You'll need:
- ☐ ball
- ☑ rubber bands

Getting to Know You

Eating together is a great way to enjoy each other's company! If your group would like to enjoy a meal together, invite everyone to bring a favorite dish to share.

Getting to Know God
(about 25 minutes)

Today's gathering is all about having fun together and enjoying one another's companionship. With your group, choose one of these activities in advance, or decide on something else that would provide a fun way to spend time together.

- Go bowling.
- Play miniature golf.
- Go to a video arcade or play laser tag.
- Hike or snowshoe on a local trail.
- Go water-skiing or ice-skating.
- Go on a scavenger hunt.
- Play board games at someone's home.
- Play soccer or baseball at the park.
- Contact your church to find a service project, such as painting someone's home or raking someone's yard.

You may also want to use one of these optional devotion ideas before or after your fun event. Hostess, be aware that Option 2 requires some easy-to-find supplies.

Devotion Option 1

Stand in a circle with all but one woman in your group, and hook elbows to lock your arms together. The woman standing on the outside of the circle will try to get inside it, while everyone standing in the circle tries to keep her out. Whether or not the woman is successful, discuss the following questions.

🍃 **What were you thinking and feeling during this activity?**

🍃 **What did this activity illustrate about companionship and friendship?**

🍃 **How can we relate these insights to our relationship with Jesus?**

❋ **Devotion Option 2:**

Stand in a circle. Use the rubber bands to join each person's wrists to their neighbors' wrists so that everyone is connected wrist-to-wrist around the circle.

Toss the ball back and forth across the circle for a minute or two. Have everyone stay connected while you discuss these questions:

🍃 **What were you thinking and feeling while we played this game?**

🍃 **What does this game teach about friendship?**

🍃 **How can you relate these truths about friendship to our relationship with Jesus?**

Getting Real ✐

Keep growing in fun and friendship! Before the night is over, make plans for another fun outing. Be sure to look up the Getting Real challenges below when you get home. Or if women brought their books to your outing, find someone to partner with and choose your challenges at the end of your event. Write what you plan to do in the space provided. Make plans to connect with your partner sometime in the next week to check in and encourage each other.

Choose at least one challenge to do this week.

- I'll make a date with a special friend just to hang out together.

- I'll rent a favorite movie, pop popcorn, and get some theater treats to share with a group of several friends.

- I'll ask a friend to help me plan a "just because" surprise party for someone who needs cheering up.

- I'll set aside an hour just to imagine Jesus as a close companion. I'll read and reflect on Matthew 28:20 as I sit with him.

Because friendship with Jesus and others is a priority, I'm going to:

_____

_____

_____

_____

_____

_____

_____

_____

_____

_____

_____

_____

_____

_____

_____

_____

_____

_____

Closing

Close your time together reading Ecclesiastes 4:9 aloud.

> "Two people are better off than one, for they can help each other succeed."—Ecclesiastes 4:9

Stand in a circle, hold hands, and stay connected as your hostess closes your devotion time in prayer, asking God to help you deepen your friendships with others and with Jesus.

Week Five

Helpful Hints for the Hostess

To facilitate relationship building, have everyone find a partner to stick with during the get-together. Have partners work on getting to know each other better.

Have everyone be on the lookout for friendship in action during your get-together. At the end of the event, invite everyone to share how she saw friendship being expressed throughout your gathering.

Invite women to draw names, and then at some time during the fun, have them express love and appreciation for the person whose name they've drawn.

If your fun event involves teams, minimize any feeling of competition by having each team do something to serve and love the other team at some point during the event.

Friend *Me!* 🖤 6 Get-togethers to Build Faith and Friendship

Week Six

Getting Centered on Jesus

Discover what it means for friendships with others to be an overflow of friendship with Jesus.

Key Verse: John 15:9-16

❧ Hostess Prep ❧

Other than preparing the meeting space and providing food, there is no additional prep for this week. Celebrate the success of your weeks together!

You'll need:

☐ fresh fruit tray

See the hostess helps on pages 70 & 71 for additional tips and food ideas!

Getting to Know You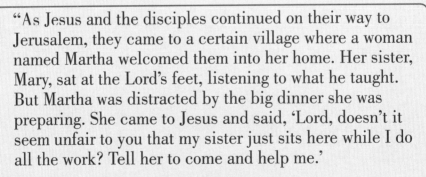
(about 15 minutes)

Enjoy a time of eating and casual chatting. Then begin your get-together with this discussion question:

🍂 **What could the food we're eating today symbolize about friendship?**

Today we'll be talking about the fruitfulness of friendship and about producing fruit that lasts through our friendship with Jesus.

First let's check in on the Getting Real challenges from last week.

Share with the entire group how you followed through with your commitment and what happened as a result.

Getting to Know God
(about 25 minutes)

During our first get-together, we explored Luke 10:38-42. Let's read it again.

Read aloud the passage below.

> "As Jesus and the disciples continued on their way to Jerusalem, they came to a certain village where a woman named Martha welcomed them into her home. Her sister, Mary, sat at the Lord's feet, listening to what he taught. But Martha was distracted by the big dinner she was preparing. She came to Jesus and said, 'Lord, doesn't it seem unfair to you that my sister just sits here while I do all the work? Tell her to come and help me.'
>
> "But the Lord said to her, 'My dear Martha, you are worried and upset over all these details! There is really only one thing worth being concerned about. Mary has discovered it, and it will not be taken away from her.'"—Luke 10:38-42

Gather in smaller groups of 3-5 and discuss the following questions. Feel free to jot down your thoughts as you're talking.

Q: What insights about this passage do you have now after exploring friendship with this group for the past few weeks?

Q: How will you be a different friend because of what we've discovered?

Form six groups, and number them 1 through 6. (A "group" can be one person if you have a smaller gathering.)

Each group will use the section on the following pages that corresponds to their group number. In your group you'll talk about an area of your community that might look different if everyone lived according to the friendship principles we've discussed over the past five weeks. Follow the instructions in your section, and be prepared to share your thoughts with the larger group. Take about 3 minutes for this discussion.

Group 1: My Workplace
Consider how your own workplace might be different if everyone applied the friendship principles we've learned and practiced over the past few weeks. Share your thoughts with your group, and jot down your notes here. If it helps, draw a picture of what would be different!

✳ Group 2: Courts

Consider how courts in your community might be different if everyone applied the friendship principles we've learned and practiced over the past few weeks. Share your thoughts with your group, and jot down your notes here. If it helps, draw a picture of what would be different!

✳ Group 3: Churches

Consider how your own church and other churches in your community might be different if everyone applied the friendship principles we've learned and practiced over the past few weeks. Share your thoughts with your group, and jot down your notes here. If it helps, draw a picture of what would be different!

Group 4: Stores

Consider how stores, malls, and other shopping areas in your community might be different if everyone applied the friendship principles we've learned and practiced over the past few weeks. Share your thoughts with your group, and jot down your notes here. If it helps, draw a picture of what would be different!

Group 5: Neighborhoods

Consider how your own neighborhood might be different if everyone applied the friendship principles we've learned and practiced over the past few weeks. Share your thoughts with your group, and jot down your notes here. If it helps, draw a picture of what would be different!

Group 6: Schools

Consider how schools for all ages of students in your community might be different if everyone applied the friendship principles we've learned and practiced over the past few weeks. Share your thoughts with your group, and jot down your notes here. If it helps, draw a picture of what would be different!

After 5 minutes, the hostess will invite each small group to share one or two key thoughts from their discussion with the rest of the group. Then discuss these questions as a large group:

🍂 **How are our lives changed if we believe that God is a friend who wants to be actively involved in each and every part of life?**

🍂 **How does friendship with Jesus change our friendships with others?**

We can learn about our friendship with Jesus by watching how he related to his friends here on earth. The night before Jesus was crucified, he met with his disciples to celebrate the Passover. Just imagine how he must have felt and the things he must have wanted to express. He knew what would happen the next day. He knew this was his last opportunity to teach and encourage his best friends. Let's read aloud a portion of what Jesus said to his disciples.

The hostess will read aloud the passage below while everyone else follows along.

> "'I have loved you even as the Father has loved me. Remain in my love. When you obey my commandments, you remain in my love, just as I obey my Father's commandments and remain in his love. I have told you these things so that you will be filled with my joy. Yes, your joy will overflow! This is my commandment: Love each other in the same way I have loved you. There is no greater love than to lay down one's life for one's friends. You are my friends if you do what I command. I no longer call you slaves, because a master doesn't confide in his slaves. Now you are my friends, since I have told you everything the Father told me. You didn't choose me. I chose you. I appointed you to go and produce lasting fruit, so that the Father will give you whatever you ask for, using my name.'"
> —John 15:9-16

🍂 What can we learn from these words about how we're to live our lives?

God has chosen us! And he wants us to love others passionately and to produce lasting fruit. Our friendship with Jesus can pour into our friendships with others—and that's making a friendship with lasting fruit. Now let's end our time by deciding our next steps and praying together.

Getting Real
(about 10 minutes)

This is the last week of *Friend Me!* Talk with
your group about what you'd like to do now
that you've finished this series. *Friend Me 2!* is
a great resource to follow this series!

**This session is a great reminder that God
wants us to go and have fruitful friendships
that help people grow closer to him. Look
at the options below, and select the one
you'd like to take on this week—or beyond!**

When you've decided on a Getting Real action, share your choice with a
partner, and write what you plan to do in the space provided. Make plans
right now to connect with your partner sometime in the next week to check
in and encourage each other.

- ✦ I'll reach out to my circle of friends with the principles I've learned
  through *Friend Me!* I'll even consider leading a new *Friend Me!* group
  with my friends.

- ✦ I'll set aside at least 10 minutes each day this week to be alone and
  deepen my friendship with God by reading the Bible and praying.

- ✦ I'll give thanks to God for his friendship—and the human friends
  God has given me who show me what Jesus is like. I'll dig into
  Philippians 2:1-11 as a model of being the kind of friend Jesus wants
  me to be.

Because friendship with Jesus and others is a priority, I'm going to:

_____

_____

_____

_____

_____

_____

Closing

As we end this series we know our friendships will change because of what we've learned and experienced. The passage we read in John 15 said that Jesus calls us his friends. And we have gone deeper in our own friendships too. Let's remind each other of that in a personal way.

Stand or sit in a circle. If you're comfortable doing so, you can hold hands or link elbows. The hostess will begin this activity.

Turn to the woman on your right, and complete this sentence, "[Woman's name], Jesus has called you his friend. I'm thankful that you're my friend too." Continue around the circle until every woman has been affirmed. (It's OK to add hugs if you're comfortable doing so!)

There's always enough of Jesus to go around! His love and grace are available to all. And as Jesus' good friends, we have the privilege of sharing his love with others and inviting them to be Jesus' friends too. Spend some time silently praying for a friend you need to share Jesus' love with.

Pray silently for a few minutes, and then your hostess will close the session in prayer, asking God to bless each member of the group as you seek to be better friends with others and with God.

Week Six

☙ Helpful Hints for the Hostess ❧

Thanks for leading *Friend Me!*

For extra impact: Give each woman a candy apple with a note attached reminding her how sweet her friendship is.

☙ Recipe Options ❧

Today women will explore the fruitfulness of friendship. All of today's food has a fruit theme.

Easiest Option:
❧ fresh fruit trays

Purchase already prepared fresh fruit trays from your grocery store's deli. Or provide a variety of fresh fruit such as grapes, strawberries, and bananas.

Easy+ Option:
❧ fruit smoothies

Set out vanilla yogurt, bananas, and a variety of fruit juices. Also set out frozen strawberries, blueberries, peaches, and raspberries. Provide one blender for every three to four people. Invite everyone to make a fruit smoothie by blending her choice of juice, yogurt, and fruit together.

Make It a Meal:

* grilled chicken and pineapple sandwiches
* mini fruit "pizzas" (or serve frozen fruit and juice bars)

Make grilled chicken and pineapple sandwiches using the following:
skinless, boneless chicken breasts (1 per person)
pineapple rings (1 per person)
½ cup teriyaki sauce
1 tablespoon honey
1 teaspoon grated ginger root
sandwich rolls
honey mustard dressing

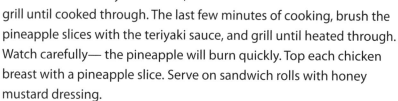

Mix the teriyaki sauce, honey, and ginger root. Heat a grill. Brush chicken breasts with the teriyaki mixture, and grill until cooked through. The last few minutes of cooking, brush the pineapple slices with the teriyaki sauce, and grill until heated through. Watch carefully— the pineapple will burn quickly. Top each chicken breast with a pineapple slice. Serve on sandwich rolls with honey mustard dressing.

Make mini fruit pizzas using the following:
1 tube of sugar cookie dough
8-ounce package of cream cheese, softened
⅓ cup powdered sugar
½ teaspoon vanilla extract
½ cup apricot preserves
1 tablespoon water
fruit (sliced strawberries, fresh blueberries, banana slices, kiwi slices, and
     mandarin orange sections)

Bake the sugar cookies according to the package directions. Combine the cream cheese, powdered sugar, and vanilla extract. When the cookies are cool, spread each cookie with the cream cheese frosting. Arrange the fruit on top. Heat the apricot preserves and water in the microwave. Brush the glaze over the fruit. Refrigerate until ready to serve.

Journal